FERAL INSTINCT

GIL MASON BOOK 3

GORDON CARROLL

The genetic drive, when reaching a crisis point, to revert to the state of the wild beast.

-Feral Instinct

1

WHAT WENT BEFORE

Seven Years Ago

Majoqui Cabrera was not nervous when he saw the flashing red and blue lights in his rearview mirror. He wore the sacred amulet that protected him from bullets and knives; it even protected him from machetes. The witch-woman had slain the chicken and chanted the rites, blessing the medal as she prayed the rosary and asked favors of the Virgin Mother on his behalf. No, he was not afraid, but he did wonder if he would have to kill this Americano police officer. The warm metal of the five-shot snubbed-nosed Ruger rode the flat muscles of his stomach beneath the button shirt he wore. The sleeves were long, hiding the tattoos that inked both arms.

He pulled to the right side of the street, careful to activate his turn signal, and came to a gentle stop. It was eleven-thirty at night on a Tuesday, and the Colorado streets were nearly deserted.

Majoqui had spent his time in the United States and knew the law. Two years when he had come of age and made his first kill, he was nine, and then for several months when he was fifteen and again when he was seventeen. He liked America. The women were pretty, and there was always excitement for a brave young man. He'd never killed an American police officer. Many in his group bragged of killing police, but Majoqui found that it was almost always bad business. Once he'd killed a policeman in Mexico, but that had been on orders; to set an example, and even then, it had been tricky. The dead cop's police friends had hunted him, and he'd had to hide in a sewage ditch for three days.

A spotlight splashed his side mirror, but he expected it and watched only peripherally so as not to ruin his night vision. The other light, aimed directly at his rearview mirror, effectively blinded him to everything behind his vehicle.

Majoqui watched for the shadow of the officer as he walked between the light and his car, and so he was surprised when the voice sounded close to his ear.

"Sergeant Gil Mason, Cherokee County Sheriff's Office. May I see your driver's license, registration, and proof of insurance, please."

The officer must have approached in an arc, staying out of the light until the last second. It was a good move, and even now, he stood behind Majoqui, making him stretch his neck back and to the side, which was uncomfortable. It made it impossible to get a good look at him. But what he saw registered instantly; average height, muscular, crisp green uniform with stripes on the upper sleeve, highly shined leather gun belt and boots. Majoqui decided he would not kill the officer if he didn't have to. The deputy appeared well trained and on guard, and although Majoqui held complete faith in the Virgin's blessings and the protection of his medal, he had found in his years that it was best not to test fate or the gods more than necessary.

Majoqui handed the officer his documents. His license, a printed temporary, was real, but had no picture and was issued to a Juan Martinez. The registration and insurance were also real, belonging to the dead woman in the trunk of the car.

"The reason I stopped you is your license plate bracket light is out," said the officer. He sounded confidant, professional.

"I will have it fixed right away, thank you," said Majoqui.

"The car doesn't belong to you?"

"My aunt's. She is loaning it to me."

"What's her name?"

"Emma Cotton." Majoqui had memorized it after strangling her and stuffing her into the trunk. She had been in her sixties and reminded him a little of his Aunt Lucinda, whom he had always loved, but he needed the car. Another thing he'd learned in his years was to take advantage of that which the spirits provide.

"Do you have a picture I.D.?"

"I'm sorry, but no."

"Do you have a green card?"

Majoqui was ready for this. "I'm a citizen. I was born in Texas." He knew American police officers had to be careful. The term was '*politically correct*,' and all kinds of trouble could be had if an officer breached protocol.

"Here's your insurance back," said the officer. He handed the card to Majoqui, who reached over and back with his right hand for the document. His sleeve pulled up during the movement, showing the bottom half of the black inked "MS" at his wrist.

"Mara Salvatrucha," said the officer. "We don't get a lot of 13rs here in Colorado."

Majoqui nodded slowly. "I was a child then. Now I am a man. I have a wife and children. I have no time for gangs."

"For some gangs, maybe, but MS-13? I've heard it said, 'once in Mara always in Mara. Death is the only escape'."

"That is true, but as you say, there are not many of us in Colorado, and so I am safe."

The officer glanced at the piece of paper that acted as a license. "How old are you?"

Here again, Majoqui had memorized the false birth date. His real age was twenty-three. "I'm twenty-nine," he lied smoothly.

"Wait in the car," said the officer as he backed away. Majoqui strained his eyes as far to the side as he could, watching the man's retreat. He did not like this. He knew the driver's license description to be a close match, but was it good enough now that the officer's suspicions had been raised? Majoqui absently fingered the charm beneath his shirt, mouthing an illegitimate version of "Our Father" as he considered his options. There was the gun, but there was also the machete under his seat. He could drive away. Many American police agencies were not allowed to give chase, and he might be able to escape. But the police officer would radio his vehicle's description and license plate to other police agencies, and he would have to play cat and mouse all night. This he could not do. He had a mission to complete. The picture of the bank president and his family rested in his front shirt pocket.

The officer was taking too long to return; was he waiting for backup to arrive? Majoqui sighed. He pulled the pistol from his waistband and slipped the machete from under the seat. He opened the door and swung his body out, facing the blinding lights. Without hesitation, he charged, using the same tactic as the deputy and arcing out away from the spotlight so he could acquire his target. And then he saw him, already out of his vehicle, kneeling behind the door and taking aim with a pistol of his own. There was a flash and a roar, and something hit him in the chest. But it didn't matter, he was protected, and he could not fail. He threw the machete and fired the gun, still running at the police officer. The machete shattered the window the officer was hiding behind, and holes plunked into the door and roof. Majoqui was almost upon him when something fast and massive flew at him from around the front of the police car. It was dark and frightening, and before Majoqui could react, its mouth was open with bright white teeth that covered his face; its hot breath like scalding water. And then the impact, blunt and unstoppable and the pain, as the fangs crushed down on his face like some inescapable trap of metal jaws. He tried to scream, but his words were choked with blood and splintered teeth. All he could do was wish that he'd asked for a blessing from the witch woman that would have protected him from this. But how could he know that a monster would attack him and that he would need to be protected from more than just bullets and knives, but from teeth as well?

Wet warmth flooded down his chest, and then his head and face were being jerked horribly from side to side. Someone was screaming so loud and filled with pain that just hearing it hurt his soul. He felt his jaw wrench, and then something in his neck popped. There was a pain so bright and sharp that it exploded into a rushing darkness that engulfed him and carried him away from the screams and the pain and the hot and the cold—carried him away from the police and his mission—carried him away from Mara Salvatrucha and his duty—carried him away to a place that was so dark and so isolated that only the Virgin herself could hope to bring him back.

2

Pilgrim watched from the back-kennel area of the Sheriff's K9 Patrol SUV as Majoqui exited his car. Pilgrim knew the man would attack before the Alpha knew ... even before the man himself fully knew. His incredibly keen canine ears picked up the sound of the man's heart as he considered, the slow even *thump—thump*—thump changing gear to a *thump-thump-thump-thump* and then up to a *thumpthumpthumpthumpthump* as it surged harder and faster. Pilgrim's motion-sensitive eyes saw the change in posture and the slight hitch to the shoulders as he reached his decision and opened the door. Pilgrim's nose caught the subtle but exciting shift in pheromones as adrenaline and endorphins pushed scent molecules out through the pores of Majoqui's skin to mingle and carry on the night wind.

Pilgrim's massive jaw rested on the Alpha's shoulder as he punched data into the computer, his attention diverted. A low growl grated deep in Pilgrim's throat, vibrating into the Alpha's body. The Alpha looked up instantly, seeing the driver turn toward him with a gun in one hand and some kind of sword in the other. The man charged out into the street and then in toward them. But Pilgrim's warning came just in time. The Alpha pushed his already open door out with his knee and stepped behind it as he simultaneously drew his gun. He hit the rear door popper, snapping the hydraulic gear into action and releasing Pilgrim out the passenger side.

Pilgrim came around the front of the vehicle as shots exploded into the night. He launched from nine feet away, his one hundred and twenty pounds of muscle and teeth soaring at close to twenty miles an hour. He hit with the concussive force of an exploding torpedo, his two-inch canines crushing in and through the flimsy flesh of the man's face and head.

The man fought.

But he had tried to hurt the Alpha.

Pilgrim loved the Alpha.

The man stood no chance at all.

I LEANED against the front panel of my lieutenant's SUV, admiring the bullet holes in the door and roof of my patrol car sitting across the street from me. The suspect—the guy that shot at me—was long gone on his way to the hospital. The paramedics said he was still breathing when they left, but I'd put two forty-fives center-mass and my K9, Pilgrim, did a job on his face and head. If he did wake up, he was gonna be hurting.

A lab tech laid a ruler next to the machete sticking out the side of my driver's side front seat and started taking pictures. That thing missed me by about an inch; some of the bullets had come closer.

"You doing okay, Gil?" It was my Lieutenant, Mike Braden. He's a big guy with a barrel chest, close-cropped red hair, and monkey arms. I think maybe God got a little distracted when he was putting him together.

"I'm okay, Mike. What's next?"

"The shoot team's on their way. So is the Sheriff. I'll need your gun and mags; that goes for your spare too."

"Already on your dash," I said, indicating with a head jab toward the inside of his rig. "Any word on the bad guy?"

"They say he's going to make it."

That surprised me. "Really. Did I miss?"

Mike grinned. "Were you aiming for his heart?"

"Yes."

"Then, you didn't miss." He double-tapped the center of his chest with a thick finger. "Dead center. Only one of the bullets hit this." He dropped an oval silver charm that hit at the bottom of its beaded chain, swinging back and forth. It was maybe a little bigger than a quarter and creased in the center.

"A Saint Christopher Medal?"

"That's what it is," said Mike. "The bullet bounced off and angled down into his hip and out his thigh."

I shook my head. "A .45 hit that and bounced off?"

"Hey, it's St. Christopher, patron saint of travelers. He was traveling when you stopped him, right?"

I shook my head. "What about the second bullet?"

"Punched through his sternum and deflected to his left shoulder. Your dog did more damage than you did."

"Well ... that's something, I guess." I shook my head again. "I need bigger bullets."

"Yeah, messed his face, shattered some teeth, made mush of his right cheekbone. He might lose the eye."

"We figure out who he is yet?"

"Not yet," said Mike. "The lab's working on prints, and we'll get a DNA sample going as soon as possible, but you know how backed up CBI is. Could take a while."

He held up a plastic bag with a photograph inside. The picture showed a middle-aged businessman with a family; a wife, two young kids, a boy, and a girl. It was a nice looking family. "He had this in his shirt pocket."

I took the baggy and turned it around. There was an address on the back. I raised my eyebrows in question.

"Yeah," said Mike. "I've got dispatch working on it."

I nodded. "What about the woman who owns the car?"

"I had Denver go by and check her house; nobody home."

"So why did he come out shooting like that?"

Mike shrugged. "Gang bangers. Maybe he was trying to make a rep for himself. MS-13 does that sometimes."

I shook my head again. "He was too cool—too calm. He's an OG somewhere."

"Old Gangster?" laughed Mike. "The kid's barely in his twenties."

"He might not be old in years, but in experience—in experience is another matter."

"Maybe," said Mike. He looked down the street. "Here come the detectives."

Jim Black and Randy Nolan were walking toward us from outside the crime scene tape. Cherokee County is big, but not so big that I didn't know most of the cops and detectives. Jim, I knew really well; he was on K9 when I first joined the unit. Randy I'd only known a little. Both were good guys.

Jim came right up and stuck out his hand. "You okay, Gil?"

"Not a scratch," I said, shaking his hand. "Sorry to make you guys get out of bed."

"I'm not," said Randy, also stretching out his hand. "It's overtime, and I've got a vacation coming up." We shook, and he said, "Gil Mason, right? We met last year on the shooting range."

"I remember. You had a nice new Sig with a laser sight."

He grinned and patted his coat high on the left side. "She's a sweetheart." He looked at my empty holster. "And you had ..." he pursed his lips, "... a Smith and Wesson 4506."

My eyebrows raised. "Very good. I'm surprised you remember."

"How could I forget an antique like that?" he laughed. "There's enough metal in that gun to build a battleship."

Jim looked around. "Pilgrim okay? We heard he got a bite."

"He's fine," I said. "He's sleeping in back of my car."

"Lucky dog," said Mike. We all laughed.

"Well," said Jim, "are you ready for the interview? We can wait till you get your legal counsel if you want."

The smart course of action was to have a lawyer present after a shooting, but I've always trusted in the department's legal process. "No, I don't need a lawyer. I'm ready when you are."

Jim nodded. "Okay, we have to read you Garrity."

Garrity is a departmental advisement informing the employee that he has to cooperate fully with an investigation. It basically tells you that if you decide your actions might result in criminal charges being leveled against you, that you can opt to assert your Fifth Amendment Constitutional right to remain silent, but that doing so could result in departmental disciplinary actions being taken against you up to and including termination.

"No problem," I said.

"Holy crap!" yelled one of the CSI techs as he stumbled away from the rear end of the suspect's car. He'd just popped the trunk, and it was still standing open. The Lieutenant, me, and both detectives hurried over. Inside was the body of an elderly woman.

"Emma Cotton," I said.

"That'd be my guess," said Mike.

The two detectives looked at me.

Jim said, "Looks like the interview's going to be a breeze, Gil."

"Yeah," said Randy. "Shootin' a guy that would murder a little old lady's likely to earn you a medal."

"Too bad you didn't kill him," said Jim.

"Yeah," said Mike.

"Yeah," said Randy.

I had no idea how right they were.

3

Majoqui opened his eye—his right eye. Something was wrong with his left eye, and his whole face hurt. There was pain, but pain was an old companion. His mother was a whore in San Salvador, and it had not been uncommon for customers to kick or hit him when he wasn't fast enough to get out of their way. Until the day he became a man—the day he joined Mara.

He was nine when he was "jumped" into Mara. He'd stood in the circle as the five were called out—the strongest five—and then they had attacked him, punching and kicking as brutally as they could—nothing held back as the leader counted—slowly counted—to thirteen. There was no thought or possibility of fighting back; none of the five were younger than fifteen, and two of them were barely shy of twenty. He curled into a ball and absorbed their kicks and punches as best he could, crying out only twice—once when a boot clipped his kidney and again when his nose was crushed into his face.

When they finally lifted him to his feet, he felt much the same as he did now, like a giant bruise. He'd peed blood for nearly a week, and his nose would forever after hitch to the right. He could hardly stand as they pushed and pulled him to a shallow cave dug into the side of a weedy hill where a rival gang member was tied and gagged.

They dragged him out and gave Majoqui the choice of a gun or a machete.

The man, he was about twenty, stared at Majoqui, breathing hard. He'd been beaten, his nose smashed flatter than Majoqui's and his lips pulped. Both eyes were puffed nearly closed. Majoqui bent toward him and stared into his eyes. The man stared back, his swollen eyes hard and filled with hate. Majoqui reached out and pulled the gag free. The man spat in Majoqui's face and laughed. He reminded Majoqui of all the men who slept with his mother. He took the machete in both hands and buried it as deep into the man's head as his nine-year-old muscles allowed.

That same night, Majoqui received his first tattoo, a small cross surrounded by the letters 'MS' over his heart. That had been pain too, but there was something else—there was pride and a sense of family —something he had never felt from his mother.

The men of Mara were so impressed with the boy that they gave him a gun. It was a cheap, homemade thing that fired shotgun shells, but no customer of his mother's ever kicked him after that night. He was given the nickname "The Crow" because of the calm way he had dispatched the rival gang member. Over the next few years, his reputation grew until he was known as a man to fear, a man not to cross. Majoqui had killed twenty-seven men since that night and was considered Mara's most deadly assassin.

Majoqui tried to reach up to touch his eye, but his wrists were handcuffed to a bed. Machines were whirring and beeping around him, and the lights were dimmed. His head felt big and soft and tender, and he realized his left eye was bandaged. And then it all came back—the police officer, the monster, his mission.

He turned his neck slowly, and again there was pain. Something clicked, hot and bright in his neck at the movement, and he saw the room was empty, that there were no windows and only an open bathroom and one door leading out. He moved his feet and was surprised to find his legs unshackled. In Honduras or even Mexico, he would have been lashed down from head to foot.

His chest hurt, but his hip and leg hurt worse, which was strange because he remembered being shot in the chest. Majoqui concentrated on flexing the muscles of his chest. A dull ache radiated throughout his left side, but it didn't seem debilitating.

The door to the room opened, allowing light to spill in as a tall, elderly doctor carrying a folder with pages paperclipped to it entered, followed by a police officer. He let his muscles relax and closed his eye. The doctor approached the bed, felt for a pulse, laid the folder near his leg, and shined a light in his eye.

"You're awake," said the doctor. "How do you feel?"

"Tired," said Majoqui through aching, clenched teeth. "Sore."

The doctor laughed. "I'd consider that an understatement. You took two bullets to the chest and had a police K9 chomp your face." He wagged a finger toward Majoqui's lips. "Your jaw's cracked. You lost a couple of teeth too. Almost lost the eye, but we were able to save it. It's going to feel weird for a while because we had to stitch it closed. You have an orbital fracture, a broken nose, a cracked vertebra in your neck, a punctured sternum, and we had to dig around in your chest a bit to get the other bullet out." He pulled the sheet down and looked at Majoqui's leg. "The first bullet ricocheted off your Saint Christopher medal, dug into your hip, and ripped out your upper thigh here. The damage was superficial, but it's going to hurt."

Majoqui watched the doctor as he pulled a pair of scissors from his white coat pocket and snipped through a section of tape that held the bandage in place on his leg. The police officer stayed out of the light so that he was only a silhouette.

"Good," said the doctor. "Very little bleeding." He taped the bandage back in place and picked up the folder. The pages slipped off the folder and floated to the floor like miniature gliders. The doctor shook his head and scooped up the papers. He looked back at Majoqui. "Get as much rest as you can. I'll check in on you in a few hours." He left the room, the police officer following and closing the door behind them.

Majoqui used his thumbnail to straighten the paperclip, and the handcuff was off his right wrist a few seconds later. His chest ached when he reached over to undo the second cuff, but he ignored it, already planning his next move.

He stuffed the pillow under the sheet and moved the IV stand and monitor as close together as possible on the door side of the bed so the guard would not be able to see there was no one in the bed when he entered the room. Majoqui found the little catch pins securing the adjustable tray that had held a water pitcher and a Styrofoam cup and separated it from its base. Finally, he pulled out the IV needle from his arm and ripped off the monitoring wires from his chest. Then he waited behind the door, the sturdy tray and shaft of metal clutched in his hands. When it opened, a short heavyset nurse bustled into the room, the police officer following closely. Majoqui pushed the door closed behind them and smashed the tray, edge side, against the base of the police officer's skull. The man went down but tried to get back up. Majoqui changed his grip and brought the flat side down square on his head. The police officer collapsed, his arms and fingers twitching.

The heavyset nurse turned, her eyes wide and her mouth opening as she stumbled backward into the IV and monitor. She tripped and fell, hitting the bed and knocking over the IV stand. Majoqui was on her before she could scream. He stuck his bare foot against her throat and pushed down with all his weight, cutting off her air. The woman fought, but Majoqui stomped down hard, balancing himself on the rails of the bed. He felt bones pop and grind beneath his foot, and then there was a snap, and the nurse went limp.

Majoqui was breathing hard now, and the room was spinning. Nausea rolled in his stomach and sweat ran down his face.

He went to the police officer and took his gun and extra magazines. He also found a Taser, some pepper spray, and an Asp—a small collapsible baton—and the officer's radio. There was a wallet with thirty dollars and a cell phone, all of which he took. Blood soaked the man's shirt, but Majoqui stripped it off so he could get to the bullet-proof vest beneath. Majoqui made a quick search of the room but could not find his own clothes. He put on the officer's pants, which were too short, his shoes, which were too big, and the nurse's shirt, which was just right to cover the vest. He also took the nurse's cell phone.

Majoqui called a cab from the dead officer's phone and took the elevator to the lobby. The taxi arrived a few minutes later, and Majoqui got in.

He still had a job to do.

4

The scene at the hospital was grisly. The dead cop was a Denver Sheriff's Deputy I didn't know. His head had been bashed in, and there was a lot of blood. The nurse was worse. Her neck had been pulped. There was discoloration, and it was terribly swollen, but the angle was what made it really bad. That and the look on her face.

We were all there; my lieutenant, both detectives, and a boatload of Denver cops. It was their jurisdiction, and they were hopping mad about losing one of their own.

Couldn't blame them.

Denver's a little different than other jurisdictions in Colorado. It's both a city and a county, so it has both a police department and a sheriff's department. But unlike most counties, there is no actual sheriff. Sheriffs are elected officials, whereas police chiefs are appointed either by the mayor or a city council. In Denver, the Sheriff's Department is responsible for the city jail system, and the police take care of the streets. Cherokee County goes more the traditional route. Our Sheriff is elected, and we have jurisdiction over the entire county, including the cities that have incorporated within our boundaries. The Sheriff's Department takes care of both the county jail and the streets. The cities themselves may have their own police force, but they have arrest powers only in their individual cities.

My father-in-law once said that our Justice System is 'just—a—system, and it's broken.' Brother, was he right! Case in point: my shooting with the MS 13 banger happened in Cherokee County; the killing of the Denver Sheriff's Deputy and the nurse happened in Denver. It's anybody's guess where the woman in the trunk was murdered. It was highly possible that once found, the killer would be tried in three different jurisdictions, and that's not even taking into account the possibility that he might not be a U.S. citizen. *Sheesh!*

The Denver detectives let Jim and Randy take a look at the bodies, and they seemed to be filling them in on everything they knew.

Randy came over to me and Mike. "It looks like he went straight to the elevator and down to the lobby. A couple of nurses saw what they thought was an orderly up here and downstairs, and a security guard saw him walk out the front doors. The tats didn't give him away, not with how everyone gets inked today. But the bandages struck everyone as a little odd. He got the deputy's gun, nightstick, Taser, pepper spray, vest, and shoes."

"So he's on foot?" asked Mike.

"Far as we know. Denver's got a twenty-block perimeter set up and all their K9s out looking for him."

"Was any of his personal property in the room with him?" I asked.

Randy shook his head. "Nope. We took every stitch into evidence."

"No cell phone?"

He shook his head again. "Nada."

"What about the dead sheriff's deputy and the nurse? Any cell phones?"

He started to shake his head again but stopped. "I don't know. Let me check." He went back into the room and came out a minute later. "None on them, and the cop's wallet is missing too."

"We should start pinging," I said.

Randy jabbed his head back toward the room. "They're on it."

Cell phone carriers have the ability to 'ping' cell phones and get a GPS location on them. Once we found out who the providers were and the cell phone numbers, there was a good chance we could get a bearing on our murder suspect.

"How about the picture with the address?" I asked.

"I've got Billy Mack there now, and Denver's sending a squad car. According to Billy, they don't know anything about anything."

A Denver detective walked over and acknowledged us with a nod. He spoke to Randy. "We have a master list of all our officer's cell phones. The provider's pinging Craig's now. We should know something any ..." he broke off, listening to the earpiece hooked to his radio. His eyes got big, and he held up a finger. "He's right out front, must be hiding in the bushes or under a car. K9 and SWAT are all converging." He touched a finger to his ear, concentrating on what he was hearing. "The ping shows him right by the front doors, near the lobby."

"Let's go," said Mike.

We all rushed for the elevator.

By the time we made it down to the ground floor, the place was crawling with cops. Three K9 officers were checking the front outside area with their dogs. Uniformed and plainclothes detectives were swarming the lobby, checking bathrooms, closets, storage, and electrical rooms, even under the couches.

I turned to the Denver detective that was with us. "Do you have the dead officer's phone number?"

"Sure," he read the number to me from a small steno pad.

I dialed it. "Everyone quiet, please." Everyone went quiet, looking our way.

The song was muffled but distinct. It was the theme song from the TV show 'Cops,' and it was coming from the trashcan by the lobby doors. A uniformed officer pulled off the lid and dug through some stuff before coming up with it. I hit 'end' on my phone, and the 'bad-boys whach-ya gonna do when they come for you,' stopped abruptly.

I looked back at Mike. "Like I said, an OG. This guy isn't stupid." I pointed at the trashcan. "There should be another one in there; the nurse's."

The cop pulled out the plastic bag and tore through it. No phone.

The detective said, "We don't have the nurse's number yet, but it shouldn't be long."

"Have you tried the cab companies and RTD?" I asked.

He went back to his radio and told dispatch to give them a call.

"Mike, do we have a picture of this guy we can send out?"

"No pictures. They rushed him straight to surgery."

I thought for a minute, looked around. "They took him through the ER. There are cameras everywhere. Maybe the security video caught a shot of his face. If that doesn't work, I can give Denver's artist a description."

"Good idea," said Mike. "Then again, how many guys have their eyelid sewn shut? It's a pretty good identifier."

I couldn't argue with that.

"Oh, and another thing, Mike."

He raised his eyebrows in anticipation.

"I'm going to need my gun back."

5

T amera looked at the clock; five till two. Good! She was tired, and her feet hurt. She'd worked a twelve-hour shift at the diner today—tonight—whatever, and she was ready to go home and snuggle her kitty, Miranda. She had found the little thing digging in the dumpster for scraps of food in the alley behind her apartment building. It was nearly starved and had a nasty scabbed-over gash on its side. She'd taken it in, bathed it, and cleaned its wound. She fed it with a bottle she bought at the drugstore. That was three weeks ago. Now it was fine, and she loved it like crazy.

She picked up the coffee pot and went around the counter, checking her tables. There were only three; a small group of teenagers with bibles, a hooker taking a break, and a doctor or nurse with a bandage over his eye who had tattoos running up and down both arms.

The bible thumpers all thanked her, and the hooker held up a hand saying she'd had enough. The doctor—or whatever—looked pretty rough. His badly swollen face was about as pale as the yellowed cream on the table.

"You okay?" she asked as she filled his cup.

He looked up at her, his one eye a gentle brown. "Yes."

"You sure? You look like you're going to puke."

He smiled, and it was a very nice smile, even with the swollen face and the bandage. "I had some surgery today." He touched the bandage.

"Wow, a doctor having surgery! Did you do it yourself?" He looked puzzled, so she touched the purple medical shirt he was wearing. "Are you a doctor?"

"No," he said, smiling again. His voice was quiet and smooth and tainted with a Spanish accent. "It's just comfortable."

She laughed. "It does look comfortable. Sometimes I stay in my PJ's all day." She turned her head from side to side, preparing to tell a secret. "Once I even went to the store in them, and you know what, no one noticed."

"Yes, America is funny that way."

She sat across from him in the booth. "You have a lot of tattoos. Did they hurt?"

He nodded. "Yes, some of them."

"I have a tattoo," she said, holding out her arm and turning up her wrist. On the inside was a bright butterfly about the size of a penny. "It hurt so bad I almost peed my pants," she said. She looked at his arms again. "I don't know how you could stand it. You must be very brave."

He pointed at her tattoo. "Why a butterfly?"

She smiled. "They're pretty."

"Yes," he said, "yes, they are."

She looked up at the clock. "I'm getting off now. Maybe we could ... you know ... go somewhere. I've got some pot at my place."

"I have something I have to do."

"Oh," she said, "that's okay. I understand. I mean, it *is* after one in the morning." She took out her order pad, wrote down her phone number, and handed it to him. "In case you want to call me sometime."

"Thank you," he said. He put the number in his shirt pocket and took a last sip of his coffee before pushing himself to his feet. He looked tired.

"Are you sure you're okay? I just live a couple of blocks away."

"Again, thank you," he said, "but I will be fine." He turned and started for the door.

"My name's Tamera," she said. "Tamera Sun."

He stopped, turned so that he could see her with his un-bandaged eye. "A pretty name. It suits you." He left the diner.

Tamera stood up. She felt as tired as the man looked. She brushed off the table with a rag and took his cup behind the counter. She was ready for home.

Miranda was waiting for her.

MAJOQUI CAUGHT THE LAST BUS. He was leery of cabs. He'd left the nurse's phone in the one he took from the hospital, hoping to throw the police off his trail for a while. Once he was far enough away, and after he changed his appearance, cabs would be safe again, but he would stick to busses and walking for now.

The gun was in his waistband beneath the shirt. The rest of the weapons were in a plastic bag he'd found by the bathroom in his hospital room. The bulletproof vest was big for him, but the baggy shirt hid it well.

He no longer had the picture with the address, but he'd memorized it long ago. He couldn't know if the police would realize that he was heading there, but he always assumed the worse.

It was almost three in the morning when he arrived at the house. He'd found an unlocked bicycle on a front lawn several miles back and made good time with it. He saw the police cars in the driveway and stayed behind bushes on the other side of the street.

There were two of them; a marked Denver Police car and a black SUV with red and blue lights in the front grill and back window.

Majoqui's face ached, as did his neck, hip, thigh, chest, and shoulder. Whatever pain medication they'd given him was wearing off fast.

Staying to the shadows and dark, he made his way across the street and up to the side of the house. The moon was only a sliver, and the yards were huge, with streetlights spaced far apart. He peeked into a window and through a break in the curtains. He saw a police officer in uniform and another man dressed in a business suit seated at a table with a man and woman, drinking coffee. The man was his primary target, and the woman, his wife. The two children were not in the room.

Majoqui, although he could be the most patient of men when necessary, was not one for elaborate plans. He liked to do what he had to do and leave as quickly as possible. But he was hurt. He felt weak and fuzzy and slow. His depth perception was ruined, and worst of all, he did not have his machete or his amulet.

Still, there was the job to do.

Sighing, he went to the back door that led to the kitchen and quietly tried the knob. It was locked. He set the plastic bag down, reached inside and retrieved the Taser, then took the pistol from his waistband. He winced as he raised his leg and kicked the door just beside the knob, the stitches from the bullet's entry and exit tearing with the strain. The wood molding splintered, and the door crashed open. He stepped inside and saw all four stunned faces gaping wide-eyed at him. He shot the detective wearing the business suit twice in the chest with the pistol and then fired the Taser at the uniformed police officer. One of the harpoon-shaped prongs hit the cop in the throat while the other struck about mid-chest. He was in the act of drawing his gun when the electricity hit. His body went rigid, and he fell to his knees. Majoqui dropped the Taser while it was still sending its electric power into the police officer's body and shot him in the forehead with the pistol. The man's brains speckled the wall behind him in high-velocity splatter, and he crumpled—the five-second charge of electricity still causing his limbs to twitch and jitter.

Majoqui turned to the man and woman. "Don't move," he said, and they didn't.

He scanned the counters with his one eye. Time was of the essence now. Still, the message must be sent. His machete was gone, but kitchens always held knives.

6

"Cute," said Lieutenant Mike Braden as he held up the nurse's cell phone he'd dug out from behind the cushion of the taxi's backseat.

They were in the city of Gunwood near a strip club called Elephant Guns.

"Dead end," said Detective Randy Nolan.

"What now?" asked Braden.

"Now," said Jim Black, "we get busy trying to figure out who this scumbag is."

"Mike," I said, "I'd like to head over to the house from the picture and see what Billy's come up with."

Mike nodded. "Sure, go ahead. I'll liaison with Denver and see if they've come up with anything from the security feed at the hospital."

I went back to my car, hopped in, and felt Pilgrim nuzzle my shoulder with his nose. "Hey there, buddy. Thanks for saving my bacon back there." I rubbed his nose and scratched under his chin. He's a big Shepherd from Czechoslovakia with teeth like a crocodile and the sweetest disposition in the Universe—unless you make him mad—then he's like Bill Bixby when he played the Hulk on the old TV show— *"You wouldn't like me when I'm angry."*

Pilgrim rides in the back of my patrol car. There's no backseat. Instead, there's a platform with a cage across the windows, a back windshield, and a slider between the front seats so I can let him see what's going on while I'm driving.

I looked at my watch, ten minutes after three, and started driving toward downtown Denver. The man in the picture, Gerald Meyer, was the president of Denver Community Bank. He was fifty-seven years old, with a thirty-one-year-old wife and two kids; a boy seven and a girl ten. The house was east of Colorado Boulevard on Eighth Avenue, not too far from the Governor's Mansion.

I radioed my destination to dispatch and tried to bring the suspect's face back to mind. His license said his name was Juan Martinez, but I was sure that was bologna. This guy was too good to give out his real name.

I've been a cop for six years and a K9 handler for five, plus four years working dogs in the Marine Corps before that. I did two tours in Iraq and another two in Afghanistan. We lost a lot of good men and good dogs to IEDs and snipers, but we took out a lot of bad guys and sniffed out a lot of bombs that saved troops' lives too.

Pilgrim's my second dog since joining the Sheriff's Office. My first dog, Sampson, died in the line of duty while saving me and a bunch of middle school kids.

I'm married with a three-year-old daughter. My wife, Jolene, is the best thing that ever happened to me. And then she did one better by giving me a daughter, Marla.

My cell phone vibrated in my pocket; it was my lieutenant, Mike.

"Got a couple of pictures from the security cameras," he said. "They aren't great, but they're something. I'm having them sent out to every agency in a four-state radius. Should be on your computer in a few minutes."

"Thanks," I said. "Hey, what's Billy Mack's number; he's at the house, right?"

"Yeah, him and a Denver cop." He gave me the number. "If you get there and you think he might show up, let me know, and I'll send a few uniforms over to help."

"Will do," I said and hung up. I punched in Billy's number. He's a good guy, made detective about a year ago, and solved some tough cases right off the bat. His phone went straight to voice mail. Oh well, I was only a few minutes out.

MAJOQUI HAD FINISHED with the pepper spray and the Taser and graduated to the knife. He'd cut out both their tongues and the woman's eyes—after the pepper spray, of course. He left the old man his eyes so that he would have to watch what Majoqui did to his wife and children.

The knife was a Global, eight-inch Chef's Knife. Majoqui had seen one in a fancy store in Los Angeles years ago. It was priced at over a hundred dollars. At the time, Majoqui had thought it ridiculous, but now that he'd used it on meat, he had to admit it was well worth the money. He'd just taken off the old man's thumb with it, and even the joint hadn't given him the least bit of trouble. The man had screamed and blubbered through the dishtowel stuffed in his mouth, but the sound was too muffled to make it much beyond the enormous kitchen. The woman was nearly played out, so Majoqui slapped the man hard across the face to make sure he was paying attention. He then walked behind the woman's chair and jerked her head up by the hair. He laid the knife to her throat and slid it across. The man screamed and shook as his wife bled out before him. Majoqui let her lifeless face drop to the table—the same table where she and her husband had been drinking coffee just a short while before.

It was time for the children.

Majoqui sighed. He did not take pleasure in the suffering and death of others. But in truth, it did not bother him greatly either. It was merely something that had to be done. Majoqui had not made this man cheat Mara; that had been his own choice. And choices—all choices—have consequences.

He laid the knife on the table in front of the man, fresh with his wife's blood, and looked up toward the stairs in the other room. The stairs led to the children's rooms. The man saw the look and screamed louder, his voice going guttural as he rocked his chair back and forth. Majoqui couldn't make out the man's words due to the gag and only a stump of a tongue, but he understood the sentiments well. The man's face was flushed with blood—nearly purple—with thick veins standing out on his forehead and at his temples. Sweat slicked his skin and soaked his shirt. Good, the message was getting through. He would take the knowledge to Hell with him.

Majoqui turned his back on the man and started for the stairs. It was as he passed the island in the center of the kitchen that he heard the sound—just a rustle of clothing—but it was enough—because there should have been no sound. He started to turn when the first bullet hit him, low in the back, square in the kidney. It felt like a hard punch, and he spun with the force of the impact. The second and third bullets plowed into his stomach, stealing his wind and blanking his mind. He doubled over and to the side, hitting the cold granite of the counter and bouncing to the tiled floor—not quite sure how he'd ended up there or where or who he was. There was more gunfire, the small pieces of copper-jacketed lead sizzling over him at scorching velocity.

Clarity forced itself over his befuddled state—it was the detective —the one in the business suit—who he'd shot in the chest—*had he been wearing a vest? No.* Majoqui had seen the blood. But Majoqui *was* wearing a vest, and it suddenly dawned on him that most or possibly all of the hits he'd just taken had probably been stopped by it. He shook his head, pulled the gun from his waistband, and dragged himself across the floor by his fingertips, careful to keep the island between the downed officer and himself. It was hard because he only had the one eye, and he had to crane his neck at an impossible angle to see the island. When he was on the other side, he struggled to a kneeling position. Quickly he checked himself. His fingers came out from under the vest with slight smears of blood, but nothing else. If the bullets had punctured him, his blood would be pouring out just as the banker's wife's blood had poured from her throat.

The counter was only about four feet high, and Majoqui

hazarded a peek over the edge. The bark of a gun and shattered pieces of granite sprayed his face, stinging his forehead and tapping against the bandage over his eye. He ducked down. This was taking too long. So many gunshots might be heard, even through these walls. Police might be on the way.

Majoqui got down on his belly and crawled to the edge of the island, thinking that if the detective were still on his back, he might not be able to see over his own body to where Majoqui was. He saw the man; there was much blood—too much blood for him to still be alive—stupid American police—why couldn't they die like they were supposed to? He was lying on his back, just as Majoqui had thought. He was breathing hard, his chest and belly rising and falling fast and shallow. He held the gun with one hand, the barrel swinging back and forth weakly. At that angle, the detective would be able to see him if he stood, but not while he hugged the floor on his stomach.

In the prone position, Majoqui took careful aim. He fired five times. There was more blood, and then the detective wearing the business suit was still. Taking no chances, Majoqui crawled over to him. When he was close enough, he shot him again, this time in the side of the head.

Standing, Majoqui pulled the magazine from the butt of his gun. There were three bullets left and one in the chamber. The spare magazines were in the hospital bag on the other counter. He pried the gun from the dead detective's fingers, then stripped two other magazines from a leather holder on the man's belt. These bullets were nine-millimeter, whereas the gun he'd taken from the police officer at the hospital was a forty caliber. They were not interchangeable. Still, two guns were not a bad thing.

Majoqui saw that the bank president had overturned his chair and was struggling to get free. Majoqui had no fear of this. The tape that bound him was strong, and the man was not.

The guns felt heavy in his hands. He was very tired, and he ached everywhere. Still, there was more to be done. He would not be able to take the same amount of time he had with the wife—no—he would have to do this quickly now.

The acrid stench of cordite and blood hung heavy in the air. He sighed again, shook his head, and took a deep breath, hoping to clear his head. He put both guns in his waistband and started up the stairs for the children.

7

Tamera Sun threw off the covers and sat up in bed. She was tired—bone-tired—and her feet still hurt, but she could not sleep. Every time she closed her eyes, she saw the man with the doctor's shirt and the bandage. He had looked so sad, so hurt and lost. Or was she just projecting?

Miranda snuggled up close to her, purring. Tamera picked her up and rubbed her cheek against the downy-like softness of the kitty's fur.

Kansas and her family were just one state away, but they might just as well be on Jupiter. She was dead to them, ever since she drove away with Kyle. He was two years older than her and had been kicked out of his parent's house after he was arrested for dealing some fake meth to an undercover cop. Tamera didn't take drugs. Oh, she'd experimented, some pot, a little coke, a couple of X-pills at raves and the like, but no meth, or crank, or ice, nothing that would turn her into a junky or meth whore. If Kyle had been into real meth, she'd never have gone with him, but the phony stuff didn't really bother her. That had been almost two years ago, and Kyle was long gone, taken up with that fake blond, Susan Fletcher, with her pouty lips and perfect bubble butt. Her mom and dad wouldn't take her calls, and all her letters had been returned unopened. She'd thought about hopping a bus and just showing up on their doorstep, but the thought of her father's stern face and her mother's shaking of the head put an end to that. It wasn't that her father was mean or that he'd beat her, but she knew she'd disappointed them and that they felt betrayed. They were proud people, and proud people took things like that hard.

At least she had Miranda. Miranda loved her, and she loved Miranda back. Miranda kept her from being lonely. Only there was another kind of loneliness, a loneliness that Miranda couldn't help.

He seemed so gentle, so kind. His voice was soft and his eye, that smooth, mellow brown. She didn't feel foolish for giving him her number like she had. She didn't even feel shame at his rejection. She was just sorry that he wasn't interested, sorry that they would never get the chance to see where things might have gone. Tamera hated missed opportunities. She felt that most of her life had been made up of just that, and she didn't want to spend another minute missing what might be. She'd always been a good judge of character, except maybe for Kyle, and she'd gotten some kind of vibe from the guy in the doctor's shirt that made her feel … safe. At least he could have told her his name so she wouldn't have to keep thinking of him as the *guy in the doctor's shirt* or the *guy with the bandage* or *the guy with one eye.* She decided to make up a name for him. She would call him … Simon … Dr. Simon.

She hugged Miranda close to her and said the name over and over.

I PARKED a few houses down the street from the banker's place. Cops never park right in front of anyone's house. It's an ambush thing—we don't like them. Of course, seeing the Denver car and Billy's black SUV in the driveway made a lie of my claim. *Kids!* I just shook my head and started toward the front door, keeping to the shadows as much as possible, because … well … just in case … habit. I walked up the three stairs to the front porch and angled myself off to the right of the door before knocking softly. It was after four in the morning, and I didn't want to wake the children.

No answer.

I knocked again, a little louder this time.

Still nothing, only ... I thought I heard something, like maybe a footstep. I listened closer. Outside, morning birds were starting to chirp and whistle, and crickets still sounded off. But inside, all was quiet, all except ... I stepped closer to the door ... my head inclining in, trying to listen ... my ear close to the ornate wood ... closer ... closer ...

A hole punched through the door just above my head, splinters of wood peppering my forehead and face. I jerked back as three more holes filled the space my head had just occupied. Light from inside poured out through the neat round holes like laser beams. Somehow my gun was in my hand, and I fired two shots back in answer.

I toggled my radio mic and demanded the air for 'shots fired.' Dispatch already knew my location and would be sending Denver cars.

Tactics required that I wait for backup, but the reality was, a friend and colleague was in there. And if he wasn't fighting, he was either dead or hurt, not to mention there were children inside.

No more holes were punching through the door, so I clenched my teeth, took a step back, and smashed into it with my shoulder. The door was solid, but I'm five-ten and a little over two-hundred pounds —none of it fat. The door frame gave, slapping the door inward hard. I was inside, scanning with my gun sites. There was a flash to my right, and I ducked as a bullet shattered a floor lamp next to me. There was another gunshot, and I fired at a blur of movement as it darted out the back door on the far side of the kitchen. I was about to give chase when I heard the whimper from the stairs. I made my way over, trying to cover everything with my gun as I did. What I saw made my mouth go dry. A little boy and a little girl, both lying on the stairs, dropped like sacks of grain, their hands, feet, and mouths duct-taped. It looked like the girl's arm was broken. They both stared at me, their eyes big and filled with fear.

I held my finger to my mouth, trying to keep them quiet, hoping my uniform and badge would let them know I was here to help. I plucked them up from their haphazard positions on the stairs and laid them on the landing. The girl cried out when I set her down, probably because of her arm. Then I left them. It was hard, they both started crying and screaming beneath the tape, but I had to make sure it was safe. And I had to see if there was anyone else I could save.

I called dispatch again, telling them I had one suspect that ran out the back door toward the East and to have Denver start setting up a perimeter. I made my way to the kitchen, sweat running down my face, my heart racing in my ears. I wasn't scared—not then—not till later—*I was mad.* Enraged. I thought of my own daughter.

Billy was first. He was shot to pieces. Then the Denver officer, most of his face was gone. The banker was next. His ears had been cut off, and one of his thumbs was missing. He'd been shot point-blank in the top of the head; his thinning hair showed gunpowder stipple burnt into his scalp. It looked fresh; blood still oozed from the wound.

But then I saw his wife ... and suddenly ... I *was* scared. I was used to bad stuff—the aftermath of battles—I'd been through two messy wars and seen plenty on the streets—but this—this was something completely different. This was like something from a nightmare— like something from Hell.

Sirens sounded in the distance, coming closer. Good. Because suddenly ... I didn't want to be alone in that kitchen anymore.

8

Tamera had just drifted off to sleep when her phone jingled the Lady Gaga song that she reserved for unknown callers. She picked up and heard Dr. Simon's voice. She knew him instantly because she'd been replaying their conversation over and over for the past few hours in her head.

"Hello," he said. "I'm the man you met earlier tonight, the one with the bandage on my eye."

"I know,' she said. "I was hoping you'd call."

"I'm sorry it's so late ..."

"I don't care," she broke in. "Do you want to come over?"

"Yes," he said. "But I'm in trouble ... I ... need help."

Tamera closed her eyes and smiled. "I can come get you. Where are you?"

He gave her an address. "Don't tell anyone," he said.

"I won't. It'll take me about half an hour to get down there."

"Good." He hung up.

Tamera threw on some clothes and grabbed her purse and keys. She lived in Gunwood, near Colorado Boulevard and Cherry Street, just a few blocks from the diner where she worked. She kissed Miranda on the nose and locked the door of her apartment behind her. Gunwood was a rough neighborhood. It was the smallest city in Colorado, only one point six square miles, but it had more bars, strip clubs, and massage parlors than any three cities in the state. She hopped into her 1991 yellow VW Beetle and pumped the gas pedal five times before starting her up. The engine backfired twice, and then she was off and running. A large, round peace symbol made of purple plastic hung from her rearview mirror, swaying back and forth.

She was so happy and excited. Just before drifting off to sleep, she had prayed to the universal deities of the cosmos that she would meet him again. And just like that, he'd called. Vaguely, she wondered what kind of trouble he was in, not that it mattered; everyone was in trouble from time to time. Most of the time, she was in trouble herself. If it wasn't her parents or Kyle, it was rent or the utilities, or the Beetle's engine acting up, or Miranda sick or coughing up hairballs. In her few short years of living, she learned that trouble was the natural state of humankind and that suffering was the consequential result of that trouble. Tamera considered it her job to help stop some of the suffering whenever she was able, just like she'd done for Miranda, and look how well that had turned out.

She was out of Gunwood in no time and into the city of Denver. It was getting close to five in the morning, and the first of several stages of rush hour was starting. There seemed to be a lot of cops out. She'd already passed three police cars, and she'd seen several small groups of police officers walking past stores and along the sidewalks.

Tamera turned east from Colorado onto Seventh Avenue, stopping at every stop sign, and there were a lot of them. To the north, she saw more police cars, their lights flashing like exploding flowers.

They were pretty.

MAJOQUI LAY beneath a jumble of bushes in the backyard of a large house about seven blocks from where he had run. He checked the cell phone he'd taken from the banker. It had a password, but the banker had told him what it was even before Majoqui sprayed the pepper spray into his wife's eyes and mouth.

The woman, Tamera, said she would be there in thirty minutes; it was almost time.

It was amazing all the things cell phones could do. They acted as clocks and calendars and notebooks and ... practically everything. Amazing.

His left kidney hurt where the detective wearing the suit had shot him. So did his face. He still wore the bulletproof vest. It had served him as well, just as the Saint Christopher amulet had. Perhaps the old witch woman's spells were still working for him. He would have to leave her a gift when he returned home, perhaps some chickens, maybe even a goat, along with some money, of course.

Majoqui had been surprised when the police officer smashed through the door of the banker's house. He'd heard the knocking and dropped the children; then, he had shot several times through the door. He expected to have killed whoever was standing there. He was an excellent shot, after all, with natural talent. But instead, the man had crashed through the door and, surprise of surprises, it had been the same police officer who had shot him in the chest earlier that evening. The one who had a monster the others called a K9.

The sight of the police officer had unnerved Majoqui, and that was not something easily done. He had barely had time to kill the banker before running out the back door and into the darkness of night.

Twigs tickled the back of his neck, and some form of insect was making its way across the bare skin of his ankle. But it was better than lying in a ditch filled with human excrement and the stench of rotting animals. Still, the experience had only reinforced his earlier belief that killing police officers was generally bad business. He hardly thought that this much would be made of killing a simple banker and his family. No. He knew that the swarm of police was because he had killed one of their own and that they would not rest until they had exacted vengeance; until they had made an example of him. It was the same in every culture; Mara was no different. It was the reason he'd been sent to kill the banker and his family. The only difference was that Majoqui knew himself to be the best. He had never failed, and he had always escaped. Tonight would be no different. The spirits watched over him, and if they proved to be too busy to watch over him, he would do what he had to do himself.

His eye was the worst now. He kept trying to open it without thinking, and the stitches would pull and tear at his skin. He no longer wore the bandage; white was not wise to wear when hiding in the dark, and he had found it made him look most frightening while torturing the banker and his wife—that and talking through his teeth added terror. Majoqui had looked at himself in the banker's bathroom mirror after he had tied them up and gagged them, but before he'd cut out their tongues. He hoped he would look more like himself when the stitches and wires came out, and the swelling went down. He had always been considered quite handsome by the señoritas, and he would not want this to change. Of course, most women were like his mother—whores. Giving their bodies away to men—but never for free—no, they always wanted something in return; money, jewelry, food, gifts, even time—but always—always something. Still, he enjoyed them and would not be happy if he were left horribly scarred.

Majoqui held his breath. Something was coming. Something quiet was hunting him, and although he hadn't felt fear since the day he'd become a man, he felt it now. Because something about what was hunting him was familiar. It was familiar, and it was close.

9

P ilgrim is the best tracking dog I've ever trained. Most of the dogs I schooled in the Marines were bomb dogs, used primarily to sniff out IEDs, but there were a few that I'd trained for tracking and good old police work. We call it apprehension training, meaning that the dogs could track suspects and then take hold of them at the end of the track—take hold with their teeth, that is. Pilgrim is a dual-purpose dog, trained in two separate philosophies of K9 work. Apprehension and narcotics. Pilgrim can sniff out drugs like nobody's business—that's one philosophy. Right now, I was using him for the other one—tracking.

It didn't take long for backup to arrive at the banker's house. About a thousand Denver police cars poured into the scene. My Lieutenant, Mike Braden, showed up just a couple of minutes later. Once the kids were taken care of, I leashed up Pilgrim and took two Denver SWAT cops with me for cover and started a track from the back door of the house where I'd last seen the suspect.

~

PILGRIM WAITED AS PATIENTLY AS he could as the Alpha slipped his harness over his head and clipped the metal clasp of the leash to the tracking loop. It wasn't easy. Pilgrim lived for the track. His body quivered with suppressed anticipation as he barely managed to hold himself in check, awaiting the Alpha's command.

Prey.

The hunt.

He knew the spoor. He'd smelled it as the Alpha approached the house. Pilgrim tried to warn him, but as powerful as the Alpha could be, he sometimes seemed to have trouble discerning the simplest of things. Pilgrim growled, just as he had when he'd warned the Alpha about the man preparing to attack earlier. The Alpha hadn't been far away, just a hundred yards or so, but the Alpha hadn't heard him. And then he'd gone right up to the door, and the fight was on, with Pilgrim locked in the car and not able to help.

That was about to change.

Now it was Pilgrim's turn.

THE SWAT GUY on my left carried one of the new Commando rifles with the stubby barrel and .223 ammo that could shoot through a brick wall and still take out the bad guy. The cop on my right sported a custom Browning 12-gage shotgun. As for me — my Smith and Wesson .45 caliber 4506 was in its holster. My job is to watch the dog while my cover officers watch everything else. Me and Pilgrim are considered the less-than-lethal part of the trio. Only I don't think Pilgrim quite understands that aspect of his role. Theoretically, our job is to take the suspect out without killing him, if possible—if not— well, that's what SWAT's for.

We went straight to the fence, a six-footer. Pilgrim climbed it like it wasn't even there. I followed him. It was a little harder for the SWAT guys, what with all their gear and everything; they wore Kevlar helmets, Kevlar gloves, Kevlar goggles, and extra-thick Kevlar vests that could withstand anything less than a tactical nuke, but like most SWAT guys, they were supermen and made up the time quickly.

Pilgrim went halfway through the yard—stopped—jerked his head to the left—trotted over to an upscale doghouse that probably cost more than my actual house, and sniffed. He sniffed long and hard, then turned and went up the stairs to an elaborate deck that must have commanded a magnificent view of the mountains.

I had one SWAT guy look in the doghouse while the other came upstairs with me. If the guy had actually been *in* the doghouse, I'm sure Pilgrim would have eaten him up—still, even dogs make mistakes, so it's always best to double-check. Trust but verify is the K9 motto.

Pilgrim gave the deck a quick once over—nose to the wood—then scampered back down the steps and to the far end of the yard.

The message was clear; the suspect had considered hiding in the doghouse—decided against it—tried the deck—ditched that idea too, and made his way to the opposite side of the yard.

The gate was standing open. In K9, we consider that a clue.

Pilgrim checked the track—quartered back and forth—went through the gate and to the west. Pilgrim doesn't track fast, but he's incredibly accurate. Tracking is tough work. The dog sniffs a combination of ground disturbance and human scent, constantly filtering out conflicting odors like food, trash, animal spoor, and all the non-disturbed ground.

We curved to the north—went through another gate—through a backyard with a gurgling water feature and over another six-foot fence. We passed through a narrow greenbelt with an asphalt bike-path running the center, and then over another fence that showed fresh damage where one of the boards had splintered, and into a backyard roughly the size of Inverness Golf Course. The grass rolled in gentle hills up to a covered patio with twin barbecues and a retractable awning. I could see a couple of footprints in the dew-kissed grass just ahead of Pilgrim. He was right on target, and we were getting close.

We rounded the corner, passed through the open gate to the front yard, and made it almost to the sidewalk when three black males, all wearing hoodies, jumped out a first-floor window from the residence across the street. One of them tripped, did a somersault in the grass, and came to his feet looking right at us. The other two stumbled into him, coming up short.

"Let me see your hands!" yelled the SWAT guy holding the shotgun.

Now I'm no genius, but when a fully kitted SWAT guy points a shotgun at me and tells me to show him my hands ... I'd show him my hands.

The burglar that somersaulted immediately stuck his hand down the front of his pants.

Go figure.

The shotgun and the Commando sounded in unison, and the guy with his hands in his pants just sort of flew back into his friends, knocking them both down. My SWAT guys advanced, flashlights beaming from the front of their smoking barrels.

Neither of the other men wanted any part of that. Both were quick to show their empty hands and prone out on the lawn.

Pilgrim watched, whining, every muscle taught with anticipatory longing to join the battle. I tightened up on the lead and stroked his head as the SWAT officer with the Commando cuffed all three of them. I called dispatch over the radio and told them shots were fired, we had three detained, and that we needed rescue for gunshot wounds to a suspect.

Commando reached into the shot suspect's pants and pulled out a black .25 caliber Italian job. He finished the pat-down on him, then did the same for the other two, coming up with a switchblade and a .38 special with the serial number filed down. There were also three pillowcases that I hadn't even noticed, filled with jewelry, coins, cash, cell phones, and a laptop.

Burglars alright.

But not the guy we were looking for.

When Commando finished with the frisks, he moved back to the injured suspect and turned him over. The bluish-white cast of his

LED flashlight showed a horrible mess where his chest should have been. A slug of lead, roughly the length and width of a grown man's thumb, had wreaked havoc on his muscles and bones.

The beam of light moved up, and I saw a much smaller hole in the center of his forehead. I looked back at Commando, and he nodded. A perfectly placed shot. Commando pulled off a glove and placed two fingers on the man's throat, but he was just going through the motions; heart and brain both obliterated before he could pull the gun from his pants.

That's why I like to take SWAT with me when I'm on a track.

Shotgun was standing to my right, and he said, "We've been looking for these guys for a while. They've been hitting houses all over Denver; raped a seventeen-year-old girl after they tied up her parents. Bad boys."

Well, there was one less now. That was something. But our murderer of old ladies, nurses, bankers, and cops was still out there, and we were stuck waiting for backup and rescue.

PILGRIM STARED at the two men, smelling the dead man's blood and wanting to add theirs to it. But more than that, he wanted the Alpha to continue the track. They were close ... so close. The night air brought his prey's fear scent to him.

Strong.

Close.

He could taste it. The man that had tried to hurt the Alpha.

Twice, Pilgrim tried to pull the Alpha toward their target, and twice, the Alpha ordered him to stay.

Pilgrim complied ... but his loving, animal brain didn't like it. Pilgrim wanted ... no ... he needed ... to protect the Alpha.

So yes ... he complied ... against all his instincts ... he obeyed the Alpha.

No ... Pilgrim didn't like it at all.

10

———

Majoqui heard the yelling and the gunshots. They were very close—maybe fifty yards over on the other side of the block. He was trying to decide if he should stay put or move when he saw the small, yellow, round car come down the street toward him. The headlights were off, just like he'd told her. He jumped from the bushes and ran to the car, waving his arms for her to stop. She must have seen him because the car lurched sharply and then died.

Sirens sounded from every direction, all getting closer. Majoqui opened the passenger's door and squeezed his way into the cramped seat.

"What's going on?" asked the girl.

He shook his head and held up a finger. "No time, señorita. Drive—out of here—quickly." He wasn't sure what her reaction would be, and he was ready to break her neck or suffocate her if necessary. But she just smiled, her eyes big and excited. She raised her eyebrows and said, "Okay." She pumped the gas pedal five times and started the car.

They passed two police cars and a fire engine on their way out of the neighborhood. Majoqui slouched down in the seat, hiding his face with his arms and hands. He didn't sit up until they were far away and could no longer hear the sirens.

Once they were in her apartment, she led him to her bedroom and sat him on the edge of the bed. She took out a first aid kit, knelt beside him, and cleaned his cheek and eye. The stitches had torn, and there was some blood, so she dabbed the area with antibiotic cream and covered it with a big square of white gauze that she secured with medical tape. She went to a dresser and brought him a joint.

"For the pain," she said. She lit the small marijuana cigarette for him and waited until he was done.

She asked him if he was hurt anywhere else, and he stripped off his pants to show her where the stitches in his leg had ripped. She treated them just as she had his eye, showing no reaction to his nakedness.

"Who is the doctor now?" he asked. But his lips smiled.

She smiled back at him and smoothed down the last of the tape.

"You must have questions," he said.

"Only if you want to tell me."

"Why are you helping me?"

She closed the kit and looked up at him. "Because you need it—and because I can."

Majoqui leaned over and kissed her. She kissed him back.

Later, when they had finished, he lit a joint while playing with her hair with his free hand. Her bed was small, but with half her body draped over him, it was big enough.

Majoqui took in the room. It was neat, with a small end table and a dresser. Multi-colored bears danced along the walls bordering the ceiling. There was a poster of some grungy looking rock star that Majoqui didn't recognize. A large water bong rested in a corner, and candles decorated the top of the dresser. A beat-up radio with an expandable antenna sat on the end table, quietly spitting out some tune that sounded like a mixture of Joplin and static. The apartment was sparse, with only a few items of furniture, but they were in good repair and tasteful.

The girl herself was like the room, a strange mixture of eras, blending today with the sixties. She was pretty, not beautiful, but attractive, comfortable ... in the same way the room was comfortable and pleasing to the eye. Her body was soft and light, small-breasted, with rounded hips and smooth thighs.

She stroked his hairless chest, teasing the edges of the white bandage with her fingernails. They were tapered, but not long, and painted green.

"Will you stay?" she asked.

"Yes, for now."

She rubbed her cheek against his ribs. "Good. I like you."

"Are there any others?"

She looked up at him. "You mean men?"

"Yes."

She shook her head. "No. Not anymore. My last boyfriend, Dashon, was a jerk. He wanted me to quit my job at the diner and turn tricks for him. He used to smack me around when he was high. I hate mean drunks."

"If I stay, there can be no others. You understand?" He looked down at her so she could read his eyes.

"Sure," she said, reaching up and brushing his cheek with her fingertips. "Sure, I understand. There won't be any others. I promise."

Majoqui nodded, kissed her gently. "My name is Majoqui."

She scrunched her eyes and smiled. "Ma-hoe-kee?"

He smiled back and touched the tip of her nose playfully. "Yes."

"It's beautiful." She kissed him, soft and deep.

"You will be safe with me," Majoqui said.

Her lips again found his as she breathed the words, "I believe you."

11

B y the time I got home, it was after ten in the morning. I was dead tired. My wife Jolene sat at the kitchen table watching my three-year-old daughter, Marla, eat pancakes and eggs.

Pilgrim padded into the room ahead of me and nuzzled first Jolene then Marla. Marla giggled and slipped him a forkful of eggs. Pilgrim nibbled off the fork without touching the tines.

Jolene shook her head. "Pilgrim."

He looked at her, his ears flattening in guilt, and wagged his tail. He scampered out through the doggy door into the backyard. Big tough police dog.

Jolene looked back at me, smiling. "Tough night?"

"Brutal," I said, bending over to kiss her. Her lips were fresh and soft and helped to wake me up.

"Sit down," she said, "before you fall down. I'll get you some coffee."

I kissed my daughter on the lips, tasting maple syrup and butter, and collapsed into the chair next to her while Jolene got my favorite mug and filled it from the pot. I take my coffee the way I did in the Marines; black, bitter, and hot, no preservatives.

Jolene pointed toward my hip, her eyebrows creasing, looking worried. "Where's your gun?"

I was carrying a spare the department armorer had issued me, but it was a Beretta. Nothing gets past my wife.

I stretched my neck and took a sip of the coffee. "The department's doing some ... tests on it."

"Tests? Ballistics? Were you in a shooting again?" She sat down and took my hands in hers. "Are you okay?"

"I'm fine, dear." I told her about my night, careful not to give too many details with Marla sitting beside us. When I was done, she got up and hugged me tight, kissing my head and crying softly. I hugged her back and told her everything was okay. Marla asked why mommy was crying, and Jolene told her that mommy was just being silly and that everything was alright. She cleared her throat, wiped her eyes, and told me to stay with Marla while she started a bath for me. I tried to tell her it was okay and that I just needed some sleep, but she ignored me and went upstairs and started the tub going. When she came back, she took Marla to our bedroom and set her up with a coloring book and crayons. Pilgrim napped in the corner. She left the bathroom door open a crack so she could keep an eye on her while she helped me out of my uniform and into the tub.

Not that she really needed to. Pilgrim loved Marla more than he loved steak. And he loved steak a lot. King Kong couldn't get within a football field of Marla with Pilgrim guarding her.

The water was nearly blistering, just like my coffee, and felt like heaven. Jolene took a washcloth and dribbled water over my hair and face, then dipped it back into the water and repeated the process over and over until I was so relaxed, I slipped into a gentle doze, half awake, half asleep; very peaceful. When the water started to cool, she toweled me dry, led me by the hand to our bed, and tucked me under the covers as if I were a little boy. She kissed me on the forehead and told me to call if I needed anything. Then she took Marla and left the room, closing the door behind her.

I looked at the clock, 11:45.

I tried to sleep.

When I closed my eyes, I saw the bank president's wife's face.

I pulled a pillow over my eyes.

I heard the little girl cry out as I set her on the landing. It jerked me awake. I didn't even know I'd fallen asleep.

I closed my eyes again. I saw the kitchen table, smelled the blood. The children started screaming behind the duct tape covering their mouths as I left to chase their attacker.

I sat up in bed, breathing hard. I looked at the clock, 11:51.

I lay back down, staring at the ceiling. *I should have killed him. If I'd killed him, those children would still have parents. The nurse and the Denver cops and Billy Mack would all still be alive.* I saw him coming at me, felt the machete slice past my face, heard the metallic *thunk* of bullets punching through metal around me, felt the heavy recoil of my Smith and Wesson as it bucked in my hands. I saw the calm determination in his eyes through the muzzle flash—determination to kill me. I saw Pilgrim attack, only this time, the man snapped Pilgrim's neck with ease and kept coming at me, my bullets hitting him square on but bouncing off his chest like he was Superman. And he kept coming—closer and closer as I pumped round after round into him —closer until he was on me—reaching—reaching—reaching for my eyes and my tongue and my ears—and the children cried, only this time it wasn't the bank president's children—it was Marla—my Marla—crying for her daddy.

I sat up again, sweat beading my forehead. The clock blinked 11:59. I could still smell blood—taste it in the back of my throat.

I was still sitting there when Jolene came into the room.

"Are you okay?" she asked.

I looked at her, feeling my hands start to shake. "Maybe not," I said.

She came to bed, gently pushed me back, and lay down next to me.

"I put Marla down for a nap."

"Those poor kids," I said. "I should have killed him. I should have ...."

She pulled my face to her chest, stroking the back of my head and whispering softly. "You did what you could. Now you rest—rest and remember we love you. Marla and I love you."

I tried to be strong, to hold back the tears, but then I remembered Billy Mac had a wife and three young children—children like the little boy and girl on the landing—children like my Marla—and then I wasn't strong—I wasn't strong at all. And she held me and rocked me and loved me and finally I did sleep. I slept, and I didn't dream at all.

12

Majoqui Cabrera met with three members of MS-13 in the diner where Tamera Sun worked. All three were tatted and packing and looked like trouble just waiting to happen. And all three paid total respect to this, a most honored member of Mara. Each listened intently to his instructions. Each memorized the details of what was required of him. None of them spoke out of turn, waiting for him to address them before offering any insight or information or asking qualifying questions.

Majoqui made sure they understood the importance of his instructions. They were Mara, but they were not from El Salvador; they were from California, the land of Hollywood and movie stars. Majoqui wanted to impress upon them that Mara's reputation was at stake and that no deviation would be tolerated.

He looked at the television screen, seeing the face of his nemesis. The man with the monster dog, the police officer Majoqui had missed with his bullets and his machete, a thing he would not have believed possible. Because of this man, he had failed to deliver the message that was to be sent in the way it was meant to be sent. The children had survived, which could be construed as weakness. Mara must never be thought of as weak.

A blurry picture of Majoqui appeared on the screen, taken from hospital security cameras. It was followed by an artist's rendition of how he would look with his eye sewn shut. Majoqui was not worried about being recognized. He had died his hair blond and spiked it with gel. He had removed the stitches gluing his eyelid to his cheek. The vision in that eye was severely blurred, but he felt confidant it was only temporary. He wore garish eyeliner and black eye shadow on his lids and under his eyes, and he looped a ring through a set of the holes left on his cheek from the stitches. He wore a long-sleeved shirt, buttoned to the collar to hide both his injuries and his tattoos.

To the first man, he said, "The rifle must be able to be assembled quickly. It must be lightweight, and the scope must be accurate."

To the second man, he said, "The motorcycle must be fast, but not too loud; I do not want to draw attention."

To the third man, he said, "The witch must be powerful. She will be expensive and should require a blood sacrifice. I will meet with her myself to receive the blessing. She is to have the blade for at least thirteen hours, to pray over and chant and mark."

He looked each in the eye, piercing them to the soul to make certain they truly understood the importance of their tasks. Americans had mostly forgotten the power of the old religion, but Majoqui knew better. He needed only to touch his chest or his leg to remember the Virgin's blessing and protection.

The TV flashed to a video feed of the banker's house, the trees and light posts circled by bright yellow police tape. The house looked different in the daylight, but Majoqui could just make out the bullet holes in the front door if he squinted his bad eye.

Looking back at the men, he asked if they had any questions. They didn't. They seemed like good, dependable men. They had brought him money, disposable cellphones, and a new identity, driving all night from California to Colorado non-stop. Still, they were from Hollywood, the land of corruption and laziness; could they be trusted? Strange, he felt less sure of them, his brothers, than he did of Tamera Sun. He decided to wait to see how they carried out his orders. If they did well, then good. If not—not.

After dismissing them, he finished his coffee and walked back to Tamera's apartment, careful that no one was following him. Outside her door, he waited, listening. Inside, he heard a male voice. *The police?* No, not the police. He opened the door, stepped inside, and closed it quietly behind him. They were in the bedroom.

Majoqui opened the door and saw the man standing over Tamera. He was tall, a mulatto, with grayish skin and striking, blue eyes. Tamera was cowering on the bed, a red handprint flaming her pale, freckle-dotted cheek. Tears ran down her face.

"Who are you?" asked the man, turning and squaring his shoulders, making himself look even bigger than his already impressive size.

Majoqui said nothing. He simply reached down and snapped the antenna off the radio from the end table. Casually, he popped off the rounded ball of metal at the end, leaving a jagged point, and stretched it to its full length, about three feet.

"Oh, really?" said the man. He reached into his pocket and pulled out a butterfly knife. With a flip of his wrist, the handles slapped back, and the blade appeared.

"Dashon, don't, please," cried Tamera from the bed.

"You wanna turn around and walk right outta here, little man," said Dashon.

The antenna flashed, and Dashon was no longer holding the knife. He grabbed his wrist as blood welled around his fingers and streamed to the floor.

Rage flooded the big man's face. He took a half step forward but stopped as the antenna flashed again, opening his cheek under his left eye.

"Ow!" he said.

Another flash, and this time a section of his upper lip flapped loosely, as though no longer supported. More blood flowed.

Majoqui moved with liquid smoothness, coming under and in so that he was behind the big man before he could react, the jagged point of the antenna piercing an eighth inch into his throat.

"If you move," said Majoqui, "I will kill you. Do you understand?"

Dashon started to nod, thought better of it. "Yeah, yeah, man. I got you."

"This woman is no longer yours. She is mine. You will leave, and you will not come back. If you come back, you will die."

"Okay, man," said Dashon, "okay. She ain't worth it. I'm gone. Just let me go. Cool?" A fine mist of blood sprayed from his lip as he spoke.

Majoqui stepped away, the slender rod of steel resting along the seam of his pant leg. He had no fear of the bigger man. If he did not leave, Majoqui would kill him.

Dashon raised his hands, showing surrender, and edged around him. When he got to the door, he looked back as if to say something, but instead gripped his bleeding wrist and quietly left the apartment.

Majoqui put a finger to the red mark on Tamera's face. "He will not come back."

"I didn't invite him," she said, the words catching in little hiccups as she spoke. "I swear I didn't. He just came in and said I was going to work for him and that I just had to accept it."

"I know," said Majoqui, "I believe you." He looked at the end table with its broken radio. "I am sorry about your radio. I will buy you a new one." He collapsed the antenna and slipped it into his pocket.

13

Z iggy was his monicker, and it suited him perfectly, the way most street names do. He was a major doper ... user that is ... not a dealer ... heroin being his drug of choice and couldn't stay still for more than a nano-second. Usually, heroin mellows people out ... slows them down ... not Ziggy.

I took a sip of my coffee and pushed his closer to him. He slurped it noisily and set it back on the table. His head jerked about on his long, skinny, black neck as though he thought someone was going to pounce on him at any second. Maybe someone was.

I wasn't in uniform, just jeans and a tan, short-sleeved t-shirt. In the movies, cops in uniform meet with snitches all the time. In real life, that would cause a sharp decline in snitches.

"This dude is bad, Ziggy. He killed cops, women; he even broke a little girl's arm."

Ziggy held up a hand, his fingers shaking like he had palsy. "I don't like nobody messing with kids," he said. "But I don't know nobody with an eye stitched to his cheek. Man, somebody like that would stand out big time."

"Okay then, what about MS 13 activity?"

His head bobbed up and down like a bobble-head toy. "Heard say a tre of Mara's boys zipped down from the land of fruits and nuts, real fast like. Heard say they was showing tats and colors like they was real proud. Heard say they was fronted by a couple of brothers, Crips, just outside of Sin City and that they messed the brothers up real bad like. Everybody knows Mara's boys. They don't play good with others."

"Any word on why they're making the trip?"

Ziggy poured more sugar into his coffee, which was already roughly the consistency of syrup. "Heard say they was helping one of their own, but that's all I heard say on that." He finished his coffee and started the bird-like twitching of his head again.

I pulled out a twenty and laid it on the table. "Thanks, Ziggy. You hear anything else on these Mara's boys, or on stitch cheek, you give me a call."

He nodded, or at least I think he did—it might have been a twitch —and held up the trembling finger again. "Ziggy'll be listening, that he will, yes sir."

I left the coffee shop and drove to the banker's house. There was crime scene tape stretched from tree to tree all around the place, and Denver detectives and crime lab techs moved in and out and about the house. I sat in my car for a few minutes, trying to recreate the events of last night in my mind; the knock, the bullet holes appearing as if by magic through the door, the gun battle inside the house, the chase, the track, the second gun battle— this one with the burglars— and finally, the culmination of the track.

I swung around to the next block, roughly following the course Pilgrim had taken me on, until I arrived at the point where we lost the track.

After backup took the living burglars away and rescue hauled off the dead man, I had continued the track with two new SWAT guys, and we ended up here. Last night, in the dark, I could only see so much, even with powerful flashlights.

It's amazing how the sun can shed new light on a situation. I knelt down by the bush where Pilgrim had tracked to and searched the grass and dirt beneath and behind it. Obvious signs that someone had lain here were evident. I even found some dried blood on the grass. It wouldn't help catch Stitch, but once we did, it would certainly help convict him. I was hoping for more, maybe a note with his current address and phone number and a picture ID, but there was nothing.

The flattened down grass and disturbed dirt showed that he'd been bedded down for a while, but where'd he go after that? Pilgrim tracked from the bushes to the street, but here the track ended. Usually, that would mean a car picked him up, but the area had been swarming with police, and besides, MS 13 just wasn't that active here in Colorado. It didn't seem likely he'd have a ride set up in advance. Then I remembered his little phone game at the hospital and with the cab.

I called dispatch and had them patch me through to the lead Denver Detective working the case. I told him who I was and where I was and asked him to send a lab tech over to collect the blood evidence. Then I asked him to check all the bodies for their cell phones. I explained how Stitch had played bait and switch with us and how I suspected he might have done the same thing with either the banker's phone or one of the dead cop's phones. Sure enough, none of the bodies had phones with them. He said he'd send the tech to relieve me and that he'd start a search for the phone numbers so they could begin pinging them to try and get a location.

After I hung up, a thought struck me. I had Billy Mac's number. I tried to call him last night when I was on my way over, but there'd been no answer, probably because Billy was already dead. I pulled up my recent calls, and there it was. I knew I should turn it over to Denver so they could ping it, but I figured Stitch had probably already tossed it. *Or maybe he hadn't.* I went ahead and called. He picked up on the first ring, almost as if he were expecting it.

"I have been waiting for you to call," he said.

I recognized the voice instantly. "Who are you?"

"I am going to kill you—you and everything you love."

"Is that why your buddies from California came to visit? Feel like maybe you need a little help?"

Silence.

"That's what I thought," I said. "I'm going to catch you."

"No, you will die. Mara is to be feared, and your death will bring that fear to all your brother policemen."

"I've already beaten you twice. Third time's going to be a charm."

There was a pause like he might be thinking I was right.

"You have strong magic," he said. "I have seen this. But Mara is stronger. Mara and the saints. The next time we meet, you will die."

I was about to say something else, something clever and witty to show he didn't scare me, but he hung up.

I called the Denver detective and gave him Billy's number so they could try a ping. I knew it was too late, that I'd blown the chance by making the call, but they'd have to try anyway. I didn't bother telling him about the call; I felt bad enough already.

After that, I called a buddy of mine from the Marine Corps that worked the streets in Las Vegas named Ron Mobile. Ron was a bomb tech in the war and took some shrapnel from an IED that exploded while he was walking up on it. If he'd been a little closer, he would have been vaporized, bomb suit and all. As it was, he just about died. The pulse wave broke a bunch of bones, and they had to dig out over forty pieces of metal and Kevlar from his chest and legs. One piece of shrapnel had severed his ring finger mid-knuckle, even through the glove. When I visited him in the hospital, he held his stump up under a nostril and said, "I bet you can't get your finger this far up your nose." That's just the kind of guy he is.

"Gil Mason," he said. "How's sleepy town Colorado doing for you? You about bored enough to come out here where the real action is?"

"Pilgrim doesn't like the heat out there. What is it today, like a hundred and ninety degrees?"

He laughed. "Yeah, well, let me think. When was the last time I had to scrape ice off my windshield? Oh yeah, never." He laughed again. "So, what's going down?"

"We had a bad run-in with an MS 13er, and a little bird told me you guys had some Crips tangle with some boys that might be related."

"I don't know about the related part, but we definitely saw some Mara action early this morning. Used a sword or something. Cut one of the Crips so bad he's going to lose an arm, which is a real shame because he has some award-winning art tatted on there that will be a loss to all mankind."

"Got any info on the suspects?"

"Oh yeah," he said. "This is Vegas, baby! We got cameras on the cameras. Got the whole episode from three different angles and in living color."

"Any chance I could get a copy?

"Do the words 'Semper Fi' mean anything? I've got a friend up in investigations who's working it. He'll be glad to know about the connection. He should be able to send it right out."

"Great. Thanks, Ron."

"Anything for the great and terrible Gil Mason, Marine Corps legend and trainer of soft furry things with big sharp teeth. Try not to fall asleep out there, pal."

Sleep, I could use some more, but that wasn't going to happen. I looked at my watch, nearly three. My shift started at seven, which left me just enough time for a quick workout, a shower, and some dinner with the family. But first, I called Jim Black and let him know about the Vegas connection so he could get in contact with them and get the video.

I am going to kill you—you and everything you love.

Too bad he was wearing that Saint Christopher medallion when I shot him.

14

Tamera Sun lay in her bed, smiling. He was the most wonderful man in the world. He even liked her cat. She had been so afraid when Dashon showed up, telling her he'd waited long enough and that she was going to start working the streets tonight. She told him no, and he slapped her hard, so hard the room had tilted, and she thought she might throw up or pass out or both. And then Majoqui had come into the room, and she was afraid all over again, this time for him because she knew how big and strong Dashon was, and she'd heard stories about how he'd messed up guys that got in his way. But Majoqui hadn't been scared at all, and he'd moved so fast and smooth, like Jet Li in that old Lethal Weapon movie. He could have killed Dashon, but he didn't, and she loved him all the more for it. Tamera hated violence; although she had to admit, she did feel a thrill at what he had done to Dashon. She'd seen the fear in Dashon's eyes and a part of her, way deep down, was glad that he had to feel a little bit of what he'd made her feel. Maybe he would realize how terrible it was to do that to someone else and become a better person because of it. She hoped so.

She could tell that Majoqui really hated violence and that he would only use it when he had to, and even then, only for good.

Everything was turning out just as she'd hoped, just as she'd prayed. The universal goddesses were smiling down on her—on both of them.

After Dashon left, they made love again, and he was so gentle, so caring. She hugged Miranda to her, remembering his passion and warmth. She had been right to feel safe with him. No one would hurt her while he was near, and she felt confident that her heart was in no danger. He just didn't feel like the kind of person to play with someone's emotions. He wasn't like her old boyfriend, Kyle. He was real and genuine and good.

Not only was he brave, but he trusted her. He told her about his childhood and how he had to join the gang in order to survive. He told her about his mother and the men and how he protected her from them once he was old enough. How he supported her so she wouldn't have to be a prostitute anymore.

She'd seen the awful things the news said about him, about killing the man and woman and the police and the nurse, but he'd explained that it was all a lie. That they were trying to set him up for what they, the police, had actually done. He said they did things like this all the time, blaming the gangs for their crimes. He was just in the wrong place at the wrong time, so they were using him as cover.

Tamera had seen a thousand crime shows on TV and at the movies where the police and the government did things just like this. Even Kyle used to say how everything was a conspiracy. Kyle used to take her to parties where the pot was plentiful, and the discussions sooner or later always turned to politics. Nearly everyone at these parties would say that 911 was an inside job sponsored by the Bushes. They'd show videos and pictures proving no airplane hit the Pentagon, and they'd say that fire couldn't burn hot enough to melt steel, and there had to be explosives secretly hidden throughout the Twin Towers for them to fall the way they did. They even showed scientific proof of how the wispy lines of vapor in the sky from jets weren't contrails like she'd learned in school, but instead were chemicals the government had been secretly spraying for decades to give people cancer and to keep them pacified. Chemtrails they called them. It was weird stuff, but they had lots of proof for what they said, and Kyle believed it, and even though Kyle was mean and hurtful, he was very smart. Smarter than she was.

Majoqui was even smarter than Kyle, and he was nice. If he told her the police were lying, then they were lying. She trusted him.

Tamera gave Miranda a final hug, then jumped up off the bed and started getting dressed. She had to work tonight.

MAJOQUI SAT outside the Cherokee County Sheriff's Office, parked in Tamera's yellow VW. He had purchased a laptop with a wifi device so he could search the Internet. With just a few keystrokes, he had learned the shifts and times of shifts of the commissioned deputies and where headquarters, as well as the scattered sub-stations, were. Even better, he had found an app that turned his also recently purchased smartphone into a police scanner, complete with the Cherokee County SO's radio frequencies.

He didn't know what kind of personal vehicle the sergeant drove, or even his name, but he knew the face. That and the fact that he was a K9 officer and that he would have to have a specially equipped police vehicle for animal transport. Also ... Majoqui never forgot a face. And he would certainly never forget this man's face.

So he waited and listened, and before it could even get dark, he saw the blue and gray minivan pull up to the front entrance and pass a card before a sensor, opening the gate. It was him.

Majoqui typed in the license plate of the minivan, and after punching in the stolen credit card number he'd gotten from his brothers from Hollywood, the sealed record on the sergeant's personal information opened up. He now had his name, address, and home phone number. A few more keystrokes, and he even had a visual image of the man's house from Google Maps.

Majoqui rubbed his cheek, feeling the thin metal ring he'd looped through the stitch holes. There was pain. The bones in his cheek and jaw seemed to be healing, but his eye still drooped, and the vision was bad. This Americano police officer had stood between him and his goal. Twice he had thwarted him. He had caused him pain and disfigurement, but worse even than all that, he had made Mara look fallible. And that could not be tolerated.

An example was to be set with the banker and his family. This sheriff's deputy ... this Gil Mason ... he had stopped that. It seemed only fitting to Majoqui that the example be made with him instead.

And so, it would.

15
***

As sergeant of the K9 Unit, I set up the schedule and training regimen for my people and their dogs. There are eight K9 handlers other than myself; six men, two women, and a mixture of German Shepherds, Dutch Shepherds, and Belgian Mals.

We have a complete training field on the north forty of headquarters, with an obstacle course, jumps, an indoor kennel, and even a mock house to practice things like attic insertions and building searches. It was a training night, so all the guys were waiting for me when I finally showed up. I had to stop off at the firing range to qualify with a couple of my spare guns since my primaries had been confiscated ... again ... for the shoot team's analysis and ballistics report, so I was a little late.

Athena Marie walked up to me, a quirky grin on her lips.

"Glad you decided to show up, boss. We weren't sure you were going to. Heard you had a rough night."

She was wearing a shroud over her badge; we all were, in honor of the officers that had been killed last night. The shroud is a black band that fits diagonally across our badges.

"Pretty rough, yeah," I said, thinking back to the mutilated face of the banker's wife and hearing the muffled cry of the little girl as I jolted her broken arm.

"I read the report," she said, the smile gone. "You did everything right."

"And still there's seven dead people and two kids without parents."

"Not your fault," she said. Athena was like a daughter to me. She put a hand on my arm. "You want to talk about it?"

I shook my head, my eyes feeling wet, as I remembered how I'd broken down with my wife. "Not now, not yet, thanks." I did a mental headshake and forced a smile. "So, what do you have going on here?"

Athena nodded. "We started without you." She pointed to the hurdles where Tom Boilenger was running his dog, Cobra, through a set. Her dog, a spiffy little sixty-pound Mal named Brutus, sat at her side, looking up at me with fearless eyes.

"I see Tom working," I said, "what about you?"

"Somebody had to take charge, Sarge."

"I knew you were bucking for my job."

"Ha! Have to deal with these morons for a lousy six percent raise? Forget it."

"Ah, but you forget the power."

"Double ha," she said with that same quirk. She was all of five feet, five inches tall and weighed maybe a hundred and ten. But she was a giant when it came to confidence. "I've got Greg and Matt suiting up and Brian and Cliff laying tracks." She pointed to Paul Graves, who was out in a field maybe fifty yards out. "Paul's setting some evidence, and Cassandra is scoping out some places down by Inverness for area searches later."

"Wow, maybe I should be late more often."

"Maybe you should."

"You sure you're not bucking for that extra six percent?"

She laughed again and looked down at Pilgrim. "Hey, boy, you're looking a little fat," she looked at me, tapped my stomach. "I guess what they say about masters and their dogs starting to look alike after a while is true."

I held out my hands. "It's the vest. Besides, any healthy animal would look heavy next to that starved mongrel you call a dog. You ever feed that poor beast?"

"You're just jealous," she looked down at Pilgrim again, "both of you. What are you feeding him anyway?"

It was my turn to grin. "Malinois."

"That big honker couldn't catch Brutus if he ran on two legs."

I couldn't argue with that. Brutus was quick as lightning.

"How about drugs? Any set out yet?"

"Let's see," she said, "there's meth, coke, and pot in the house, and we've got X, heroin, and shrooms in the cars."

I nodded. "Nice job. Let's start with the cars. Pilgrim hasn't worked narcs for nearly a week."

We headed over to the house. There was a built-on garage that was really more like a barn. It held the shells of three cars set on dolly-like wheel systems so we could easily move them around. There was no glass, and the seats, door frames, center consoles, airbag holders, radios, speaker compartments, and dashes were all removable for easy access to hide things in.

I put Pilgrim in a sit in front of the first car, then gave him a hand signal and said, "kilo." He went to the front license plate and began sniffing. He searched the whole driver's side front panel, sniffing the outside air around the car, moved to the rear, and came up the other side, finally finishing back at the front license plate. Without waiting for another command, he started on the second vehicle.

"That one's a blank," I said. We mix up cars with and without drugs, so the dogs don't start thinking every car has drugs in it.

Pilgrim was paying a lot of attention to the next car's passenger's side wheel well. He stuck his head deep into the well, just above the tire, and then sat with his nose pointing toward the space.

"I'll call it there," I said.

"So would I," Athena said.

I went over and said "yes" and dropped his yellow knobby ball toy in front of his nose. The ball is attached to a sturdy nylon cord with a handle so I can play tug-of-war with him, which I did briefly. He's a

strong dog, and it takes a lot to play tug-of-war with him. I gave him
the out command, and he released the ball. I took him to the front
license plate of the last car and sent him to find the drugs again. This
time he went back and forth several times between the driver's front
side door seam and the rear side door seam. He finally settled on the
front door, and I opened it for him and sent him in to search the inte-
rior. I taught him to search a car in sections, beginning with the door
panel that is open. Pilgrim sniffed it and continued inside, methodi-
cally checking his patterned sections. He finally alerted on the radio,
really sniffing it hard, and then indicated by sitting and staring at it.

"The radio compartment," I said.

"Close," said Athena. "Get him to sniff closer to the steering
column." That's the way it is in K9 training. I'm the trainer and have
the final say, but we all help with every dog and with every handler.
That can be hard sometimes because cops tend to have an ego to
begin with, and when you're on an elite team like K9, the egos can
sometimes swell outside of skull capacity. I make it a strict rule to
check our egos at the door when we come in for K9 training because
it has to be all about the dogs and reading them correctly. When I
trained dogs in the Corps, a missed IED would get Marines killed.
Out here on the streets, it's no different. You miss a bad guy and he
could shoot you in the back as you walk by.

I pointed toward the dash near the steering column, and Pilgrim
obediently followed with his nose, sniffing in quick little huffs that
allowed the alar fold on the inside of his nostrils to open, forcing air
to flow through the upper area of the nasal passages. When a dog
exhales, the air takes a different path, blowing out the side slits and
keeping the scent still trapped in his nose for better detecting. Pilgrim
followed the scent up the column to the wheel and finally over to the
center, sniffing along the small seams where air escaped from around
the airbag compartment. He sat and stared at the steering wheel.

"What's in there?" I asked.

"Point six grams of heroin."

"That was a little tough for him."

"Yeah, a lot of the dogs hit it right where Pilgrim did, by the radio."

I looked down at Brutus. "Let's see Brutus run it." Brutus was pure money on drugs, by far our best narcotics detection dog.

Athena grinned. "Find drugs," she said to her dog. Brutus bolted to the car and started his circle of the vehicle. He sniffed the seam of the driver's front door and started pawing it.

There are two disciplines of narcotic dog indicators; passive and aggressive. Pilgrim is a passive indicator, in that when he finds the strongest odor of narcotics, he sits and stares and maybe pokes his nose at the spot. An aggressive alerter, like Brutus, doesn't sit. Instead, he starts pawing, biting, or scratching at the spot. Both disciplines are equally effective, but each suits different dog psychologies. The only trouble I've found over the years is that aggressive alerters make finding training locations more difficult because the dogs are a bit more destructive. Oh, and we never, ever train bomb dogs to indicate aggressively; for obvious reasons ... those reasons being—boom and BOOM!

Athena let him in, and he went straight to the steering wheel and started digging at the center pad.

"Show off," I said.

"When you got it, flaunt it," she said.

My phone vibrated. "Sergeant Mason."

"Hey, Gil, it's Jim Black. I just got done talking to Las Vegas PD. Looks like your three boys, if they are connected with our suspect, did get in a tussle with some Crips down there."

"How'd it happen?"

"From the security tape, the Crips were inside a convenience store —four of them. One of the Thirteens came in and got some beer. He was tatted all over, and one of the Crips flashed him a sign, just looking for trouble. He found it. The Thirteen was wearing an open vest, showing his chest and arms. You'd never expect a weapon on him. But he had one alright. He undoes his belt buckle, snaps his wrist, and the darn thing turns into some kind of sword. He nearly takes off the sign flasher's arm and then whips right into the other three. Cuts two of them pretty bad, then robs the teller and picks up his beer, and leaves. Very slick ... scary slick."

"A belt sword? Never heard of that. Thirteens usually go for machetes and Saturday night specials."

"Yeah," said Jim, "weird. The dude was good and fast. It was like a magic trick, only gory."

"Any pictures?"

"Plenty on the guy with the sword, and some blurred photos of the guy in the front seat, nothing on the guy in back. We got the plate too. Turned out to be a steal, but off a different car. They were in a green SUV, and the stolen plates come back to an Accord."

"Okay, send whatever you've got to my phone. Who knows, maybe I'll run into them."

There was a pause.

"Gil, don't take this the wrong way, but your part in this is done. You should leave it up to the Denver Dicks and us now."

There was another pause, this time from me.

"Look, Jim, there are a lot of people dead here, people that maybe wouldn't be dead if I'd shot a little straighter or a few more times. I'm going to have to live with that, and it's going to be tough, but maybe it'll be easier if I help you put him away before he hurts anyone else."

"I understand all that, Gil, I do. But this can't be a personal vendetta thing, or you could mess up the whole criminal case."

"It's not, Jim. I just want to help catch this guy, that's all."

"Alright, Sarge, only keep me posted on anything that comes up."

"Absolutely."

A few minutes later, my phone vibrated, and I downloaded the pictures of the guy with the sword and the fuzzy picture of the man in the passenger's front seat of the green SUV. Jim even sent me the entire video from the convenience store. I love technology, maybe even more than Kip from Napoleon Dynamite. The guy with a sword also had a tattoo of a tear dripping from the corner of his left eye, showing that he'd done time somewhere. That meant he was in the system. And if he was in the system, I could find him.

16

The rifle was better than he had asked for. It was a custom Les Baer .308 with a twenty-four-inch barrel and a Mag-Pul adjustable buttstock. It was also equipped with a Vortex 6.5 20X50 mm PST tactical scope and the standard Harris bipod on the front underside of the handguard. Three twenty-round magazines, all filled with Federal 168 grain Gold Medal Match ammo, were included. The heavier bullets would ensure a straight, flat trajectory with maximum penetration, which was important since they would need to punch through the heavy glass of a car's windshield.

The motorcycle was a bit flashier than he'd wanted, but it would do. It was a 2009 Kawasaki Ninja ZX-10R with a stack design liquid-cooled 998 cc inline four-cylinder engine and could go from zero to sixty in 2.84 seconds. It was glossy black and looked like pure speed.

The brothers had done well. They had secured both items quickly and efficiently. And the witch woman sitting across from him was best of all.

She was the real thing. He knew it the instant he walked into the room. A priestess of the highest order, a Lyanifa. He crossed himself and whispered a quiet *Hail Mary* under his breath. Her right eye was blind, staring about in a gummy sea of opaque cataract, but her left was midnight black and could pierce to the soul. She was ancient, her wispy hair as white as her dead eye, with gnarled fingers and arthritic knobs for knuckles. Her dentures were a size too big for her shrunken gums and hideously white against the nicotine color of her skin. Wrinkled lips, smeared lavishly with bright red lipstick, left pinkish stains on the butts of the filtered cigarettes she chain-smoked as she read his palm, the cards spread out before them.

Power radiated from her like waves of heat, and Majoqui basked in it as she blessed him and chanted over him and said the secret words that would shield him and give him protection from those who would do him harm.

Her wrist was a withered stick, covered in leathery sinew, as she picked up the knife and slit the chicken's throat with practiced ease. The blood flowed hot and fast into the bowl, the fowl's talons twitching as she dropped it to the floor, and stared with her one eye as the contents told their futuristic tales.

Majoqui feared no human, no weapon. He had stared "señor death" in the face many times and never looked away. Only the supernatural held the mystery that was able to spark fear in his soul. He felt that fear now as she smeared her fingers in the mixture of goat and chicken blood and entrails. She had severed the goat's genitalia, as well as his heart and liver. She added them to the bowl, along with three medallions that she first prayed and chanted over before laying them carefully next to the dead animal's manhood, the source of his strength and pride.

The old woman painted a cross on Majoqui's forehead, the blood feeling oily and cold, and then ran her fingers across his cheeks, painting them both the color of her lips. She prayed the old prayers, chanting and singing, as her voice rose in volume and speed, escalating upward until she was screaming, her body convulsing into tight spasms that shook her frame and brought near terror to the heart of the great assassin. Her words became guttural barks that exploded from her throat, and her tongue spit out and in like a poisonous snake searching its prey.

Majoqui's heart hammered in his chest as she flicked drops of blood onto his face and hair, baptizing him in the blood of power. She gripped the sides of his face in her hands and screamed her inarticulable words to the heavens and to Hell, calling on the saints and the demons to grant him his desire, no matter the cost. At last, she sat back, exhausted and spent, her red lips slack and a line of drool stringing to the table. Her dead eye floated absently as her living eye shook in its socket as though she were dreaming.

And perhaps she was, thought Majoqui. Perhaps she was searching through the nether world of sleep and dreams, trying to regain the strength she had just passed to him.

He kissed her hands, slipped the bloody charms from the bowl, kissed each in turn before pulling them over his head, and then left.

The three brothers from Hollywood drove him out east, past Byers, to a dirt road that led down and around to a grove far back from the highway.

Majoqui had them set a series of beer cans at hundred-yard intervals. He drew the rifle from its hard-plastic case and seated one of the twenty-round magazines. He bolted in a .308 cartridge and snugged the buttstock into his shoulder. The first can grew large in the scope as he sighted in. The supersonic crack of the missile, as it pierced the sound barrier, hurt Majoqui's ears, despite the wadded-up bits of paper napkin he'd stuffed deep into his ears. The beer can exploded and frothy liquid sprayed in all directions. Carlos, the brothers' leader, picked up the can and held it out for him to see through the scope. The entry hole had punched dead center, proving the sighting to be right on target.

Majoqui waved him off and sighted in on the second can a hundred yards downrange. The Vortex scope was equipped with mil dots for wind and elevation adjustment, but Majoqui had never used them, preferring instead to use his natural talent for judging lead time and bullet drop.

Releasing a third of his breath, he pulled steadily back on the trigger until the familiar kick to his shoulder told him the bullet was on its way. He saw the can spray as it went spinning downrange. He'd hit it high, near the lip. He made a mental adjustment and sighted on the next can another hundred yards down.

Then came the buck and the *crack* as the bullet slid through the sound barrier, and this time, the beer can buckled at the center before exploding its contents into the air in a white spray.

The recoil was very slight, about the same as an AR-15, little brother to the M-16. Majoqui had not been in the armed services, but several of Mara's members had, bringing their experience and knowledge back to the group for dissemination. Majoqui had learned much of his gun knowledge from them, and he had learned even more from the Internet, but of course, hands-on was the greatest teacher of all. Majoqui was a good shot with a pistol, but he was deadly with a rifle. He'd spent many a day with a .22 up in the hills of San Salvador, shooting rats and birds and virtually anything that ran, crept, or flew past his purview. Since those long-ago days, Majoqui had killed nineteen men with the rifle from great distance. He had missed only once, and that was a very far shot indeed. Close to a thousand yards. The bullet had struck a wall a few feet away from the man. Majoqui had seen the bricks chip at the bullet's impact. The man had jumped and looked around but had no idea he had just missed death by a yard. Majoqui adjusted, aiming more than a foot over his head. This round caught him in the chest, and it was as if he were a puppet whose strings had just been cut. His body went instantly limp, and he fell as loose as water to the street.

Remembering, Majoqui held the picture of the last can several inches above the upper rim. There was a breeze now, from the east. He let the barrel drift to the right in compensation, and then came the *almost* surprise of the *kick* to his shoulder and the sharp report that assaulted his stuffed ears. The beer vaporized as it vacated the metal canister that had an instant before safely housed it.

The Crow had not lost his touch.

Majoqui nodded as the three brothers whooped and cheered his marksmanship. He had what he needed, and now the example must be set.

Putting the rifle back in its protective case, he motioned for the others to return. The sun was slipping behind the mountains to the west, and he had to pick up Tamera's VW for his next job. It was wise to know the prey's habits, and since observation was the best teacher ... he had a car to follow.

17

I was tired. It had been a long day of training, and I'd suited up and caught all the dogs. Sweat soaked my shirt and had dried on my skin, making me feel clammy and itchy. I needed a shower and bed.

No word at all on Stitch or his buddies from California. Jim Black had put a BOLO out on the SUV, along with the plate and descriptions on everyone we had, but nothing had turned up yet. I knew Denver would be out in droves. Nobody killed one of theirs and got away with it.

Pilgrim slept in the back of my patrol car. There's no backseat. Instead, there's a platform with a rubber mat and a sort of metal cage that covers the back and windows. I have a slider that I keep open so he can stick his head through, and I can pet him. I also have an automatic door popper that hydraulically opens the passenger side rear door at the push of a button so I can call him to me if I'm on a traffic stop and things go bust, like they did the night before with Stitch. Pilgrim snored loudly, and I could hear his paws scrabbling against the rubber mat as he chased a rabbit or a bad guy in the world of dreams. Good. He'd earned the rest. First with Stitch last night, and again tonight in training. Three different decoys had put on the bite-suit to catch him. Cassandra took the first hit. She stood out about thirty yards away and screamed and yelled at him as he came at her, her arms waving with a bamboo snap stick in one hand. Pilgrim never even slowed. He hit her on the inside left shoulder near her chest, and even though she turned expertly with the blow, his sheer 120 pounds weight, combined with his momentum, maybe 30 miles an hour, bowled her over. She hit the grass hard, and I heard her breath whoosh out. But she recovered like the pro she is and started ground fighting immediately, wrapping his body as best she could with her legs, keeping him on the bite until I called him off.

Matt Shunt and Brian Floss were the next two victims. Matt caught him on a runaway, Pilgrim hitting him in the center of the back and knocking him face-first to the ground. Brian's catch was easier. He was hiding under a bush, and Pilgrim sniffed him out and bit him on the right bicep after a seven-hundred-yard track across parking lots and through a golf course. Even through the suit, there's a good deal of pain with the pressure of Pilgrim's jaw strength.

Pilgrim had had a full night, and I envied him his ability and opportunity to be able to sleep while I had to make the trek home. It was like I was his chauffeur or something. *Sheesh.*

I pulled into my driveway a few minutes later, yawning as I activated the garage door opener. We live in a small, two-bedroom house in Littleton, off of Bowles and Lowell. It's an older house with a few problems, but the yard's pretty big by today's Colorado standards, which gives Pilgrim plenty of room to romp. Not that he's that big a *romper.* He's never been a high energy dog, being as big as he is, but what he lacks in speed and energy, he more than makes up for in scenting ability and brute strength—less of a sports car ... more of a tank.

It was nearly three in the morning as I shut off the car and pushed the button to close the garage door. Just then, a yellow Volkswagen drove past. It was too dark to see the driver, but I didn't recognize the car as belonging to the neighborhood. It wasn't the paperboy either, and it sure wasn't the milkman. I craned my neck to try and catch a glimpse of the license plate, but it didn't have a bracket light, and the door closed too fast anyway.

I let Pilgrim into his kennel. I have two. The one in the garage has a doggy door to the house and another to his outside run where he can do his business and get sunshine whenever he wants. There was no sunshine at this time of the morning, but he went out anyway ... to take care of business.

When I got inside, I looked out the living room window to make sure the VW wasn't cruising through again. It was a pretty safe neighborhood, but no neighborhood is so safe as to be immune to burglaries or theft from motor vehicles.

Nothing.

I yawned again and made my way to the kitchen. Jolene left a note on the fridge telling me there was a burrito in the microwave, and all I had to do was hit the minute heat button and then remember to take it out before I fell asleep. *What a gal.* I hit the button, grabbed a soda from the fridge, and then sank into my favorite chair, the recliner. I popped on the TV, kept the volume low, and flipped through the channels until the microwave *dinged.* I grabbed the burrito, a fork, and a paper towel and went back to my chair. Nobody made green chile like Jolene, and she'd loaded it with pork, just the way I like it. I hadn't even realized I was hungry, but I plowed through it in record time while still flipping through the channels.

I had to wonder why I was paying such high cable bills for the privilege of having some two hundred paid advertisements hogging up all the channels. I finally settled on an old John Wayne flick. It was one of my favorites, McLintock.

Somebody ought to belt you in the mouth. But I won't. The H... e... double toothpicks I won't!

Nobody punched anybody in the face as good as the Duke. Not even Chuck Norris. Chuck *kicked* people in the face better, yes, but Mr. Wayne was the best movie puncher of all time.

The doggy door clickety-clacked, and in came Pilgrim. He went to the front window where I'd stood before getting my burrito and came over so I could rub his big head. I'd been a bad handler with Pilgrim and allowed him to get into the habit of begging for table scraps. So, sue me. I cut a chunk off my burrito and let him eat it out of the palm of my hand. Once the food was gone, he lay down next to my chair and fell asleep.

After a few minutes, I set the empty plate on the coffee table and started to get up for bed, but the mud fight was still going on in the movie, and who could leave that? So I stayed where I was ... and then there was the scene where John shoots his daughter's boyfriend in the chest with a blank, making her think he'd killed him at her request and then ... well ... the next thing I knew, Jolene was smiling down at me as she pulled me from the chair and helped me into the bedroom. I shucked off my gun belt and clothes and crawled under the covers in just my skivvies and a t-shirt. I should have hopped in the shower first, but I was way beyond that now. I kissed Jolene on the lips and then kissed Marla on the forehead. She snuggled between us, her thumb corkscrewed between her pink lips, and then I was out.

I dreamed of my teenage days. My parents were good people who loved me, my brother, and my sister, but I was a bad kid. It wasn't that I meant to be bad; it was just that I was curious ... curious about the world ... that and the fact that I hated school. I ran away for the first time when I was thirteen. Oh, I know, lots of kids run away at that age. But I didn't run away like most kids. I ran away to Alaska, where I lied about my age and signed up on a crabber boat. I made it for about two months before a State Trooper spotted me and shipped me back home. But by then, of course, I'd been bitten by the bug, and I would take off every chance I got. I never went to the same place twice, and I got farther away almost every time—my poor parents.

I dreamed of that first time on the crabber boat. There was a fight. A big red-haired boy from Okie, in his early twenties, went off on a skinny Basque guy in his late fifties. The boy had huge arms and hands, and he picked the older man up off the deck with one hand, by the throat. The Basque moved so fast I hardly caught the movement at all. He swiped his hand in and down. Suddenly, the redhaired boy dropped him and clutched his forearm, blood squirting from between his fingers. He started screaming ... not like he was mad ... like he was dying. I'd never heard anything like it. The sound of it made the hairs stand up on the back of my neck. It was like that in the dream too. I could feel my hair standing up, and a chill ran through my body. In real life, the Basque and I became good friends, and I learned a lot from him. In the dream, he just turned and looked at me. There was something terrifying in his eyes. I looked down and saw I was carrying my daughter in my hands, and when I looked back up, it wasn't the Basque anymore. It was Stitch, and he was staring at Marla with his one open eye. In his hand was a machete.

I jerked awake, breathing hard and barely holding in the scream that tried to make it past my lips. Marla was still lying between Jolene and me, still sucking her thumb, still safe.

It took a long time before I could fall back to sleep. And when I did, I had another nightmare; only I couldn't remember it when I woke up.

18

Ziggy thumbed the striker on the lighter. Three jets of green-colored flame heated the small black ball of tar heroin to a liquid as it rested in the bowl of the spoon. Ziggy set a small piece of cotton over the goo and carefully drew the now filtered drug into a syringe through the cotton, his usually palsy nowhere in sight. He tapped the plastic syringe several times to raise air bubbles to the top, then gently squeezed it out the needle. The shoestring already circled his bicep, swelling his veins to thick snakes waiting to be fed. He didn't even feel the point as it slid past his flesh and into his bloodstream. The world changed. His perception changed. Time and reality changed. He could think again. Reason and knowledge flooded back in vibrant strobes that invigorated his senses. He closed his eyes, and the horrible hunger ... the need that possessed his every thought and action, subsided to the back of his consciousness where it lingered like a shallow threat.

The alley was deserted except for him and the rats. But he kept enough presence of mind to peek up at the street every so often to make sure no cops were coming his way. And it was because of this that he saw the tattooed man walk past. He knew him instantly. The way the rabbit knows the cougar. And he also knew what it could mean *to* him.

He slipped the string from his arm, and with practiced ease, quickly arranged his paraphernalia into a purple cloth Crown Royal bag with a drawstring and shoved the bag into his pocket. Ziggy hurried up to the mouth of the alley. He was just in time to see the son of Mara meet another gang member, and he watched as the two of them stepped into the nightclub.

His head bobbed back and forth as he angled down the street. It was early, only nine o'clock, and the heavy hitters wouldn't be out for another hour or so, although some of the whores were already pushing their wares. They knew better than to waste their time on a burned-out junkie like him. But there had been a time, not so long ago, when he would occasionally spend his money on them. That was before heroin had replaced his need for women, or sex, or booze, or even food ... most of the time. She was a jealous lover, heroin, and she didn't like sharing her conquests with anyone or anything.

Ziggy didn't go into the club. This month it was called *El Azul Muerta (The Blue Dead)*. They charged a five-dollar cover, which he didn't have and wouldn't have paid even if he did. Last month, the same place had been called *Head Bangers* and had catered to the white, punk crowd. Now it was inhabited by Chicanos and other South and Central American peoples.

Half the street belonged to Denver. The other half, the south side, belonged to Aurora. Police cars of both persuasions cruised up and down Hampden looking for troublemakers.

Ziggy was half black, half Asian. His father, an Air force pilot who married a Japanese woman, brought her with him back to the states. His father was a big David Bowie fan, hence the name Ziggy, which he had hated all his life. Ziggy had been a decent soccer player back in high school in Chicago. He'd had a nice build, one that women liked, but that was nearly three decades ago. His once lean muscles had long since been eaten away by age and the heroin so that he was now barely skin and bone. And the skin his body was able to hold onto was thin and easily breached. Ziggy knew what he looked like, but he also knew that his muscles would grow back quickly once he dumped the drugs and started eating proper. And he was going to do that, sure enough, just as soon as he was ready. Just a few more hits with the lady, and he was going to be all done with her, oh yes. He knew he could do it anytime he wanted to—anytime he *really* wanted to. That was the key, of course, to *really* want to. And he would, eventually. He just wasn't ready yet. Not quite yet. Not when he knew Gil would be good for at least a Grant, and maybe even a C-note, if he wanted these guys as bad as it seemed he did.

Ziggy didn't have a cellphone. If he did, he would have sold it anyway, and the closest payphone was at the gas station a half-mile down the street. He bobbed his head back and forth, trying to think. If he left to call Gil, the tattooed man might leave without him knowing. If he didn't go to make the call, the tattooed man was sure to leave eventually, and Ziggy had no way of following him except on foot. Following an MS 13 gangbanger on foot was a sure way to get your throat slit.

What to do?

He ran back to the hookers and singled out a short, fat, white girl with pimples and hot pants. Her plump thighs bulged out of her shorts, the cellulite looking like dimpled curds of cottage cheese.

She chomped a wad of gum noisily.

"Could I use your phone?" he asked as politely as he could.

She shook her head, more streetwise than her age made him believe. "So you can run off with it and make enough for a hit? Beat it, doper."

"No-no little miss, please, this is an emergency."

She cocked her head and stuck a hand against an ample hip. "You don't look like yer dying, honey."

"No-no, see, I got some information I've got to get to a fella, and it's real important."

"Information? What kind of information?"

"It's secret, like. Ziggy say he can't tell, no ma'am, he can't do that."

"Oh yeah? If it's that important, it must be worth something."

"Well now, little miss, Ziggy say that if you let him use your phone, the man Ziggy calling would probably give you a nice five spot for your trouble."

"A nickel? Old man, my minutes cost more than that. I'd need at least a dime, and even then, I want some collateral before I hand it over to you. Something to make sure you don't beat feet out of here the second you get it."

Ziggy was a little taken aback by her calling him an old man. After all, he wasn't old. Still, he needed the phone.

"Okay-okay, little miss, only we gotta hurry, and Ziggy ain't got no collateral, but you can hold on to me if you want while I call him."

She squinted her eyes at him, then reached out and took hold of his sleeve with one hand while she fished out a flip-phone from between her large breasts with the other.

"Make it fast," she said, tightening her grip on his sleeve.

She had surprising strength for a girl, and to be truthful, she made him a little afraid. He punched in the numbers as quickly as he could and smiled at her with his blackened nubs of teeth while he waited for Gil to answer.

"Sgt. Mason."

"Yes, sir, this here is Ziggy."

"You have something for me, Ziggy?"

Ziggy could hear the intensity in his voice over the phone and thought that maybe he could get even more than a bill if he played this right.

"I hear say that I do. I hear say that the man with the tattoos is down here."

"Where?"

"Ziggy's going to need the promise of some cash before he can tell you that. Lots of cash."

Ziggy's eyes darted in their sockets as he tried to calculate what he could get. "Two ... three hundred dollars," he said, his voice breaking on the last word.

"And an extra fifty for using my phone," the fat hooker yelled into the phone.

"If he's there, Ziggy, and we catch him, I'll give you five hundred dollars. Now quit screwing around; where is he?"

Ziggy could hardly contain himself. "Hear say he's in a club called El Azul Muerta on Hampden."

There was a pause.

"Did you hear it, or did you see him yourself?"

"Oh, Ziggy done seen him, alright. Seen him his own self, big as life and twice as scary. Seen 'em walk inside and watched ever since, and he hasn't left, no sir."

"Where are you?"

"Just down the street, a bit to the west, standing next to a fa... uh... nice little miss who done let Ziggy use her phone."

"Stay there. I'll have a Denver car there in a minute." He hung up.

Ziggy smiled at the hooker.

"What did he say?" she asked. "About my money, I mean."

"Hear say he'll give you twenty-five and not a penny more."

The whore grinned. "Better than ten."

"Yes, ma'am, little miss," said Ziggy. "That it is. That it is."

Old man indeed.

19

M ajoqui pulled the chair back for Tamera and then sat beside her. Carlos and the other two sat opposite them. The music was loud, the lights dim, and the drinks expensive. Tamera had a beer, she didn't like hard alcohol, while he ordered a tequila with lime.

He had the Americano police officer's pattern down now, after following him the last three days. Better than that, though, he'd learned about the award ceremony on the Internet. Tomorrow night, the police officer and several other officers from congruent jurisdictions were being given medals for a narcotics bust they had made earlier in the year. Majoqui spent a good portion of the day plotting the possible routes to and from the ceremony and was nearly certain of the path his prey would take. The rest of the day, he spent driving the route on the Ninja motorcycle, scouting for the best possible location for the ambush.

He found the perfect spot.

Tamera held up her beer mug, and he obliged her with a gentle clink of glasses before taking the tequila in one gulp. It was smooth and hot and hit his stomach like a ball of fire. He felt it swim through his veins with incredible speed.

Carlos had gotten here first, checking for police presence and then calling and giving the others the okay to come in. The place was beginning to fill up. There were around ninety or so men and women dancing and drinking and generally milling about. Nearly everyone was Latino, although he did spot a few whites and two blacks in the mix. Other than the four of them, no one else sported Mara signs. He was surprised MS 13 hadn't infiltrated further into Colorado, it being so close to California and Nevada. He made a mental note to bring it up when he got back to Salvador. One should always take advantage of business opportunities.

A clamor sounded at the front doors, and people started to shout. Carlos jumped to his feet.

"La Policia. Ejecuta!"

Majoqui didn't even turn his head. He grabbed Tamera's wrist and jerked her down under the table. Carlos and the other two were already headed for the back door, shoving people out of their way, but just as they got there, the door opened, and three Denver police officers rushed through the doors straight at them.

Majoqui pulled the gun from his waistband and fired three quick shots into the floor. The sudden shots shocked the crowd into silence, and in that instant, Carlos whipped the belt from his waist and slashed the closest of the police officers across the shoulder. Bedlam erupted. People were screaming and yelling and running; bodies pushed and trampled. Majoqui pulled Tamera out from under the table and led her to a wall where they made their way toward the front doors. Police positioned there were now pushing through to where the gunshots had sounded, looking for a shooter. Those in the back were engaged in a battle with Carlos and his two brothers. Majoqui saw an officer shoot Carlos point-blank in the chest. Carlos didn't seem to notice. He slashed out with the sword, and a red line appeared across the officer's cheek and jaw. Blood sprayed. One of the other cops took a beer mug to the head, and the third one began firing into the Mara brother that had wielded the mug. He went down heavy and loose, and the cop turned and shot twice more into the third brother, hitting him in the face and shoulder.

Carlos swung the sword again, striking the cop in the thigh. The man screamed as he was lost in the swarm of bodies pushing for the exit.

Insanity. The room was dark and packed and loud and smelled of booze and gunpowder.

Majoqui changed direction immediately, pulling Tamera to the back door, shoving people away from them. He stayed as close to the wall as he could to keep from being knocked down or trampled.

He reached Carlos, who was bent over one of the brothers, trying to get him to his feet, but the man was dead. Majoqui grabbed Carlos and shook him, screaming for him to come with them. Carlos stared at him with blank eyes as blood ran in a steady stream from the small bullet hole in the center of his chest, right where the vest ended, showing his tats. Carlos fell to his knees and toppled to the side. Majoqui knew death when he saw it. He pried the belt sword from Carlos's fingers and dragged Tamera from the nightclub.

Outside, the air tasted remarkably fresh and cool. People were running, women in skimpy dresses were crying, police sirens were screaming toward them from every direction.

Majoqui buckled the sword belt around his waist, just as he'd seen Carlos do, and the two of them made it to the front and started down the street as a sea of police arrived on scene.

Tamera was crying, her shoulders trembling like a little bird. He put his arm around her and led her to her car. The Kawasaki Ninja was across the street and a little to the east. He gently pushed her inside and told her to drive home, where he would soon meet her. She didn't want him to go, but he stopped her with a raised finger and told her to leave. She did as he said, although it took her several tries before she managed the right ration of pumping the gas pedal to get the engine started.

Majoqui watched her drive away and then scanned the area. The Americano police officer was there somewhere. Majoqui could feel him. And then he saw him, across the street in front of the club, his uniform different from the Navy blue of the Denver police. He wore green BDUs, with the pant legs bloused at the top of his black boots, just as he had on their other meetings. Majoqui had learned this was the standard for K9 officers in Colorado.

The deputy, Gil Mason, suddenly stopped talking to the skinny black man and looked in his direction. At least ten people were milling around him, but it seemed as if he were staring straight into Majoqui's eyes. Because of the distance and the dark, Majoqui was confident the man wouldn't recognize him in his disguise, but a shudder ran up his spine just the same. It was a shudder like he had only known when confronting the powers of the supernatural. Without realizing it, he reached up and gripped the three blessed charms that hung from his neck. He turned, shaken, and tried to lose himself in the crowd, suddenly sure that somehow, someway, the man had known who he was and even now was coming toward him. But when he dared a glance back, the deputy was only talking with the black man and not looking at him at all.

He made his way to the bike, feeling foolish and a coward but still shaking. The vibrating power of the Ninja beneath him helped him regain some semblance of composure, but he gunned the throttle a little too hard, making the cycle pop up and forward and then shoot down the street with an ear-splitting sound. He saw the deputy look in his direction a final time and again felt that supernatural dread sweep across him. It made his skin crawl and his limbs tremble, as though he were a child afraid of the dark.

Majoqui hated Gil Mason all the more for it.

20

I stripped out of my uniform, careful not to wake Jolene or Marla, who was sleeping next to her. I unstrapped the bullet-resistant vest and pulled it over my head. It's way lighter than the flak vest I had to wear in the war, but even this light-weight Velcro felt heavy after ten or fifteen hours, not to mention the thirty-plus pounds of gun belt with all its gadgets. Batman's utility belt has nothing on the modern-day cop's belt. Gun, extra ammo magazines, handcuffs, flashlight, nightstick, Taser, pepper spray, rubber gloves, leather gloves, radio, pager, cell phone, keys. *Holy overload, Batman!*

I pulled up my pajama bottoms and slipped under the covers beside my two girls. I gave them both a kiss then lay back, exhausted. It had been a long day, and something was bothering me. I couldn't quite put my finger on it, but whatever it was, I could feel it nagging at the back of my mind like a piece of food stuck between my teeth. Of course, the fiasco at the club hadn't helped.

I'd told Denver to hold back until I got on scene, but they didn't. Instead, they rushed right in, and if Stitch had ever really been there, he'd gotten away. Worse, all three of the Mara boys from California were dead, and three Denver cops injured, one of them pretty seriously. By the time I got there, it was all over but the crying.

I met up with Ziggy out front, and he was able to identify one of the bodies as the gang member that met Stitch at the door. The other two bodies were sporting plenty of MS 13 tats, so I was confident they were our boys. Only Stitch wasn't with them. And since the dead guys were exercising their right to remain silent, I was back to square one, no closer to catching him than before I even knew about the other guys.

The little girl's cry echoed in my ears, and her dead mother's eyeless face stared at me from the table. *If only I'd emptied my magazine into him when I'd had the chance. If only he hadn't been wearing that saint's medallion. If only ... if only ...*

I closed my eyes, praying for the images to go away, and fell almost instantly asleep. I got my wish; the images my waking mind couldn't let go went away. But the dreams ... the dreams were worse ...

a sleeve pulled back revealing the fatal faded letters and numbers
eyes black and soulless
the machete spinning and spinning through the dark
the little girl
the little boy
the blood
a medallion
bullets punching through wood
the sting on my face
a motorcycle
everything flash—flashing across the dreamlike strobes from a camera
sounds crashing like God's thunder
screams, gun blasts, sirens
the dead Denver cop lying on the kitchen floor, his face mostly gone
the eye
one eye
devoid of mercy
so black
the black of eternity

the black of Hell
the banker
his wife, his wife, his wife
the children
Marla
the small arm bent in a way the human arm does not bend
the nurse
all of it coming so fast, so fast
flash—flap—flash
the noise
the screams
the cries
the plunk of bullet's hitting metal
the fear
the excitement
the loss
yellow Volkswagen
the nurse, her neck pulped and swollen
the cop, his head sopped and soggy, blood pooling
the banker's wife
flap—flappity—flap
stitches holding the eye closed
whimpers behind duct tape
three burglars
the crash and smash of shotgun shells and automatic weapon's fire
the blood
the children
the smell
the taste
flap—flash—flap
the face staring at me
piercing high on the cheek
spiked blond hair
Ziggy twitching and talking and bipping and bopping
yellow Volkswagen

Pilgrim hot on the trail
so close
so close
bloody hole surrounded by tattoos
tongues on the table, eyes on the floor
children crying ... whimpering
VW at the PD
VW at my house
spiked blond hair, pierced cheek
stitches
stitches
stitches
blood everywhere
machete
eyes black and soulless
faded tattoos sliding back under the sleeve
numbers
letters
and always, always the whimpers of children

21

Jolene traced her finger along the long 'Z' shaped scar that rode the upper ridge of Gil's right chest muscle. A piece of shrapnel from a roadside IED had almost ended his life before she even knew him. A thought flitted across her mind, *what would her life have been like if she'd never met him.* The idea frightened her. She loved him so much.

Marla wiggled, fussing between their grown-up bodies, and noisily sucked at her thumb. She'd been sleeping with them since the day she was born. Jolene had breastfed Marla until she was nine months old, and sometimes she still missed the feeling, the closeness. Marla was the only thing in her life that meant as much to her as Gil.

It must have been another rough night for him. He'd undressed quietly, slipped under the covers, kissed both her and Marla very gently on the head, letting his lips linger as he breathed them in, before lying next to his girls. Then he draped his arm over them, as though his reach could protect them from whatever horror he might have seen during the night. He'd stayed that way for a long time, staring in the dark at the two most important things in his life. He finally fell asleep just before the sun rose in the east. She'd almost let him know she was awake, almost asked him what it was that was bothering him so much. But she knew him well enough to know that he would tell her in his own time, in his own way. He was always afraid to scare her, to shock her. He would sometimes say that the flesh had an evil habit of never letting go of the really horrible things that got into your head. Eventually, he told her almost everything, once he figured the best way to phrase it, to blunt its assault and cushion the effect of the actual events.

Gil didn't understand that none of it really scared her, not for her or Marla. Sometimes she was afraid for him and the effect it had on him, but not for them. She had absolute faith in his ability and his resolve to protect them.

Jolene did not hold this position through blind faith. The very first time they met, he saved her life. He had been her strength and love ever since. She could not imagine going through life without him.

She let her palm rest against his chest and felt the strong pump of his heart. It was his heart she loved most about him. Jolene's father was a pastor of a small church, and all through her childhood, she and her siblings would read the bible with him. It was always the best part of the day for her. When she was about nine years old, she had asked him about a passage in Exodus where God said that He would harden Pharaoh's heart so that he would not let God's people leave Egypt. She didn't understand. God wanted the people to go, so why would He make Pharaoh's heart hard?

She remembered her father smiling. He was delighted with the question and told her how smart she was for seeing through to the *heart* of a matter that many adults had difficulty understanding. He ran his finger along the lines of text and showed her where God said that Pharaoh would harden his own heart as well. This confused her all the more. Had God hardened Pharaoh's heart, or did he do it himself?

Early one hot summer afternoon, her father just smiled and got up. He went to the kitchen where he rummaged around for a few minutes before coming back with a small yellow tub of Play-Doh with a blue lid, a short fat heart-shaped candle that he had bought for their mother on Valentine's day, and two paper plates.

He put the candle on one plate and set it in the window. He popped the lid off the tub of Play-Doh, quickly molded a simple blue heart, put it on the other plate, and placed it next to the candle. Their living room had a southern exposure with high windows, so the sun blazed straight down onto the windowsill at this time of day.

Her father picked up the bible and said, "Some people have a heart for God, meaning that they love God, and they know He only wants what is best for them. They want to do what He instructs them to do. But other people, selfish, prideful people, don't care what God thinks or wants; they just want to do what feels good to them at the time. God calls them a *stiff-necked people,* meaning they won't bow their heads to Him or His will. They won't humble themselves."

He pointed at the windowsill.

"Now, just watch for a few minutes," he said.

Jolene, her two sisters, and her brother all watched raptly, waiting to see the mystery unfold. And soon, they saw a whitish crust begin to form over the surface of the blue heart. The more it dried, the harder the shell. And soon, small cracks began to appear on it.

At the same time, the short, fat candle was beginning to soften and melt, caving in on the bowl where the little black wick stood.

Jolene's father pointed out the window. "Think of the Sun as God's power. The same power is shining on both of these hearts, the wax and the clay, but it is the nature of the heart's themselves that are reacting differently to that power. When God shines his power on the heart that loves Him, it softens and melts. But when God shines his power on the heart that hates Him, it hardens into a rock. God knew the nature of Pharaoh's heart. He knew that if He showed him that He was the true God and that Pharaoh's gods were false, his pride would harden his heart against Him. And God was right."

Gil's heart had once been like the clay, hard and in rebellion against a God that he said he didn't believe in. The war had helped do that to him, and it had taken a lot of discussion and burning of the midnight oil before she and her father could convince him of the truth of God.

But Gil was honest above all else, and the night finally came when he saw that his arguments had been proven wrong, and he surrendered his life to the Lord. On that day, his heart had changed from clay to wax, and it had melted.

And now that Gil's heart was malleable, Jolene had seen the shape that the Potter was molding it into, and it was a beautiful shape, full of love and caring and generosity. He was becoming the man she had always dreamed of having and loving for all eternity. Gil loved them with a sacrificial love that made her own heart melt.

Her fingers moved to the flat muscles of his stomach, then to the defined curves of his powerful arms and shoulders, up to his throat and cheek. She played a nail around the curl of his ear. Oh, how she loved him. She hated the sin of the world because of how it hurt him, how it made him fear for them—the things he had to see, to witness, to deal with. The people ... the terribly hurt people ... the terribly mean people ... the terribly bad people. So many tragedies, so many lives in ruin and chaos.

A part of her wished he'd quit, but the other part, the larger part of her, knew that he also loved the job. That he craved the action, the chase, the hunt. He was the little boy who loved superheroes, grown up to become one himself. She also knew that if he quit, the world would be the worse for it because he was exactly the kind of man that should be a cop. The kind of man everyone would want to be a cop. The kind of man that did what was right and risked the consequences. The kind of man that would give his life to save another's. He truly was a superhero; only he wasn't bulletproof. He didn't have super strength or super speed or x-ray vision, and he couldn't fly. She loved him all the more for it. Because he was a hero *without* the super. He did what they did, even though he was mortal—a man who could hurt and bleed and die.

And one thing more.

Gil had given her Marla.

And Marla was the light of her life. Jolene had always loved God, but she had moved into a new relationship with Him now that she was a mother. Jolene had come to believe that children are God's way of showing us why He made us. Our own acts of creation. Our own acts of love. He made us because He wanted to shower us with His love and to show us what it is to be alive, to exist, and to be able to experience the beautiful bonds of relationship.

And because of God's great act of love, Jolene was able to have that bond with Marla, a relationship that helped teach her the greatest depths of love.

And Gil loved Marla just as much as she did. Marla was a daddy's girl for sure, and she had him as wrapped around her finger as any one man could be.

The two of them were inseparable, and next to God, they were the most important things in her life.

Gil moaned in his sleep, his fists clenched as his eyes moved beneath their lids.

Bad dreams, another part of the job. He deserved so much better. She wondered what was going on in that world of sleep inside his mind. He seldom spoke of his dreams, even when she asked. He said he rarely remembered them, but there was something about his eyes when he would say it that made her think he wasn't being completely honest. Some nights he would cry out. Some nights he would say things, little snippets that would give her a glimpse into his psyche. Sometimes about the war, sometimes about his police work. But always it was bad; a battle where his men were killed, a suicide he couldn't save, an accident victim crushed inside a mangled vehicle. People hurt, people dying, people hurting other people, and her husband having to deal with all of it.

A sudden rage burned through her at the thought of all the pain Gil had had to absorb through the years, both physically and emotionally.

He was hurting now; she could feel it. He *had* been ever since the night of the shooting. The night the nurse and the police officers had been killed. The night the children had been hurt.

She touched his cheek, brushed her fingers along his forehead, and he relaxed; his fists unclenched, and he quieted.

She had seen him like this before, only not as bad. Jolene thought maybe it would be a good idea to call her dad. He might be able to help Gil; to make him feel less responsible for everything that happened to everyone. Gil always thought he should be able to save everyone, and when he didn't, he took it very personally. He was the sheepdog: ever vigilant, always ready for action.

Yes, she would call her father tomorrow and see if he could come over this weekend. That made her feel better.

Jolene ran her fingers over the muscles of Gil's chest again. Such a strong man in so many ways. He was brave to a fault.

Thinking of his bravery made her remember they had the award ceremony to go to tomorrow night. She smiled. He deserved it. He deserved it so much.

Jolene's fingers tickled their way to his belly button. She considered waking him, but then Marla wiggled between them, and she decided to let them sleep. She kissed them both and closed her eyes.

How good God was to her.

22

Majoqui sighted in on the driver. He was old, maybe seventy-five, with thin gray hair and a face lined with wrinkles. He hunched close to the steering wheel, as the old often do, as though the extra few inches could help their failing eyesight. The high-powered scope brought out every detail, even from this distance. The bridge had been constructed for the Light Rail, but the next run was over an hour away. He had time.

It was almost ten o'clock, but because it was a weeknight, the street was nearly deserted. Majoqui had been lying in the same position for over four hours, killing driver after driver in his mind as they drove at him along Kipling Parkway. Most men could not have endured such a position, but Majoqui's patience was a thing of legend among the Mara community. He'd once lain upon a pile of rocks and steel for five days awaiting his target. The ordeal had almost killed him. Dehydration, the blazing Columbian sun, insects, and the sheer shock to his body's system. He lost over fifteen pounds, but the shot had been perfect and had moved him up several notches in the gang's hierarchy. Majoqui had developed his technique for patience while lying for hours on end, perfectly motionless, as his mother rutted with her customers. He'd learned early on that drunk, lustful men could be dangerous, even to little boys of five. It was best they didn't know of his existence, so he would lay motionless, silent, barely breathing, willing himself invisible. He had become so good at this technique that he sometimes believed he ceased to be detected by humans or animals. Even insects seemed oblivious to his presence. They would crawl over him on their way to wherever they were going, but they never bit, stung, or hovered around him the way ants and spiders or wasps would do to ordinary people.

An hour earlier, a group of four teenagers walked below him, talking and laughing. They never looked in his direction, just as Majoqui knew they wouldn't. He was invisible.

Majoqui would be victorious tonight. He would kill the Americano police officer who seemed to have some strange ability over him. He would make an example of him, to both the world and to the spirits, for he was certain this man must have some connection, some protection from the supernatural realm. How else could he explain the injuries the man had caused to him or the way the man kept intercepting him? But Majoqui had gone against others who were protected. He had gone against others who were great warriors with protection as well. Always he had won. He won because he respected both aspects of the battle, physical as well as spiritual. So, he would make this police officer the greatest of examples -- to pay homage to him and to the spirits that protected him. He would also spread fear through the police community and to the spirits so that they would know not to go to war with Majoqui in the future.

A dark van came straight up the hill on Kipling, passing Colfax. A cool breeze rose the hairs on Majoqui's neck and the backs of his arms. He snugged the rifle butt in close, knowing in some strange way that even he did not understand that his waiting was over. The excitement began to build, but Majoqui held it in check. Discipline was needed here.

The van was still several hundred yards away, but as the scope came to his eye, Majoqui saw the face of his target. It was the police officer Gil Mason.

Majoqui said a quick prayer to the Virgin Mother and curled his index finger around the rifle's trigger.

23

Tamera Sun picked up the meager change and swabbed the table with her towel. It was eleven-thirty, and there were no other customers in the restaurant. The two cops who had just vacated the table were regulars and were always nice to her. They were both older, and in the past, she had liked it when they came in. The place had been robbed twice since she started working there. She'd been off work both times, but still, the idea of it scared her. Having the police around usually made her feel safe. But that was before ... before Majoqui. Now they frightened her.

They were looking for him, accusing him of terrible things. But she knew his heart, his soul. And there was no way he could have done the things they said he did. He was strong and brave, and they were trying to frame him for some government cover-up. Just like they did on 911. But Majoqui was too smart for them. They would never catch him. And best of all, the two of them would escape back to his country and be together forever.

Still, she was afraid. She'd had to witness three men being killed right in front of her. The police had shot them down for no reason. They would have killed her too if Majoqui hadn't saved her. Majoqui could have left her, saved himself, just run, never looking back. But he hadn't. Instead, he'd shielded her with his own body as he pushed his way through the mass of people, dragging her to safety and freedom.

The two police officers got into their patrol car. Tamera watched as they drove out of the parking lot and onto the street. She let out a breath she didn't know she was holding. Her fear was for Majoqui, not for herself. They wanted to kill him. He'd told her all about it after the scene at the nightclub. The banker was going to release evidence that the government was behind the collapse of the economy. The police had killed the banker and his wife to keep him quiet. They would have killed the children too, but Majoqui stopped them.

She didn't understand all of it, her mind just didn't work that way, but she understood that the cops were bad and Majoqui was good, and that was enough for her. She would go anywhere just so long as she could be with him.

Tamera had wanted to leave right away after Majoqui's friends were killed, but he said he had one last thing to do before they could go. He said he had to stop the man who had killed the banker and his wife and had tried to kill the banker's children. He said the banker had been his friend and that honor demanded he protect the children from further harm.

It was so like him. The way he had protected her.

She loved him, and soon they would be together forever, and she would never have to worry about people like Dashon or Kyle again.

24

———————

The award ceremony was nice, the dinner and dancing afterward even nicer, but best of all was the ride home. Jolene was beautiful, dressed in a black gown with spaghetti straps and the pearl necklace I'd given her last Christmas. She laughed, telling me how Mike Braden had dropped a piece of shrimp. It had rolled down his tie, over the rounded hump of his huge chest, down the curve of his stomach and somehow landed in his gun belt. She almost cried when she related how it took him forever to dig it out, fussing all the while that the smell would permanently wreck his leather if he left it.

On the radio, playing low as a backdrop to help Marla stay asleep, the Beatles rhythmically sang a song about how their world was never going to change. I liked the sound of it because, just now, everything in my life was so perfect.

Jolene smiled, her teeth so incredibly white they seemed almost to spark as we drove under the streetlights on our way home. Marla snored lightly in her car-seat, sucking her thumb and cuddling her giraffe blanket close to her face and chest. She was completely tuckered out when we picked her up from Jolene's sister's house after the party. Pilgrim guarded our home.

Jolene stretched against her seatbelt to get a look at her. She reached back and brushed a lock of hair off her forehead and beamed those luscious eyes at me.

"She's so wonderful," she said.

"Stop bragging."

"Is it bragging if it's true?"

"Good point. In that case, you'd better add beautiful, graceful, and oh so smart."

"You forgot well behaved."

It was my turn to smile. "Well, that goes without saying. Look who her father is."

Jolene slapped me lightly on the arm. "That's what makes it so hard to believe."

I raised my eyebrows. "Oh, so you're going to take all the credit?"

"Most of it." She dipped her head and looked at me from under her brows. "You look pretty sexy in your dress uniform."

"Really?"

Her smile was pure seduction. "Really."

"Is it the tie, the patches, the badge, the gun, or what?"

"Yes," she purred.

That sent a tingle through me.

The streets were nearly deserted as we approached a red stoplight at Colfax and Kipling. I slowed the car to a gentle stop.

"How sexy?" I asked.

Jolene slid a perfectly shaped arm over my shoulder and cupped the back of my neck in the palm of her hand. She pulled me to her, and her lips were soft and inviting. I smelled the delicious scent that was uniquely her, tasted the delicacy of her lips, the firm pressure of flesh against flesh.

She pulled back, and her eyes were so deep and hypnotic that I could have drowned in them forever.

"The light," she whispered.

"What light?" I whispered back.

She grinned and nodded toward the windshield. "The traffic light, it's green."

I shook my head. "No, it's not." And we kissed again.

"I love you," I said.

"I know," she said, and then she grew serious, "I know." And then she kissed me with passion. As I pulled ahead, my beautiful wife next to me and my sweet daughter in the seat behind me, I wondered how I could be so lucky.

The Beatles sang, 'Nothing's *gonna change my ....*'

I was the happiest man in the world.

25

Majoqui put the crosshairs on the woman's forehead. It was an easy shot. He'd made much more difficult ones from far greater distances. His finger was already padded around the trigger as they crossed Colfax and began to pick up speed. But he hesitated. Something ... some inner feeling was bothering him. Majoqui didn't know what it was; he couldn't quite place his finger on it, but it was there, and it was real, and it would not be ignored.

Majoqui had trusted his instincts far too long to override this strange sense that invaded his courage and stopped him from taking the shot. *How many times had this enemy thwarted him?* Majoqui's eye still lacked full movement, and its sight was not yet clear. His jaw ached, his cheek ached. There was pain in his chest and hip. Not only had his brothers been killed in front of him, the banker's children, who were to prove the power of Mara, had been snatched from his grasp.

Majoqui wanted the man to watch as he killed his wife and child. He wanted him to suffer for all the wrongs he had done to him. For daring to challenge him. Daring to pit his will against that of Mara's greatest assassin.

Yes, Majoqui wanted him to suffer long and to know that it was his fault. But whatever it was that spoke to him, a sixth sense, the spirits, or maybe the Mother herself, whoever or whatever it was, was speaking loudly, telling him that he must not play with this man. That he must kill him quickly, kill him now.

In the confines of the telescopic scope, he could capture half of their faces as they leaned close. *How perfect it would feel to see the man's reaction as his wife's blood and brains sprayed across his face.* It would be justice. The man would have to go to Hell with the memory of his woman's beautiful features erased and replaced with a gaping horror that would stay with him through all eternity. And it was right there, just a tug on the trigger, so easy, so impossible to miss.

Majoqui felt the sliver of the metal trigger begin its sway back, as though of its own accord. The target was there, big and getting bigger by the second. So easy. He could not miss, not here, not now. His blood surged through his veins, his heart a mighty drum as he stopped his breath, with half of it trapped in his lungs. The heavy copper-jacketed bullet would destroy her beauty, disintegrate her teeth, crush her bone. Her blood would vaporize, her flesh would liquefy, and her light would go out, gone forever. And the man would know—the man would know it had been Majoqui and that Majoqui had triumphed over him. He would know he had failed—failed his wife, his child, his own sense of justice, his job, his fellow officers, and most of all, himself. And he would know the cost, the price, the pain, and horrible emptiness that even death could never hope to still.

Majoqui wanted this for the man. He wanted it more, perhaps, than anything he had ever wanted in his life. But Majoqui was no fool. He was wise. He was disciplined.

The minivan had reached a speed of about forty-five miles an hour and was less than a hundred yards away. The man turned his face back to watch the road, and Majoqui moved his sight picture from the woman to the man, centering the cross on the bridge of his enemy's nose. There was an instant of elation, and Majoqui felt the heavy thud against his shoulder as the deadly missile left the weapon to fly to its target.

26

I turned from Jolene to look back at the street when something flashed from up on the bridge. My combat brain instinctively took over. I punched the gas pedal and *hard* steered to the right, sending the van into a skid. As I overcorrected, I heard the tinkle of glass from the bullet as it passed through the windshield. It grazed past my cheek and exploded through the side window, blowing the safety glass into a million fragments.

The Beatles played on as the backend of the van fishtailed, and we almost went over. I snapped the wheel back to the right, turning into the skid, and then quickly to the left, praying to find just the right touch to keep us on all four tires, but then we hit the curb. There was a massive impact, and then an eerie feeling of weightlessness as the van started to roll. We flew up and over, and everything lifted into the air—CDs, a pen, Jolene's sunglasses, Marla's sippy cup—as though the laws of gravity had ceased to exist. And in that instant, everything went silent, completely silent, and time seemed to slow as we finished the first roll through the air and began the second. But then the passenger's side tires touched pavement, and sound returned, as well as actual time. It was like being inside a tornado, the deafening roar of grinding metal and snapping struts. Rubber screamed as it shredded away, glass shattering everywhere as the terrible power of centrifugal force had its way with our bodies and limbs. Airbags exploded, smashing into our faces, as the seatbelts and shoulder restraints crushed us into our seats. I heard Marla cry; even through all the insanely loud destruction that was closing in on us, I heard her.

I thought it would never stop, but then it did, as abruptly and brutally as it started, with an incredible jolt that almost stole my consciousness.

The van lay on the passenger's side. The airbags had deflated, and I saw Jolene look at me. There was blood on her forehead and in her hair, but she was awake and alive. And then I heard Marla from the back. She screamed, "Mommy, Daddy!" in her little baby voice, and I gave thanks she, too, was alive.

My seatbelt held me tight. I punched at the release with my thumb, but there was too much weight for it to let go. I dug my pocketknife from my pants pocket, snapped it open, and sliced through the lap portion in one easy stroke.

I had to push myself into an upward position, one knee against the center console, and one foot wedged against the center floorboard divider.

And then I heard the motorcycle as it grumbled up to us. It sounded like a crotch rocket, and something in my subconscious told me it meant danger. In war, you learn to trust that inner feeling, and I trusted it now. I reached down and drew my Smith and Wesson from its holster.

I eased my head up through the shattered window and saw him. It was Stitch. He looked different. Blond spiked hair, eyeliner, a ring in his cheek where the stitches had been. But it was him. I suddenly realized I'd seen him before, at the nightclub, and even before that, in the yellow VW.

In that instant of clarity, everything came together. He'd been following me—hunting me. Tracking my patterns. I'd been too oblivious to notice, so wrapped up in my life and job that I had let my guard down. And now it was time to pay the price for my weakness. He was here to kill me: me and my family.

As if in slow motion, I saw him pull a black semi-auto from his waistband and point it at the passenger side windshield.

He looked up at me, that one eye drooping and lagging behind the other, and grinned.

My gun was up and firing before he could twitch. Two bullets into his face. Two in the chest and two more back into his face. He flopped to the ground in that unique way that the dead do, his gun still in his hand.

I was out and over the side of the van in a second. I kicked the gun from his lifeless fingers and stared down at him. His face was a mess, unrecognizable. The chest shots were perfect and bloody. No medal or charm was going to save him this time.

Marla continued to cry as I took her from the car seat. Then she hugged me and said she loved me, which seemed strange because she couldn't really talk yet. Getting Jolene out was more difficult, but I helped her through my window and set her feet on the ground just as the first of the patrol cars and rescue units were pulling on scene.

I crushed the two of them to me, so thankful they were alive and unhurt. I squeezed them so tight and held them so close that golden sparkles danced behind my eyes, and I felt like I might pass out.

I closed my eyes as I felt a strange click in my neck. When I reopened them, I was in a dream, being rushed down a corridor on a gurney, the overhead lights slapping past overhead. But why? I wasn't hurt. Or was I? Had I been shot? Or maybe I'd broken something in the crash and was just too amped up on adrenalin to notice until the action had stopped? I tried to raise my right hand, but it wasn't there. I tried my left, but it was gone too. There was nothing. No feeling, no pain, no weight, nothing. I tried to talk, but nothing came out. My lips wouldn't move. I tried to blink ... the lights overhead, blindingly bright ... but again I couldn't.

Lord-Lord, what was happening to me? Jolene! Jolene! Marla! Where are you?

I turned from Jolene to look back at the street when something flashed from up on the bridge. *Light refraction from a telescopic sight!* But that was silly; this was Colorado, not Afghanistan. There was no war here. But some inner sense told me it *was* war, and I torqued the wheel to the right as something punched hard and fast through the windshield, spraying me with glass dust. I felt a sting on the side of my neck as the high-velocity bullet singed my flesh and exploded the window to my side.

But I'd swerved too hard and now had to jerk back into the skid before it was too late. Only the van wouldn't respond, and we hit the curb going too fast. Like in the movie Superman Returns, when the jet gets too close to space, there was an instant of weightlessness. Things floated—Marla's sippy cup, a pen, CD's, a pair of sunglasses —and then gravity came back to life, and there was a terrible jolt as we touched down. Glass detonated, metal screamed as it tore apart, rubber shredded and melted sending its horrible stench at us in a wave.

The Beatles were still singing about how their world would never change—as my world was coming apart.

The van somersaulted—once, twice, three times—before smashing down on Jolene's side and grinding to a halt against a light pole.

I shook my head, glass fragments flying from my hair like sparkling droplets of water. I looked at Jolene. There was blood on her forehead, but she looked at me, her lips trembling into a hesitant smile. Marla cried from the back, letting us know she wasn't hurt too badly, which was lucky because the back half of the van had been ripped open right behind her seat. If she'd been one row back ...

The high-pitched whine of a crotch rocket raced toward us, and a sudden feeling of all-consuming fear swept through me. I tried to push myself through the window, but the seatbelt held me in place. I slipped my pocketknife out of my pocket and tried to cut through the belt; only it wouldn't cut. It was as if the blade were dull or the material of the seatbelt too dense to slice. The motorcycle came closer —closer.

Frantically, I sawed at the belt, that feeling of absolute dread pushing to near panic. The edge of the knife caught in the material and frayed it down a notch.

The motorcycle screamed to a stop a short distance from us.

I ripped the knife back and forth, snapping and tearing a strand at a time.

Jolene looked at me, her eyes big and glassy with shock and fear. She turned to the windshield, watching as something approached.

My fingers felt numb and clumsy, and I almost dropped the knife, but I held on and with all my strength sliced through the last of the cloth.

Dropping the knife, I catapulted myself up through the windshield just as Stitch pointed the gun at Jolene's face.

A horrible feeling of guilt crushed at me as I recognized the man from my dream. The man in the VW. The man from the nightclub.

I fired. Round after round after round. His face and head exploded in a red mist, and still, I fired, on and on until there could be no mistake this monster from Hell was dead. Until I was certain his evil was obliterated from the world, and there was no chance that he could take them away from me again.

When the slide locked back, I dropped the magazine and slid in another so fast most people wouldn't be able to tell there had been a lapse in gunfire. I emptied three magazines into his wretched face and body, standing directly over him for the last nine rounds.

Jolene was standing beside the van, holding Marla, when I turned back to them. Marla had a strange dimple in the center of her forehead with just a tiny drop of blood at its center, but she was smiling and holding her arms out for me to take her and hold her. A fragment of safety glass must have nicked her, but for some reason, seeing it made me feel hollow inside. It must be the thought of how close we had all come, how close to losing each other.

I grabbed them up close and cried into their hair, telling them how sorry I was—how very, very sorry. I kissed Jolene on the lips and tasted blood, and when I pulled my head back, I heard a strange click in my neck. I closed my eyes, and when I opened them, I was in the dream again. I saw people moving quickly, back and forth above me. I couldn't tell what they were doing, but whatever it was, it seemed urgent. And then I realized they were wearing blue masks over their mouths and noses, and I understood they were doctors and nurses. But why were they here, and what were they doing working on me? I wasn't hurt. I wasn't the one that needed help. They should be working on Marla and Jolene ... I tried to talk to them, to beg them, but nothing came out. I couldn't move ... couldn't speak.

Jolene looked at me from the passenger seat. So beautiful, so full of life and love. Marla sat behind me, sleeping peacefully. Something caught my attention from ahead, a flash, a spark, a reflection of light: nothing big, nothing to capture one's attention. Not here, in the USA, in America, where there was no war and people were safe and secure and you didn't need to be on constant watch—constant guard.

But there was something, that inner voice that I knew better than to ignore. It pulled at my mind, warning me that something wasn't quite right. Like something wasn't right about the yellow VW or the man from the club that got on his motorcycle. Things that I should have paid attention to. Things that could mean the difference between life and death.

I cranked the wheel hard to the right and saw the hole blown through the windshield. Something hit me in the throat, a piece of glass maybe. I felt it for an instant, and then it was gone, and the van was tipping. I ordered my hands and arms to steer to the left, but they wouldn't move. I tried to force my shoulders into action, but they rebelled. I felt the passenger's side wheels leaving the ground and, in a last-ditch effort, tried to shove my body to the left, hoping it would drag my hands in that direction through sheer momentum. But there was nothing, and the van continued to tip as it hit the curb and bounced up in the air and over so slowly. A pen danced weightlessly up from the center console, as did CD's, Marla's ballerina sippy cup, and a pair of sunglasses. They were Jolene's, and she looked like a movie star when she wore them. I would tease her about it, and she would slap me playfully on the arm laughing. And then we were spinning and slamming against the hard asphalt, the centrifugal force ripping one of the sliding side doors off and away. Glass shattered as metal contorted and ripped apart. The rubber on the tires was shorn away, and the rims and axles dug jagged groves through the blacktop of the street beneath. The sound was horrendous and came from everywhere at once. A cacophony of impact and whirling missiles and flying glass was punctuated by the sounds of grunts and moans and small cries from the fragile bodies of flesh that were helplessly captive, along for the ride. John and Paul, singing through it all that nothing was gonna change their world.

And then it stopped. We must have hit a light pole along the way because the van was ripped apart. I was lying on the asphalt. I'd been torn from my seatbelt and shot through the windshield. In my peripheral vision, I could see the remains of the destroyed driver's seat. There were several small fires where puddles of gasoline had ignited. And straight ahead, I saw into the van, the metal roof peeled back like a can of sardines. And there was Jolene, strapped in her seat, blood running down her face from her forehead and nose. The airbag had deflated. As I watched, I saw her stir. She shook her head slowly. I wanted to scream at her to stay still and not move her neck, but the words wouldn't come. And then I heard Marla cry for her mommy, and I saw that she was still in her car seat, strapped tight and sound.

I was so glad, so thankful. But then I heard the motorcycle, and an overwhelming panic sucked all the heat from my body, leaving me numb and frozen in terror. I tried to move my eyes so I could track his movements, but like the rest of my body, they were locked. And still, the Beatles sang.

The bike stopped behind me, so close I could hear the crunch of the gravel as though it were inside my head. The monster dismounted, came around, and knelt in front of me so that he could look into my eyes.

It was Stitch.

He cocked his head, first this way and then that way, like a dog that heard a strange sound. He nodded slowly and stood up. He pulled a gun from his waistband, pointed it at my head.

I tried to move. I poured every last ounce of willpower into the attempt, but it was like trying to move the ocean. There was nothing to hold onto.

"Leave him alone!" screamed Jolene.

Stitch turned. He started walking toward her.

I tried to scream, to shout, to make any sound. But there was nothing.

Stitch walked right up to her, pointed the gun. He looked back at me. He grinned.

I heard a click and closed my eyes. When I opened them, I was awake, and the nightmare had just begun.

27

Majoqui took the corner at ninety miles an hour, almost losing it but managing just barely. The sound of squad cars, wailing too close behind him, encouraged a bump, and the speedometer needle passed a hundred and kept going.

He was on Alameda heading east now, being tailed by at least three Lakewood Police cars. But this was a long straightaway, and no cruiser was going to keep up with the rocket. The speedometer pegged at one-eighty, but the wind rushed faster and faster past his face, and when he hit two hundred, reality seemed to change. It was nothing he could ever put into words, more like a religious experience than an event. The world changed, or at least his perception of it did. His vision sharpened in the center, blurred at the edges. Details sprang to life; colors vibrated their brilliance, reality rushed past on the sides like a raging river.

And then he saw the stop sticks.

The cop was ridiculously far away, and with the incredible maneuverability of the motorcycle, Majoqui would have no difficulty avoiding the trap. Only, as the thought crossed his mind, he heard the pop of the tires as they exploded and saw the police officer as he passed him by.

Impossible that he had been moving so fast.

But he had been, and now the bike was rip-sawing back and forth, the handlebars ripped from his grip. He was flung through the air as though he held no weight. There was time for him to reach out to the Mother with his prayer, and then his body struck something ... and something else ... and something else. Branches slashed at his face and hands, tore at his arms and legs and body, snapped and splintered as his momentum carried him on. He lost consciousness for an instant but then shot up to a sitting position, amazed he was still alive.

The sirens told him the police were almost on him, and he reached for his gun, even as he saw the destruction his wild flight had wrought on the long row of hedges he had passed through. It was a miracle. He touched his talismans with his left hand as his right continued to search for the gun.

It wasn't there.

He'd lost it in his wild tumble. But there was no time to mourn its loss or try and find it. He had to escape.

Majoqui pushed himself up from the thick Evergreen bushes and ran to the northeast. The street sign ahead said Harlen St. but Majoqui had never heard of it. He kept running, trying to get close to buildings so he could disappear into the shadows.

A stream of police cars was pouring into the area, their red and blue strobes splashing across the night and searching him out.

Majoqui dove behind a thin screen of bushes as a patrol car raced past. He stayed there, catching his breath and trying to think out the best route to freedom. Overhead, the whopping thud of monstrous blades beat at the air. He chanced a look upward and saw the powerful beam of the helicopter's searchlight stabbing at the ground, looking for him. Majoqui knew there was power in a stare; that some men could feel when eyes were on them. He had this ability himself and so did not question it in others. He turned his face to the dirt and waited for the horrible insect to fly away. But it did not fly away, and suddenly he heard cars screeching to a stop close to him. The sun went supernova, blinding the area around him, sending its awesome rays through the scant bushes so that he became visible for anyone to see.

He jumped to his feet and started to run when the first police officer hit him with a flying tackle on his left side. The cop was young and thick in the shoulders and chest. The impact was brutal, and Majoqui slammed into the ground hard, losing his breath, spots dancing behind his eyes. Majoqui grabbed the young officer by his testicles and squeezed as hard as he could. He jammed his thumb into the officer's eye, then punched down at the young man's nose. There was a snap, then a crunch, and he was free of the man's grip. Majoqui grabbed for the officer's gun, but the young cop held it locked in its holster with both hands. Majoqui wished he had worn the sword-belt. He could have split the man in two with it, but he'd left it with Tamera, wanting to stay light and flexible.

An arm snaked around Majoqui's throat, and hands seemed to grip him from every direction. The cold metal of a gun barrel dug into the flesh of his forehead, and he heard someone say, "Do it, please do it!" Majoqui released his grip on the cop's gun. He was pulled away from the young officer and shoved roughly to the grass. Someone's knee ground into his neck. His arms were dragged behind his back, and handcuffs snapped painfully tight around his wrists. Someone kicked him hard in the side. He tried to see who it was so that he could repay him sometime in the future, but a fist struck him on the jaw, breaking his still damaged bones and momentarily blanking his vision. Next, he was hauled to his feet and half carried, half dragged to a patrol car, and shoved into the backseat.

Majoqui felt a trickle of blood make its way down his chin from his mouth, the flesh hot and swollen. But that was okay, a small price to pay. They had captured him, but he had been captured before and by men far more brutal and dangerous than American police. They would not hold him. He would escape. Of this, he was certain.

Majoqui had given the witch woman an extra hundred dollars to ensure it.

28

They were doing things to my body. I knew this because my field of vision would jerk this way and that. I couldn't move my eyes, couldn't close them. They stared up at the bright lights, faces darting in and out of their view. I couldn't feel what they were doing, but I understood I was in a hospital, that they were trying to save my life. But I didn't care about my life; I only cared about Jolene and Marla. They were all that mattered.

I tried to speak, tried to move. I could hear, but everything was muffled and warped and confused. Doctors and nurses continued to slide in and out of my sight; their movements seemed urgent, harried, but it was as though they were working on someone else's body. I wanted to close my eyes. I wanted to sleep. I wanted to sleep forever. I reached out to God. *Please ... Please.*

Please what? I wasn't sure. I knew there was something ... something horrible ... something I needed help with. Help that only God could give. But the weirdness of the sounds and actions going on around and above me made it too hard to think, to remember.

An instant of pain, there and gone. That surreal feeling of weightlessness as the van flipped and rolled. Marla's cry; the blood in Jolene's hair. And the high whine of the motorcycle as it came for them. And something ... something else ... something my mind didn't want to face.

No, God ... Lord God, no.

Someone moved my head back marginally enough that my line of sight changed. A tube snaked past my vision and into my mouth. Again, there was no feeling, only the vague understanding that I was being intubated.

"Blood pressure's dropping fast," I heard someone say to my right. "We're losing him."

I didn't care, just let me sleep, let me forget.

Forget?

I saw the reflection, up high on the bridge for the Light Rail. Such a small thing, hardly noticeable, only I did notice, I did. And I should have reacted—or did I react? Did I? I moved—I tried to move—only it was too late. And I felt ... pressure, a sting, so small, just a touch and then ... nothing. And I saw the hole in the windshield. I saw the hole, and a part of my brain knew what that hole was. I tried to turn—I tried, but nothing ... there was nothing. And then the flipping, the rolling. Marla's sippy-cup and the pen and CDs and sunglasses. The sounds, the smells, the world spinning, tumbling. Lying there, awake, seeing, hearing. And then he came, and I knew who he was and realized how I had failed them. How I should have known; how I should have put it together. How it was staring me in the face all that time. He knelt in front of me, staring into my eyes. I saw it, and he knew that I saw it. He knew that I knew. And that was enough. He took out the gun, cocked his head as if considering, then pointed it at my face. I heard my sweet Marla's baby cry from inside the van, Jolene's voice telling him to leave me alone.

No, Jolene, no, stay quiet, stay hidden, please, baby, please.

And then he stood. He stood.

"Flatline!" I heard the words, as though from outside of time, but I still saw what I saw. He stood.

And he turned.

There was a flash, and I saw the paddles, slick with a clear jelly, as they moved out of my sight.

"He's back," said the same voice. "Steady rhythm. Pressure's increasing."

Please, God.

"Put him out," said another voice. "We may have to open him up."

Yes, put me out! Put me out before ... he turned ... *no, no put me out. Put me out* ... and he walked toward them ... *no no no* ... he walked to Jolene, the gun bouncing along the seam of his jeans. The van was on its side, on Jolene's side. She was still strapped in, but the windshield was gone. I could see her ... her beautiful face ... she was awake ... staring at him.

"I love you, Gil. I love you, Marla," she said.

He pointed the gun.

PUT ME OUT!

I heard Marla cry a final time. The medicine was starting to work, but it was too slow—too slow—I heard—I saw.

Please, Lord.

Only it was too late.

And then I went to sleep. And I didn't wake up for a very long time.

29

Tamera Sun sat down on the stainless-steel stool. She picked up the phone and held her hand up, palm touching the inch-thick bulletproof glass, fingers splayed. On the other side, Majoqui pressed his hand opposite hers.

He looked good to Tamera. His bruises had healed, as had his droopy eye. His jaw was wired shut, but he'd written her that the wires would be coming off soon. Tamera thought it was cute the way he had to talk through his teeth. He sounded funny.

"I've missed you," she said.

Majoqui smiled at her, showing two rows of silver bands. "I've missed you too," only it sounded like *I've misshed you too.*

So cute.

"How are they treating you?" she asked.

"Fine," said Majoqui. "American jails are very easy."

Tamera thought how much more handsome he looked now that his eye didn't droop anymore. He'd put on a few pounds as well, all muscle. He was still thin but lean and wiry. She saw that some of the inmates rolled up the sleeves of their shirts to show off their arms, but not Majoqui. He was too modest for that. But she could still see the definition in his forearms and at the top of his chest. He was easily the most beautiful man she'd ever known. And he loved her.

"I talked with my aunt last night," she said, knowing that he liked to get right to the point.

"And what did she say," he asked.

They were speaking in code, of course. Just like secret agents. It gave Tamera a squiggle of fear to talk with him like this. They were planning his escape right here in front of the guards, and they had no idea.

"She said she would be ready in five weeks." Tamera knew they were listening, Majoqui had told her so, and he knew about these things. But it didn't matter. The code would fool them. Any number she said he would subtract two from, so five weeks meant three.

Less than a month and they would be together again. And that sent another squiggle through her; only this one wasn't fear.

"What time?" he asked.

Tamera was so excited she almost blurted out the actual time but caught herself. "One in the morning," she said. Which, of course, meant eleven at night.

Majoqui nodded his head. "Very good."

"Did you get my letter?" she asked. She wrote to him every day, sometimes twice or even three times a day.

He smiled, showing the bands again. "Yes, (yesh). It was lovely."

He looked at her intently. "You will be ready."

It was not a question, and this time the squiggle was a mixture of both fear and excitement. "I will."

Majoqui nodded. "And what of the policeman?"

"According to the news reports, he's still in a coma. They don't know if he'll ever wake up."

She saw the briefest of smiles flit across his lips before he nodded again. "Very good. He sleeps with the knowledge of his failure."

Tamera knew the lies that the media was spreading about Majoqui. They said the most awful things, accusing him of horrible crimes. But he had told her the truth about how they were trying to frame him. It was the government, just like her old boyfriend had told her. They were so bad.

"Is there anything else I can do for you?" she asked. "I can put money on your account."

He shook his head. "No. I have everything I need. But it is so good to see your beautiful face. The guards here are not so ... pretty."

She laughed. He was always so funny. Tamera had heard how men in jail would often use women to bring them money and things like that. But not Majoqui. In fact, he had money sent to her. He had told her just how much she needed to save for when he got out, and the rest he told her to use any way she liked. Every week or so, there would be a knock on her door, somehow they always knew when she was home, and there would be a member of Mara, often covered in many of the same types of tattoos that Majoqui wore. They always treated her with respect, and they gave her packages. Sometimes there was money inside, sometimes marijuana, and twice there were guns. She'd also received a wallet with credit cards and a Colorado license with Majoqui's picture on it, but somebody else's name. It was like being in a movie, and it was exciting.

"I love you," she said.

Majoqui stared into her eyes. "I know. I love you."

30

The sound of the gunshot woke me up. It didn't open my eyes because my eyes were already open, but it dragged me out from that strange timeless world of coma back into reality. I would have screamed if I could, but even my vocal cords were paralyzed.

A nurse came into the room, leaned over me, and dripped some saline into my eyes. I couldn't feel her thumb on my eyelids. I couldn't feel the drops as they splashed into my eyes. I couldn't feel the tissue as she wiped my cheek.

My body was dead.

Maybe I was dead, and this was Hell. An eternity stuck inside a lifeless body.

I didn't care. It didn't matter. Nothing in all the universe mattered anymore except one thing. Hate.

I hated ... everything. Life ... beauty ... the present ... the future. I hated the man I knew as Stitch, but most of all ... most of all, I hated God.

He had failed me. When I needed Him most, when I cried out to Him, when I begged Him with all my mind, with all my heart, with all my strength, He had turned a blind eye to me and let what happened happen.

I felt the rage inside me. Felt it burn with the ice that was now my soul. I heard the gunshots, both of them. And I made myself listen ... made myself watch ... over and over again as my love, and my life were murdered before me. And the rage grew. I listened to Jolene's voice, to Marla's cry, so filled with fear. I smelled the burning gas and rubber, saw the shattered glass and twisted steel. Watched as his boots grated and clicked, coming closer. Saw his face—that face that I should have known. And I let the guilt feed the fire; let it stoke it like an out of control boiler that was fast approaching its bursting point.

My mother and father came into the room. They stood, one on each side, and each picked up a hand. I couldn't feel them, but I felt the hate. The all-consuming hate. I even hated them. My own parents, because they were alive while my wife and child were not.

And in that instant, I went to war with God. I would never forgive Him. Never. Never.

And the rage exploded inside me, so powerful I thought it would kill me. But it didn't kill me. It did something else.

My eyes blinked.

I saw the shock and disbelief on their faces.

I blinked again.

I heard my mother say it was a miracle.

It was no miracle. It was hate. And I would use it. Use it as the weapon it was.

I would kill Stitch. And I would hate God forever.

31

Majoqui stared up at the cement ceiling of his cell. Court had gone well today. His lawyer had been granted another continuance. The American court system was ridiculous. If he could stretch this out long enough, Gil Mason might die of his injuries, and there would be no eyewitness to accuse him. Of course, there was much circumstantial evidence—the rifle, the motorcycle, his proximity to the shooting. But his lawyers, the best money could buy, had assured him these obstacles were not insurmountable.

In the meantime, the food was good, the bed reasonably soft, and the entertainment—television, movies, card games, chess, checkers, dominos—made the days go by quickly. There were even weight machines to help him keep in shape. He'd even put on a few pounds since getting out of the medical ward.

The medical ward.

He touched his head where it had struck the pavement. If not for the helmet, he would be dead. The helmet and his charms.

The memory drifted over him like an old friend. He closed his eyes and let his mind go back to that night.

The shot had been perfect. It was the twice cursed man himself that had kept it from being instantly fatal. At the exact instant Majoqui's finger pulled the trigger, the man had looked directly up and into his scope, and in the thousandth of a second it had taken the bullet to travel the hundred or so yards, the man moved. He jerked and started a turn, his hands twisting the steering wheel. It was so slight, just a fraction, but it was enough. The bullet, meant to strike him at the tip of his nose, instead clipped his chin. Its downward trajectory tunneled into his throat. Before Majoqui could re-sight and get off another round, the van sped up, swerved into the curb, flipped several times, and crashed into a light pole, nearly shredding the vehicle.

Majoqui slung the rifle over his shoulder and mounted the Ninja. By the time he reached the crash site, several small fires and debris had spread over a large area. The driver's front seat had detached, and both it and the driver had been catapulted through the windshield, landing twenty or so yards from the light pole. The seat was on its side, the man facing the destroyed vehicle.

His eyes were open.

The woman was alive, trapped inside the van, blood dribbling down her face from a head wound. Majoqui had seen much worse and guessed that under ordinary circumstances, she would have survived the injury. The back of the van had been nearly sheared in half just behind the baby seat. Suddenly Majoqui heard the little girl start crying. Truly the saints must be strong with this man for all of them to have survived such an event.

Majoqui walked up to the police officer, knelt, and looked into his motionless eyes. *Was he dead?* The pupils dilated slightly then squeezed down to pinpricks.

"You *are* alive," breathed out Majoqui. The idea that this Gil Mason could be so protected gave Majoqui an instant of fear. So much so that he considered getting back on his bike and leaving and never confronting this man again. But then another thought struck him. They had not survived because they were blessed or protected, but rather as a gift to Majoqui from the Virgin and the saints and the demons.

Majoqui saw the puddle of blood pooling under Gil Mason's head, spreading out from him in a lopsided circle. He was alive, but he could not move. He was helpless. He was alive, but not for long. Just long enough for him to watch. To watch and to know. To experience Majoqui's ultimate victory.

He would have liked to take his time, but sirens sounded in the distance. So, he ended them with a single shot for each. A part of him thought he should finish the man as well, but the widening pool of blood told Majoqui that Gil Mason had very little time anyway, and he wanted him to have those few minutes to contemplate on his failure—on Majoqui's success.

And so, he had gotten on the Ninja, a smile spreading across his lips as he saw the horror in his enemy's eyes, those staring eyes, and gunned the engine. He goosed the powerful bike, popping a slight wheelie, and then screeched across the asphalt. The wind swept across his face and hair, and he was off. He'd made it to Garrison before the late nineties model Ford pickup truck almost smashed into him. He'd managed to avoid it, but in the process caught the attention of a police car. And then came the chase and the stop sticks and then the fight and capture.

He learned that Gil Mason was alive but comatose and paralyzed. He considered having some of his brothers go to the hospital and kill him, but the thought of him trapped in a perpetual nightmare, where he had to helplessly witness his wife and daughter being slaughtered over and over and over was too sweet a revenge.

The witch woman's magic had been strong. He would have his men reward her greatly. And she would bless more charms. Because Majoqui was not yet done in this place. Majoqui would stay here in the American jail for a time. He would eat their food, sleep in their beds, take their medicine. He would grow strong. And from where he was, he would coordinate the infiltration of Mara to this state. And when it was time, he would leave the jail. Fat from their food, healed by their doctors, and ready to take control of the empire he had planned and was bringing to pass.

Majoqui smiled at the thought that he owed all this in part to his enemy. To Gil Mason.

_____

32

F our weeks passed since my first blink. Now I could talk and even walk a little.

The .308 round had hit me in the throat, barely missed the carotid artery, and clipped the C1 vertebrae, chipping it and causing trauma to my spinal column, before ripping out the backside of my neck. The damage and shock to my system had instantly and completely paralyzed me.

But the paralyzation was only temporary. Once the swelling and bruising to my spinal column dissipated and the shock to my system wore off, I began to slowly regain my normal bodily functions. The doctors tell me I was lucky.

They were wrong.

If the bullet had been a centimeter to the left, I wouldn't be here at all. That would have been lucky.

My parents told me about the funeral. About how hundreds of police officers turned out for the service to show their support for my family and me. I couldn't yet speak when they told me. I could blink and move my neck a little, but everything from the top of my chest down was dead, as though it wasn't even there. That's how I felt at the news of my wife and baby's funeral. Numb, like it was someone else hearing it.

In the first days after going to war with God, the rage and hate and desire for revenge sustained me. But since then, I'd come to terms with reality. I would never leave this bed. And even if I did, it would all be for nothing.

Mike Braden, my lieutenant, came in later that night and told me how they caught Stitch. His name was Majoqui Cabrera, and he was an MS 13 assassin. The Feds had an extensive work up on him, and once they knew who he was, they'd done a thorough audit of the dead bank manager's books and found out that he'd been laundering money for Mara. He'd also been stealing from them.

I didn't care. It didn't matter.

He would go to trial, be found guilty, sentenced to twenty years in prison, or maybe even get the death penalty, and end up dying in prison of old age. Colorado doesn't like to kill her death-row inmates. Instead, she lets them live long, useless lives so they can relive their glory days while eating well, watching TV, being kept warm in the winter, cool in the summer. Where they can be medicated, educated, and live a life of what many in poorer countries would consider a life of leisure.

And none of it mattered. Majoqui Cabrera was out of my reach, and my wife and daughter were gone. The knowledge sucked away the power of my rage, leaving me feeling dull and lost.

By the second week, I could feel sensation and temperature all the way down to my toes. I couldn't walk, but I could bend a little at the waist, and my arms were starting to twitch when I fought to move them, which wasn't often. I took my first steps in week three.

And now it was week four. I'd finished my morning exercises, mostly to keep the physical therapist from haranguing me, fifteen minutes before Nathan Bale, my father-in-law, walked into the room.

He stood there in the doorway, looking at me. His eyes were red and wet. He was thick and solid, built more like a cube than anything else. He'd taken state in college wrestling a few decades earlier in his life, and as he stood there, he looked as immovable as a boulder.

I stared back at him, emotions trying to battle within me, trying to find the energy to bubble to the surface, to gain some traction, some purchase so that they could claw their way back to life. I felt a warmth of rage at my loss, a spasm of guilt for not protecting his daughter and granddaughter as I had promised, and as was my duty, and a tingle of violence at what I would like to do to Stitch. But none of these were strong enough to break through the lethargic, chronic fatigue that had settled into my bones, making me as dead on the inside as I was on the outside.

Nathan watched me for a long while. He stood there, silent, unmoving, and unmovable. Like a statue of some long-ago golem come to take me to Hell.

And then finally, he shook his head slowly and stepped into the room.

"I tried to come," he said, "before ... many times ... but they wouldn't let me see you."

"I told them not to," I said, my voice sounding dead to my own ears.

"But ... but why?"

I just stared across the room. Not looking at him. Not speaking.

"I don't understand," he said.

"No," I said, "I don't suppose you would."

"Gil," he said. "I'm so sorry. So very, very sorry." He pulled out a handkerchief from his back pocket and wiped at his eyes. And in that instant, he didn't look like an impervious rock to me anymore. He was a broken man who had lost his most precious child.

I saw the shudder as it rippled from his shoulders down through his body, like water over a fall. I saw him break and crumble until he was racked with sobs. He walked over to me and smothered my hand in both of his.

I saw all of this, and I didn't care.

"Pray with me, son," he said, and he bowed his head, his tears dripping on my hand.

"No."

I didn't say it loud or with menace or malice. Just the simple single syllable with all the innate and final power the word held of its own accord.

"No."

And that stopped him. He looked up at me from under those bushy gray eyebrows, his eyes as blue as a newborn sky, still wet from his tears.

"What?"

I looked into those deep wells of kindness, the same eyes that had looked out at me from Jolene's face, the same as Marla's, and I still felt nothing. No shame, no guilt, no anger, no sympathy. Nothing.

"No. I don't pray anymore."

I heard him sigh, saw his jaw clench. He looked down, blinked a few times, then looked back at me.

"Don't do this, Gil."

I said nothing, just watched him. My face as dead as my family.

He shook his head. "Don't you dare do this, Gil."

"I'm only laying blame where blame is due."

"God didn't kill them. That criminal did."

"God is sovereign. Isn't that what you always say?"

He nodded, still holding my hand, tears still flowing down his cheeks.

"Yes, yes, of course, but we have free will; we make our own choices."

I was in no mood for a debate, no mood for anything. I just wanted to be left alone—forever.

"Either He made it happen, or He allowed it to happen, I don't care which. My wife and daughter are still dead. I hate Him for it." I looked into his eyes, my stare and voice equally neutral. "You should too."

He squeezed my hand, and I felt the bones grind together. I didn't return the grip.

He sniffed, wiped at his eyes with the handkerchief.

"This is grief talking. I understand."

"You understand nothing."

"Gil, this isn't God's fault."

"I want you to leave now."

"No, son, not until we've talked this through, not until you understand."

With my free hand, I pressed the buzzer for the nurse. She entered the room, a smile on her lips.

"I want him to leave," I said.

She looked at my father-in-law.

"Sir?" she said.

He gripped my hand again, and again I was limp, unresponsive.

"Gil, what you are doing is wrong. You have no right to blame God. No right to be angry with Him. Instead, you should be leaning on Him, seeking comfort in the knowledge that you will be with Jolene and Marla again one day. Be thankful that they are Christians and that God has made a way for us to be reunited with them."

"Be thankful? Thankful? To the God that sat by and watched while my little girl and my wife were slaughtered right in front of my eyes? Slaughtered while I was helpless to stop it? You need to leave now."

I looked at the nurse.

She put a light hand on Nathan's shoulder.

"Sir, would you come with me please?"

"Okay," said Nathan. "Okay, only I want you to think on this. It's not okay to be angry with the God of the Universe. It doesn't matter what you might think or what you might believe, even in your grief. God is God. He's real. He's loving and merciful and kind. But He is also powerful. And He doesn't take kindly to being blamed for things that are not His fault."

He let go of my hand, and it flopped back onto the bed. He turned and started to let the nurse lead him away.

"He could have saved them," I said. "He could have, but He didn't. I'll never forgive Him for that. No matter what you say."

I saw Nathan pause.

"I'll pray for you," he said.

"I don't want you to."

He looked back at me for just a second, and I saw more tears streaming down his face. "Free will," he said and then walked with the nurse out of the room and down the hall.

Majoqui was the model prisoner. He was revered by his fellow inmates for having killed cops and hated by the guards for the same reason. He had been quiet, peaceful, humble even for his entire stay.

That was about to change.

Majoqui had healed. He had begun the infiltration of Mara into the state of Colorado. Already his brothers had begun the fear campaign against the Bloods, the Crips, and several of the Hispanic gangs.

Majoqui had initially planned on staying longer but decided his personal touch would be required to truly take over the state's crime institutions. There were people that needed killing.

It was ten-thirty, fifteen minutes before lockdown. Thirty or so inmates milled about the day room, most dressed in orange, the felon's customary color. But a few were dressed in red, like Majoqui. Red signified danger, as in assault or escape risk. When you were in red, you wore shackles anytime you were outside of the day room.

The Cherokee County Jail was less than ten years old and built along the lines of most modern correctional facilities. There was nothing like it in San Salvador or any of the countries he frequented.

There was simply no way for him to escape these walls. Even if he had every member of Mara from all over the world attacking at the same time, he doubted they would be victorious. No, the only way to escape was to do so from outside.

Majoqui considered himself a simple man. And as a simple man, he believed in using what had worked in the past.

He was sitting at a round table, a chessboard painted on its surface. Three other inmates sat with him playing cards for commissary items. Majoqui had a full house in his hand and a homemade shiv hidden in the crotch of his underwear. The black man sitting next to him was named Jamal and had some form of mild mental condition. He was slow. Back home, Majoqui would have called him a retard, but here in the states, he found that word to be frowned on. "Mentally challenged," they called it.

Majoqui picked up his plastic cup of coffee. The coffee was not hot, but only Majoqui knew that. He raised the bet, then looked up to make sure everyone was intent upon their cards and the small paper chits they used in place of the actual commissary food from their personal stocks. Gambling was against the jail's rules. When he saw no one was looking at him, he threw the contents of his cup into his own face. He jerked to his feet in mock outrage, glaring at the gentle giant still sitting next to him.

"Jamal! You puta! Nobody does that to me!"

Jamal looked up stupidly. Majoqui punched him in the face and then dove into him. Jamal wrapped him in his arms, and they both fell to the floor, rolling.

Inmates started screaming and pounding on doors and tables. The day room erupted into a frenzy of clamor. No one interfered or tried to break them up.

Majoqui waited until he heard the sally port door open, then he reached into his pants and pulled out the make-shift knife. He turned the sharpened piece of metal on himself and plunged it into his side, away from any vital organs, where a love handle would be if he had one. He yelled and flailed, breaking Jamal's grip, just as deputies reached them.

"He stabbed me," he screamed as he dropped the knife onto the concrete floor. Only, with his wired jaw, it came out "shabbed me." Majoqui fell onto his back and writhed in agony as deputies jumped on top of the dumbfounded Jamal.

One deputy scooped up the knife while two more forced Majoqui's arms behind his back and cuffed him.

It took several minutes for the deputies to get the other inmates into their cells, and by that time, an impressive amount of blood had leaked out of Majoqui. He continued to moan until the nurse showed up.

"Please, I'm dying," he groaned and then pretended to pass out.

The nurse called for a gurney and then radioed the sergeant on duty to tell him they would need an ambulance.

Inwardly, Majoqui grinned. Of course, it would be more difficult this time; they knew what he had done and would take precautions. And because they thought they knew what he was capable of, those precautions would be extensive. Only they would still underestimate him because they had no idea what he was capable of.

Within a half-hour, he was in an ambulance on his way to the closest level-two trauma center in the area. Two deputies were in the ambulance beside him, with a third following in a patrol car. Both of his wrists were cuffed to the gurney. He moaned quietly, still acting nearly unconscious.

The paramedics continued their work as the lights flashed and the siren wailed. They inserted needles and tubes into his arms and the back of his hands. They attached round sticky patches with little metal knobs in their centers to his chest, arms, and legs. They started an IV drip and began monitoring his heart and other vital signs. In the cramped space of the rescue unit, the paramedic's bodies blocked him from the deputies' view.

Majoqui could unlock handcuffs with the end of a rat-tail comb, a paperclip, even a toothpick. Tonight, he used two springs he had obtained over the past three weeks from ink pens he'd stolen from deputies at the jail. It had taken several days of patient work to twist and twine the thin metal coils into straight tools that would be sufficient to pick the locks. He'd hidden them beneath a nail, one on each hand. The jail deputies had been careful to double-lock the restraints, making them more difficult to defeat. Add to that the fact that they were in a moving, speeding vehicle that was juking and jagging its way through intersections and traffic, with paramedics jostling for position and bumping against him repeatedly. And so Majoqui did not let it affect his pride that it took him almost thirty seconds to pry the springs from his nails, unwind them and unlock the handcuffs, freeing his hands to do what they were about to do.

The deputy on his right wore a level-three duty holster, which meant it had three safeties to defeat before the gun could be removed. The deputy on his left wore a simple snap holster, much easier to conquer. Majoqui waited. His brothers from Mara should arrive at any time.

He watched through slit lids as they took a corner. Something hit them hard and fast as they entered the intersection.

It was time.

The impact threw the paramedic onto him, obscuring him from the deputy's view. The deputy was also thrown, but into the back of the paramedic. Majoqui reached under the paramedic's arm, turned into him at the same time, and gripped the butt of the deputy's gun. With his pinky finger, he popped the safety snap, and as the ambulance fishtailed and spun, he leaned back, the gun sliding smoothly free.

Majoqui had hoped neither deputy would notice, but both reacted instantly. The one on his right was reaching for his weapon when the bullet struck him in the mouth. It was a .45, causing horrible damage.

The second deputy was trying to push the paramedic out of his way, but it was nearly impossible in the cramped quarters. Majoqui reached around the paramedic and fired three times into the deputy's groin and pelvic area. The deputy screamed and continued to scream as he crumpled against the wall and then onto the floor. Majoqui shot both paramedics, one bullet each through their heads, then sat up and shot the writhing deputy through the eye.

The driver of the rescue unit slammed on the brakes, throwing Majoqui off the gurney and into the forward wall. The impact made him dizzy, but he shook his head and aimed through the small open section between his compartment and the driver's. He was too late. The driver had jumped out the door, and worse, he'd taken the keys with him.

Majoqui quickly stripped the gun from the dead deputy's level three holster and collected his extra magazines as well. He found a cell phone on the cop's belt and took it as well.

The patrol car tailing them had stopped about fifteen yards back. He would be calling in reinforcements. Majoqui opened the side door and slipped out. Instantly, the patrol car's spotlight found him. As it did, the occupants of the vehicle that had crashed into the ambulance opened fire on the cruiser. Majoqui himself pumped three bullets in the direction of the patrol car's windshield, then ducked back inside as sparks flew from the side of the rescue rig.

Another car came screeching up to the patrol vehicle, and automatic gunfire raked the car's windows and body.

Majoqui jumped out of the ambulance and started for the first of the cars when gunfire sounded behind him. Something hot and deadly burned past his face, and he reflexively fell to the asphalt. Rolling up to the front tire, he peered around in time to see a state trooper outside of another patrol car sporting an AR-15 that was aimed at him. Majoqui ducked back just as a supersonic bullet flattened the tire.

A hail of gunfire flew at the trooper from Majoqui's support vehicles, forcing the officer to retreat to the back of his car for cover. Majoqui would have to cross directly through the line of fire to get to his brothers in Mara. He would have to wait until the trooper was either hit or in the process of reloading. But more sirens were coming fast, and every second counted.

Majoqui made the decision to change his plan of escape. He fired two rounds at the trooper and ran across the street and up against a house. He slid around the corner and into a row of bushes. The bushes offered him some amount of concealment as he made his way to the north.

This was a residential area, and he ran for several blocks, staying as much in shadow as possible. Once he was a reasonable distance away, he started trying door handles. Being in the suburbs instead of downtown, he found the front latch unlocked on the fourth house he tried.

Majoqui locked the door behind him.

All the lights were out, and the home was quiet. Majoqui crept up the stairs to the master bedroom. Inside was a woman in her mid-forties sleeping soundly. On the nightstand were pictures of the woman with a child, a young boy. In the photo, the woman looked younger. Majoqui hoped that meant the boy was at least a teenager now. Majoqui was not a big man. He didn't need large-sized clothing.

Majoqui searched the room, his eyes fully adjusted to the dark. In the distance, he heard numerous sirens coming into the area. Coming for him. But he was safe.

He had hoped to find something he could use to crush the woman's skull. He had the guns, of course, but he did not want to take the chance of damaging them. In the end, he simply clamped his hand over her nose and mouth. She tried to fight, but it didn't last long. He held her for several minutes after she'd given up and gone limp, just to make sure.

He found the boy in the back bedroom. Asleep. He was around fifteen and taller than Majoqui, although more slender and with a touch of acne on his cheeks and nose. In this room, Majoqui found many blunt weapons. He finally settled on a metal baseball bat that sat in a corner with a brown leather mitt draped over the knob. Gently, he pulled the sheet up over the sleeping boy's face and head.

Afterward, Majoqui made himself a sandwich from the kitchen and washed it down with a soda. In the bathroom, he found peroxide and bandages and made short work of the stab wound. It still seeped blood, but although it was deep, he had been careful not to hit anything vital. He popped a few aspirin and dragged the dead woman into her son's room.

The woman's bed was very comfortable, and he'd almost fallen asleep when he remembered the dead deputy's phone. He called Tamera, told her he was out and that he would contact her in a few days. He hung up, took the battery out of the phone, and dropped it on the floor. He stripped, pulled the covers up over his shoulders, and was asleep before the last of the police sirens had stopped wailing.

34

Majoqui has escaped. I lay in my bed watching the newscasters on the television screen overhead. And for the first time in weeks ... I felt ... something. A spark. Life. Emotion. *Hate.*

For the first time since losing my family, I had a reason to live.

Revenge.

Revenge is mine saith the Lord.

Not this time. This time it's mine.

I *would* kill Majoqui Cabrera.

I moved my trembling fingers to the hospital phone and called my lieutenant, Michael Braden. I still had only limited use of my motor skills, and it took me three times to get the number right. He answered after the second ring.

"Hello?"

"Did you hear?" I asked.

"Yeah, the Sheriff called a few minutes ago. I'm watching the news now."

"I want on it."

"Gil, you can barely move."

"I'll get better ... fast."

There was a long pause.

"Gil, buddy, it's just not possible. You know that."

"I'll be out of here in a week."

"No, Gil, it's not just that. You're too close. You're personally involved. You have to know there's no way on Earth we can let you have any part in this investigation. It would be automatic grounds for a dismissal of the case, or even if we somehow won, for an appeal. Not to mention how it would leave us open to civil litigation. You just have to sit this out and let us do our jobs."

There was another long pause before I spoke.

"There won't be a trial, Mike."

"Stop talking, Gil. Go to sleep. I'll come see you in the morning."

He hung up on me.

I pushed the buzzer for the nurse. She appeared at my door almost immediately.

"Yes?"

"I need to speak with the physical therapist."

A puzzled expression came over her face. She looked at her watch.

"You mean now ... tonight?"

"Yes. Right now."

"I'm sorry, but they only work in the daytime, Mr. Mason."

"Then help me into a wheelchair and take me to the gym, or the physical therapy room, or whatever you call it."

She shook her head. "I wish I could help, but I have other patients to take care of. And besides, the physical therapy room is closed at night. I'm afraid you'll just have to wait until tomorrow."

I could feel the blood pumping in my temple, and I had to fight down the impulse to scream at her. Instead, I lay back and closed my eyes.

"All right. I want to see the physical therapist first thing in the morning."

She told me she would make sure he got the message and left the room. As soon as she was gone, I opened my eyes and gripped the sidebars of my bed. My muscles felt like pasta left in water overnight.

My arms, shoulders, and chest muscles shook and trembled as I pushed up, lifting my weight from the bed.

Up-down, up-down, up-down. I did five dips before my arms gave out, and I crumpled into the bed. Sweat rolled down my face, and fire shot through my triceps. The room swam before me and lights sparked behind my eyes. My breath rasped in and out of my lungs like I was some ancient asthmatic.

I waited thirty seconds and started my second set.

There was no time to waste. I had a man to kill.

35

T amera Sun reached into the bag and found the cell phone at the bottom. She took it out and looked at it. Excitement bubbled inside her. She knew Majoqui would be calling her soon. The Mara member had been a boy this time. He couldn't have been older than twelve and had no visible tattoos yet. He had dropped off the plain paper bag and left without speaking a word. But Tamera had seen the news reports.

She didn't know where Majoqui was, but she knew where he wasn't ... in jail. And she knew that nothing would keep him from getting in contact with her.

Slipping the phone into her jean's pocket, she brewed a cup of tea, pet her cat's fur, and turned on the TV. All the local stations were talking about the escape and the big shoot out. She sat on the loveseat with Miranda curled in her lap. The tea was hot, and she took it in tiny sips. She was so nervous she considered smoking some pot to calm her but decided against it because she wanted to relish the feeling of knowing that they would be together very soon.

Tamera had quit her job nearly a month ago at Majoqui's request. Majoqui never *ordered* her to do anything; he was too much of a gentleman for that. He would simply suggest to her that she do something. The idea of refusing any of his requests never entered her mind. He was the man ... and he was a real man. So unlike the other boys she had known. He made her feel like a real woman. He made her feel like a princess. She felt completely safe with him. And she would do anything for him.

The phone vibrated in her pocket.

MAJOQUI PEERED through the curtains of the woman's front window as he waited for Tamara to answer her phone. The police had been conducting house-to-house searches for several hours. Twice they had rung the doorbell, and twice they had tried calling into the house. Both times they left. There was no forced entry, no sign of a disturbance, all the doors and windows were locked, so they could only conclude there was no one home. They had left, but Majoqui was sure they would be back, and eventually, they might decide they had to get inside to make certain he wasn't there. However, that would not be until someone called the police saying the woman had not shown up for work or the boy had missed school or family members were worried about them. And so, in the meantime, he was safe.

Tamera answered the phone. He talked to her soothingly for several minutes and then gave her the instructions for where and when to pick him up. After that, he napped for several hours. He would not leave until evening. The boy's clothes would help, as would the red hair dye he found in the woman's bathroom, but the dark was his best friend now that they had pictures of him.

At three o'clock he raided the refrigerator and made himself a nice lunch. There was no beer, but he did find several bottles of red wine. Majoqui was no connoisseur, but he liked his drink less sweet than Sangria. Still, it wasn't bad, and it did give him a slight buzz.

Speaking of which, he could already hear the flies in the woman's son's bedroom, even through the closed door. It amazed Majoqui how insects could always manage to find the dead. There wasn't even any smell yet, and still, here they were.

Majoqui finished his lunch, watched some television, mostly about himself, and slept off and on for another three hours. The police didn't come back, and even before it was completely dark, their cars had deserted the neighborhood.

At nine-thirty, a yellow Volkswagen puttered its way down the street and stopped five houses down. Majoqui locked the door behind him and started toward the car.

He had an empire to build.

36

Three weeks had passed since my first set of dips. I could walk, even jog, for brief periods. I used real weights and could bench about one-fifty. Still a long way from my usual sets of three-twenty-five, but progress.

Majoqui Cabrera was still free. A middle-aged woman and her son had been murdered in their home the night he escaped, just a short distance from the crash, and it was apparent he'd stayed there for at least a day. There had been no sightings of him, and the common consensus was that he fled back to South America.

It didn't matter. I would find him. Wherever he was.

My father-in-law tried to see me twice more; both times, I refused.

I was out of the hospital and back at the house. When Jolene and Marla were alive, it was a home; now, it was only a house. A place to eat, sleep and work out. Nothing more.

I slept on the couch and hadn't gone into our bedroom or the nursery since coming back. I bought new clothes and showered in the guest bathroom.

The dreams were mostly bad. I kept reliving the event ... that's what the shrink from work called it ... *the event*. At first, it would happen almost constantly, and in the mornings, I would be more tired than before I went to sleep. But slowly it got better, to the point where I would wake up in a sweat only once or twice a night. Again ... progress.

The doctors hadn't signed off for me to return to work yet, but that didn't stop me. I started making calls and calling in debts. I had every cop I knew squeezing their snitches and contacts to get a line on Majoqui. Sooner or later, something would turn up. I have friends in the FBI, DEA, military intelligence, even the CIA, and they were all keeping tabs on their wiretaps, drug deals, and gang surveillance.

No one could remain completely anonymous, not these days, but Majoqui was doing a pretty good job. MS 13 had always been one of the toughest gangs to crack. They were brutal on snitches, and fear had a way of shutting people's mouths. But Majoqui had somehow taken that fear of talking to a new level.

My K9, Pilgrim, was bored out of his mind. At Cherokee County, we take our dogs home with us. The County owns them, but they live with their handlers. Athena Marie had taken care of him while I was in the hospital, and even now, she came over twice a day to help me feed and pick up after him. She also brought me the latest news on Majoqui and MS 13. And although there had been no news on Majoqui, MS 13 was another matter.

I finished the last of twenty pull-ups, my arms shaking like I'd done a hundred, and let my feet drop to the floor. Athena had rigged the pull-up bar across the doorway of the kitchen.

Wiping sweat from my forehead with the bottom of my shirt, I staggered over to the table and sat heavily in the chair. My heartbeat was a hundred and forty, and it felt like there wasn't enough air in the whole house to get my breathing back to normal.

"Don't die on me, Sarge," said Athena, as she filled Pilgrim's bowl with water.

"Rehabilitation ain't as fun as it's cracked up to be."

She laughed. "Isn't that the truth! I broke my wrist when I was fifteen and had a cast for three months. My wrist was as thin as a pencil when I got it off and felt like it was made of glass. The simplest things were nearly impossible, and I felt like I had to baby it all the time. The exercises they gave me to strengthen it looked so easy on paper, but they hurt like crazy."

She gave Pilgrim a pat on the head and looked over at me. "You're doing good though, boss. Last week you couldn't do five pull-ups. At this rate, you'll be back to normal in a month."

Normal. No. I would never be back to normal.

I nodded, keeping my true feelings to myself. "Thanks for the chin-up bar. It's been a real help."

She brought me a glass of ice water and sat next to me at the table. "My pleasure. Now to work." She flipped up the screen on her laptop and punched in her password.

"There've been seven different reports of MS 13 moving in on other gang's turf. And not just the Bloods and the Crips either." She navigated the touchpad and brought up a series of news reports. "Yesterday, a Sons of Silence member got half his hand cut off by a machete as he was conducting a business transaction that may or may not have involved a certain crystal substance."

I scanned the report. "Anything to indicate Majoqui was involved?"

She shook her head. "No, but none of this started until he escaped."

I nodded. "The question is—is he behind all this, or is it just a result of them seeing fertile territory when they came out to help him? If he's the brains, he has to still be in the state. If not, he could be back in South America."

"Yes, sir. That is the question."

"We have to push harder," I said. "Whether he's here or there, somebody had to have seen something. Any word on the yellow Volkswagen?"

"Our guys are stopping every one of them they can get reasonable suspicion on. So far, nothing."

Frustration was making me crazy. I felt the blood pumping at my temples. I always hated being an armchair quarterback. I work my best out in the field where I can look into a suspect's eyes and hear the timbre of his voice. Relying on others is hard. I had to get out on my own.

"Anything else?" I asked.

"Just this, and it may be unrelated." She pulled up a grainy black and white security video. "An Aurora detective sent me a video stream. He was working a gas drive-off call and checking the video surveillance when he happened to see it." She stopped the feed and pointed to a man at the counter. His face was away from them, but he had collar-length dark hair and was wearing an untucked plaid shirt and dark jeans.

"What about him?" I asked.

"Watch," she said.

As the clerk finished ringing up his items, the man reached back for his wallet, pulling his shirt up on the side in the process, revealing a wide swatch of belt.

"There," said Athena. "See the shine? How it doesn't bend? And look how wide it is."

I nodded. "The belt sword. That Aurora detective has a good eye. I wouldn't have caught that."

"Me neither," she said. "We sent out pictures of it after the night club massacre and even included a website that shows video of it in use, but still, it was a great catch."

I stared at the screen.

"What do you think," she asked, "is it him?"

I shook my head slowly. "I don't know. He's about the right height and weight. The build and stance are similar. But I can't be sure. I need to see his face. Any other angles?"

"No, that's all he had."

"Run it back and freeze on him as he leaves the store."

She maneuvered the touchpad.

"See how he never looks at the camera?"

She scrunched her lips. "Maybe, or it could just be bad luck for us."

"Could be, but he's a smart little bad guy, cunning. It's the kind of behavior I'd expect from him." I stared a little longer. I could see his neckline and a small portion of his right jaw. "There's not enough. I can't tell. When you get a chance, download it and send it to my phone."

There was nothing conclusive, but it might be him. It was something, maybe. I looked at the grainy image a final time. *If it's you*, I thought, *I will get you.*

PILGRIM LAY under the table as the two of them talked. He missed Jolene and Marla. He couldn't know what had happened to them or where they had gone ... just that they were no longer a part of his life. And that made him sad. Marla used to sneak snacks to him, and he would ride her around on his back ... she weighed almost nothing. And she hugged him and rubbed her face in his fur. He would lick her face and make her giggle and crawl away from him before returning for more. But now there was no little girl to play with and no Jolene to scratch his head, rub behind his ears, sing her quiet songs while she cooked or did the dishes, or worked around the house. Now there was only the Alpha, and he was different. His voice was different. The way he moved was different. Even his smell was different. It wasn't just his injuries; it went far deeper than that. Pilgrim could sense where he hurt ... the damage to his physical body. But his true hurt lay somewhere Pilgrim couldn't see or hear or smell. Somewhere hidden. Somewhere bad. Pilgrim wondered if it might be the same place that kept Jolene and Marla from him. If he could know where that place was, he would find them, and he would kill wherever or whatever kept them from him. He wanted it to be like it used to be, little Marla playing with him and Jolene and her beautiful voice and the Alpha watching over them with Pilgrim at his side.

Athena and the Alpha continued to speak at the table above him. Their voices were animated, and he heard something in the Alpha's voice he hadn't heard since Jolene and Marla left ... *excitement*. He listened closer. Yes, excitement, but not the type of excitement that used to often meld with his tones. Different. Filled with hate and anger. Pilgrim had never really hated anyone. He loved the hunt and the fight and the vanquishing of an opponent. But he'd never really hated anyone. So the emotion was hard for Pilgrim to fully comprehend. To make sense of. But the loss of Jolene and Marla and the change in the Alpha's behavior was affecting him as much as it affected the Alpha, planting true seeds of hatred into the nexus of his soul.

Pilgrim's animal brain explored the emotion and pain and loneliness that invaded his world, stripping away his natural confidence and happiness until a slow-burning flame flared in his heart, and he began to understand, at least on some level, what the Alpha felt. What true hatred is.

From the excitement in the Alpha's tone, Pilgrim understood that it must have something to do with the change in their lives. Something to do with the loss of Jolene and Marla. And whatever it was, Pilgrim hated it. He hated it with his newfound hatred. Pilgrim would help the Alpha find whoever or whatever had taken Jolene and Marla from them. And when they found it, Pilgrim would allow the hatred its reign.

TAMERA SUN WATCHED the four men leave the apartment. They were young and tough-looking, but they all paid great respect to Majoqui. On the table in front of her was a pile of money, over a hundred thousand dollars—more money than Tamera had ever seen in real life. In the last few weeks, millions of dollars had come in and gone out of her small apartment. And Majoqui was responsible for all of it. What a man he was. And he loved her. A goofy little waitress from Kansas, loved and protected by a man of wealth and power and courage. He was her knight in shining armor.

She saw that he was looking at her.

"What are you thinking?" he asked.

"How much I love you."

"That is good," he said. "I will be out late tomorrow."

The smile drifted from her lips. "How late?"

"All night, perhaps."

"Will you be ... safe?"

He started stacking the money.

"I am always safe. But I like that you worry for me." He gathered together more of the loose bills. "I will have men watch over you. You will be safe."

The smile came back.

"I'm not scared."

"That too is good," he said. He looked up at her, reached over, and took her hand. "The money can wait."

"Yes," she said, "it can."

37

Jim Black shook his head.

"I just can't do it, Gil," he said.

I took a sip of my coffee, set the cup down.

"Look, Jim, I'm not asking to be lead or anything like that. I don't even have to be in on the arrest. But I am going to help catch this ... this guy, one way or the other."

Technically I was still out on FMLA and would be for a few more weeks, but I felt pretty strong again, although my endurance was low.

"You know I want to help, Gil. You and me go way back, but we've got to do this by the book. Otherwise, it all gets thrown out in court. You know that better than anyone."

We were at a Caribous. Jim was drinking some foo-foo concoction that was supposed to pass for coffee while I had my usual, strong and black, just like back in the Corps.

"I do know better than anybody, and I've got more to lose than anyone involved, so don't think for a second that I'll do anything to jeopardize the case. But I know this guy. I've seen him, I've looked into his eyes. And I've got boots on the ground looking for him. It was my snitch that almost tagged him at the club."

"I understand all of that, Gil, but what do you want me to do?"

I took another sip, looked straight at him.

"I want to see the file. I want access to everything you have. On him, on Mara, everything."

Jim shook his head. "I can't do it."

"Yes, you can."

"No, Gil ...."

"Yes, you can. Look, it'll all be under the table. No one will know. Just you and me."

He shook his head again.

"Wait," I said, "just hear me out. Officially, I'm not working. I've got twenty-four-seven to devote to nothing but catching Majoqui Cabrera. I'll be undercover like no one else because, right now, I'm not really a cop. I can go places a cop can't go, fit in places a cop couldn't."

I rubbed the five-day growth of stubble on my cheeks and chin.

"I don't have to shave. I haven't cut my hair since the ... incident. I don't even have to shower. And everything I get goes straight to you."

I could see he still wasn't buying it, so I pulled out the big guns.

"Jim, I know your career goals. You want to make at least captain before you retire. You crack this case ... you catch Majoqui Cabrera, and you're guaranteed chief, maybe even undersheriff."

He stopped shaking his head, picked up his coffee, and took a slow drink.

"You don't make chief by breaking the rules," he said.

"Yes, you do," I said. "Sometimes, sometimes, you do. You make chief by getting results. And I'm going to get those results. I'm going to get Majoqui Cabrera with or without your help. It will be easier, faster, with you, but I'm going to get him either way. The only real question here is are you going to be in on it or not?"

He took another drink.

"If this got out, it could cost me my job."

"It won't," I said. "If it does, I'll say I stole the file. I won't leave you hanging; you know me better than that."

He set the cup down and looked me in the eye.

"We don't have a lot."

"Anything's better than nothing," I said.

He reached into his pocket and pulled out a thumb drive and a cheap cell phone and slid them over to me.

"Don't put this on a work computer. Buy some phone cards. We won't use work phones or our personal cells, just these. My number's already programmed into it ... only mine."

It was my turn to take a sip of coffee.

"You come prepared," I said.

He didn't smile.

"Yes, I do."

I pulled a cheap cell phone out of my pocket and looked at it.

"I guess I won't need this."

Jim smiled, but it was guarded.

"Great minds ..." he said.

"I'm going to get him," I said.

He shook his head, finished off his coffee.

"I believe you. But don't kill him, Gil. I know you're thinking you want to, but that isn't the way. You have to let the courts take care of this. You want revenge; I understand that, I do. Let him go to prison where he'll get raped in the showers three times a week, end up with AIDS, and maybe get shanked over a pack of cigarettes or a bad drug deal. Let that be your revenge. Let him suffer long and hard. Believe me, it's worse than a quick death, especially for a little pretty boy like him."

I looked into my coffee cup as I held it to my lips, letting the steam hide my eyes.

"Sure," I said. "That's what I'll do. I'll let the courts take care of it."

"I want your word."

I set the cup down, looked him in the eye.

"I give you my word."

Hating God made lying a lot easier.

38

The new car was a Cadillac Escalade, black like my coffee. I dropped the backseat to use it as a makeshift kennel for Pilgrim. I'd need him. The gun was a Beretta nine-millimeter that I'd bought off a banger in downtown Denver. The serial number was filed off, but that didn't matter to me. He'd tried to jack up the already jacked up price, but I let him see past my eyes into my real eyes ... my dog eyes ... like looking into my soul. My soul was a dark place just then, and he backed off right away, took the previously agreed on money, and beat feet out of there. Wise move. After all, I did have a fully loaded nine-millimeter with no serial number in my hand.

It was one-thirty in the morning, and I had parked down the street from a bar I knew to be a hangout of the Crips in Aurora. I recognized at least three gangsters I'd arrested over the years and a few more I thought I might have had contact with. I let them alone. I needed someone who wouldn't recognize me.

And then I saw him.

He was short, maybe five-five, with thick shoulders and rounded biceps. He had a gut, but it looked hard like the rest of him. He was black, not brown, but "black black," like a Nigerian. He was decked out all in blue. Blue baseball cap, the bill slid to the side, blue baggy mid-calf jeans that sagged halfway down his butt over blue boxers, and a blue sleeveless silk shirt that was open to his belly showing his tats. Oh, and of course, blue Nikes. He was around twenty-five, with the unmistakable round puckered scar of a healed bullet wound over his right pec. Yeah, he looked to be hard all right.

I didn't spot any weapons, but that didn't mean he wasn't carrying. He was obviously an OG, which stands for Original Gangster, which was exactly what I wanted. In ordinary life, twenty-five is young, but living the gang life is like dog years, which would make him about a hundred and seventy-five.

I followed his blue Honda Civic away from the bar at a reasonable distance. Not letting him know he was being followed at a quarter to two in the morning on a Thursday would be nearly impossible— especially when one was following a righteously paranoid gang member that had been shot at least once in his life. But I didn't plan on letting him get far. Turned out, he was better than I thought. He picked up that I was tailing him before we'd made the third light. He pulled into an ally off Chambers and Colfax and stopped the car. I pulled in behind him.

This was the dangerous part.

I exited the Escalade, closed the driver's side door, and stood next to it, watching him. I saw him looking at me in the rearview mirror, even in the dark of the alley. He seemed very calm, and that told me a lot about him.

Finally, he opened the door and stepped out, facing me. I still didn't see any weapons, but again, that didn't mean he didn't have any.

"Whatch you want, white boy?" he asked. His voice was even and calm, like his demeanor. He wasn't scared. Not a bit.

"I need some information."

He cocked his head like maybe I was crazy.

"And why would I give you information?"

"Because it will help you."

"I don't need no help from no cracker cop."

"Why does everything have to be about race?"

He just looked at me.

"Besides," I said, "I'm not a cop."

He snorted at that.

"You as cop as cop gets."

"Not right now," I said. "Right now, I'm exactly what *you* need."

"I don't need nothing."

I almost told him that was a double negative but decided against it.

He turned to get back into the Civic.

"I need some information on a group that's cutting into your territory and your profits. A south of the border gang."

That stopped him.

He gave me that head cock look again.

"And when I say 'cutting,' I mean it both figuratively and literally."

"Oh, you think that's funny? Lil BB is a bro of mine. Him getting cut like that ain't funny."

"But you haven't done anything about it," I said. "And that's because Mara is hard and dangerous to deal with, not to mention secretive. I can help with that."

"Crips don't need no help from no honky cops. We know how to take care of the thirteens."

"I'm not saying you can't, what I am saying is, why not let somebody else do your work for you? Tell me what I need to know, and I'll clear Mara out of your areas. Guarantied."

He did the head cock thing again.

"Why?"

"Why what?" I asked.

"Why you cops sticking your noses into a blood feud between the blues and the thirteens? And why you want to help us over them?"

I walked up close to him,

"They killed cops. And they're turning the streets into a war zone. That's got to stop, and they've got to pay."

He was quiet for a while, thinking, so I let him be quiet and think.

Finally, he said, "That's cool. I can believe that. Why you pick me?"

"Two reasons. First, I don't know you, and you don't know me. Second, you're no punk kid. You're not in it just for the quick cash, drugs, and girls. You're not even in it for the rep, not anymore anyway. No, you are loyal. Loyal to the Crips and what they stand for. Now, I don't agree with that particular choice, but I am also loyal, so I can relate. We belong to different gangs, you and I, but we both believe in what we are doing. And since, for the time being at least, we have certain goals that are the same, I say you and I, just us, agree to help each other to accomplish those goals."

"I ain't no snitch," he said.

"This isn't about snitching. This is about killing."

"Killing thirteens."

"Yes," I said. "Killing thirteens."

He nodded, thinking again.

"One thing," he said.

"What's that?"

"Thirteens is killing Bloods too, but they can't be no part of this. I ain't siding with no Bloods, not even to kill thirteens."

I held out my hands.

"The enemy of my enemy ...," I said. "It only makes sense to hit them from both sides. It will go faster."

He shook his head.

"Bloods killed my baby's momma long time ago. The only use I got for Bloods is target practice. So, it's me or them. You choose."

I had planned on using both the Crips and the Bloods to squeeze in on Mara, but this changed things. I had a choice to make.

"Deal," I said.

"Whatchu want to know?"

"Majoqui Cabrera."

He nodded, a thin smile stretching his lips.

"The Crow," he said. "Bird of death. Yeah, he's the one started the ball rolling. But you don't have to worry about him."

"Why not?"

He pulled out his cell phone and checked the time.

"'Cause in 'bout ten minutes he gonna be dead."

39

Majoqui Cabrera watched through the telescopic scope and saw the two Crips, dressed in blue and black, get out of the car. One of them held a silver briefcase. They were in the Bull's Eye parking lot in Gunwood, and the place was well lit. Majoqui's contacts had told him of the drug deal going down. Six Kees of coke worth roughly two-hundred and fifty thousand dollars brought in from Mexico and fresh for the taking. The Crips had the money, and whoever the cartel had paid to mule the money up from Texas had the drugs.

Some were afraid to steal from the cartels, but not Majoqui. Besides, the blame would fall on the Crips anyway.

Ten minutes later, a white SUV pulled into the parking lot, circled twice, and then stopped a short distance from the Crips. Two men got out and started talking to them. Majoqui waited, watching through the high-powered sight. Neither the weapon nor the scope was as good as those he had used to shoot the American police officer, Gil Mason. No, the police had those, but these would do.

All four of the men went to the back of the SUV. They opened the tailgate and looked in. They stayed there for a short time, talking and reaching inside the vehicle. Finally, the Crip with the briefcase handed over the case and some car keys to one of the two men from the SUV. The two men walked over to the car the Crips had come in and opened the front doors.

That was the signal.

Two groups of three broke from the bushes at the edge of the lot and ran toward the two vehicles. They were Mara, and they were armed with fully automatic rifles equipped with suppressors. Majoqui knew of the Gunwood police and their quick response time and wanted to take no chances.

But as the two groups came within twenty yards of the vehicles, something strange happened. Flashes erupted from the back of the SUV, and Majoqui's men began to fall. A barrage of gunfire exploded, and sparks chipped and danced off the vehicles and asphalt. Glass shattered, and metal thunked and plunked as heavy bullets punched their way home.

Majoqui took only a second to see what was happening. It was a trap, and he had fallen into it. He sighted in on the driver who was now out of the car and shooting at Majoqui's brothers.

Majoqui fired. A puff of red misted the air, and the Crip dropped limply to the tarmac. A slight shift and the second man fell just as swiftly. Four more piled out of the small car. Majoqui instantly understood that they had been lying down in the back seat, just as the men must have been in the SUV. How many were there, he wondered? No time for that, though. There was time only to kill.

He turned his attention to the SUV and started placing rounds through the back windows. The high-velocity .308s slid through the glass effortlessly.

Five of his six men were down, but Majoqui was not known as The Crow for nothing. He planned for every contingency.

Three cars raced into the parking lot packed with Mara members. They opened up on the SUV with a variety of firearms. No suppressors here. They were the backup, and noise was not their concern.

Majoqui turned back to the other car and sent a bullet through the forehead of the closest Crip. His next round missed its mark as the man moved at the last instant. He saw the hole that punched through the door frame just above the man's head. He re-sighted and was about to fire when something made him turn to the side. Four Crips were scrambling over a brick wall below him and coming his way. They must have been looking for him, and now that they had pinpointed his position from the muzzle flash of his rifle. They were coming hard and fast. This he had not anticipated. The Crips were learning, adapting. He would have to be more careful.

He shot the closest man through the throat. The second man hesitated for just an instant at the sight of his dying comrade and then fell like a puppet with its strings cut. A copper-jacketed slug passed through the top of his skull, through his brain, down his neck, to exit near the base of his spine.

The other two men were shooting at him now, their bullets whipping by at differing velocities, churning up grass, and burning the air as they passed.

Majoqui ignored the flying pieces of death as though they were nothing more than bothersome insects. He calmly shot both men.

Something stung the inside of his right thigh, and as he turned, a white-hot streak of lead burned across his shin. Two more Crips came from behind. Majoqui dropped the rifle and pulled out the little .380 in his waistband. He shot the closest man five times and saw small puffs of dust lift from the man's shirt with each shot. He fell, tripping the second man. The gun flew from his hand and landed close to Majoqui.

Majoqui could have shot him dead, but he didn't. It was time for a lesson. He snapped the sword belt from his waist, and as the Crip rose, he swung it in a diagonal downward stroke that took off both of the boy's hands at the forearms. Blood sprayed in a geyser, and the boy, no older than seventeen, Majoqui guessed, stood there gaping at where his hands used to be. Majoqui swung again, and the boy toppled as his left leg separated just below the knee. He hit the grass, and now he was screaming, blubbering, begging for his mother.

Majoqui scanned the area looking for any further threats. There were none. His men had killed the rest of the Crips and were quickly hacking their bodies with long machetes. In the distance, sirens could be heard. As if on cue, his men stopped their mutilation and gathered up their dead, piling them into the cars. And then they were gone. Now there was only Majoqui and the screaming boy. Majoqui picked up his rifle and, as he passed the bleeding Crip, casually swung down with the sword a final time, severing the boys remaining foot at the ankle. The boy shrieked as though he were being burned in a fire. Once again, the charms had worked, and Majoqui was safe. He did not spare the boy out of compassion; he spared him to send a message.

And the message would be understood.

40

The first call was from the Crip I had made the deal with. It was two o'clock in the morning, and he was wide awake and mad. I didn't know his name, not even his street name, and that was the way we were going to keep it. In my head, I called him 'Dog' because of the way he canted his head when he was thinking. So, Dog he was, although I would have to be careful not to call him that out loud, he might take offense. Dog called me on the cell phone I'd initially gotten for Jim Black. He told me their plan, whatever it had been, had failed and that The Crow was still alive and that he would get back with me as soon as he got any information that might help me find him. The conversation was short, and as soon as the second call came in, I understood why.

It was Jim Black, and he told me about the massacre in Gunwood. Eighteen dead Crips, all shot up and hacked to pieces. And another in critical condition with no hands or feet. It made national news—the most significant gangland killing since the Capone era. And right here in the sleepy little bedroom community in Colorado. Jim said it had Majoqui's handy work written all over it ... and in blood. I told Jim about Majoqui's secret title, The Crow. He said it fit, and I agreed.

He said he'd start a world-wide search for info on the street name of The Crow.

I went back to my computer and the file that Jim had supplied me, looking for anything they might have missed that would give me a clue to Majoqui's whereabouts.

It was nearly five in the morning, and I hadn't slept in thirty hours. The dreams were too bad. Every time I closed my eyes, I was back in the van, noticing the glint, hearing the music, and saving my wife and daughter—only to wake up with the knowledge of the truth slapping me in the face like a bucket of ice water.

And then I saw it, right there, in a picture of the listing of his personal effects. The Saint Christopher's medal bent nearly in half from the impact of the .45 I'd sent into his chest. There was blood on it. Dried blood. I did a quick scan of the DNA test and found that some of the blood had been his, probably spatter from Pilgrim trying to bite off his face, but there was other blood as well ... goat blood.

And that got me thinking.

Santeria.

A perversion of Catholicism mixed with voodoo, practiced by a lot of South American, as well as Caribbean and West African cultures. It combines worship of the saints with animal sacrifice and sometimes narcotics.

If Majoqui were a believer in Santeria, he would need a priest or priestess to bless his protective charms. And I didn't think there could be that many of the Santeria hierarchy in Colorado. I googled it using about a dozen different headings and came up with a plethora of psychics, mystics, witches, warlocks, and fortune-tellers, none of which had anything to do with *legitimate* Santeria practices. The best thing about the internet is how much information is out there. The worst thing about the internet is how much information is out there. But along with the garbage, I managed to sift out five possible candidates. Three were priests, but none had achieved a rank higher than Obas, and none, the highest rank of Babalawo, or 'Father Who Knows the Secrets.' Of the two priestesses, one was only a diviner known as an Italeros. But the other one ... ah, the other one. It took me nearly an hour to find a picture of her, but when I did, I knew my search hadn't been in vain. She was a Lyanifa, or 'Mother of Destiny,' the female counterpart to the 'Father Who Knows the Secrets,' and she looked the part. The real thing. And since Majoqui was the real thing, I felt certain this was the woman he would go to for his magic. I took down her address and phone number.

In a few hours, I would make an appointment.

BEFORE, I might have been scared—a little anyway. But now I was beyond fear. All fear. Death meant nothing to me. Hell meant nothing. I didn't even fear failure—because I would not fail. Nothing could stop me.

The house was pathetic, either by design or just lack of care. The old roof sagged, and of the tiles that were left, many were askew, and all had weathered to the point of near disintegration. The yard was an unintended xeriscape of weeds and dirt—the porch decorated with bones on strings and small statues of saints ... and other things.

The old, unpainted door creaked slowly open on my first knock. Inside smelled of ancient tar and nicotine. Cobwebs collected in upper corners and stretched from lampshades and across dipping door frames. Bruised light pushed through time-worn curtains caked with dust.

She sat at the table, smoking. The picture had made her look like a starlet in comparison to the reality that stared at me with the one good eye.

Ash, longer than what remained of the cigarette, wobbled as her wrinkled, bright red lips puckered and sucked at the filtered butt. Ridiculously fake eyelashes fluttered as a curl of yellow-gray smoke, almost the same color as her flesh, drifted slowly past them.

When she spoke, her words were not loud, but they were heavy, laden with the malignant power of disease.

"And what do the police want with an old mother of Santeria?"

I was not in uniform. I wore an untucked short-sleeved shirt and blue jeans, socks, and sneakers on my feet. I wasn't even wearing a badge. What was it with people being able to tell I was a cop?

"A reading," I said.

In the corner, I spotted a bowl with smears of dried blood in it. I sat across from the old woman.

She took another drag on the cigarette, holding the smoke deep in her lungs for so long, only a dirty shifting of the dim light was left to dribble out from her flared nostrils. A wan smile tilted her lipstick smeared lips. She reached her hand across the table, palm up in invitation. Her wrists and arms were withered sticks, the skin sagging loosely.

I laid my left hand in hers, also palm up.

She looked down into the lines of my life. She stubbed out the remainder of her cigarette in a glass ashtray next to my hand, then slid a long nail as red as her lips along my palm, tracing my journey.

"You are not a believer," she said, and it was not a question.

"No."

"And yet," she said, looking up into my eyes with her milky cataract and piercing black orb, "you do believe."

"That's not why I'm here."

"Is that so," and again, it was not a question. "You think you know why you are here, white man. You think you know." The smile widened, her overlarge dentures looking like panther's teeth. "You know nothing."

I started to pull back my hand, but she held it with a strength I wouldn't have believed her capable of.

"You walk," she said, "you talk, you breathe as though you are alive. But you are not alive. You are dead—the walking dead. Your soul is dead. I see you, *zombie*, with my dead eye, walking in the world of the dead. In the world of the damned."

Her false teeth snapped shut, making a sharp clicking sound.

"You think you know," she grinned, and it was a thing of horror to behold, "you think you do, but how can you know anything when you do not even realize that you are dead?"

I swiveled my hand in hers—fast—so fast she didn't have time to react—and crushed the brittle bones tight— so tight I felt them pop and grind in my grip. Her grin turned to an oval of agony.

"That," I said, "is where you are wrong, old woman. I know exactly what I am. And unless you are ready to join me on the other side, you will tell me everything you know about Majoqui Cabrera, The Crow."

A tear welled and overflowed her living eye and started down the curve of her cheek, but the moisture was absorbed in the dark, deep crevasses of her age before making it to her lips.

Through her pain, she spoke.

"I know that he will destroy you. I know that he has killed you already. But that, that is only the beginning. I know that what awaits you is an eternity of torment and guilt. That is what I know, white man."

I squeezed tighter.

"I don't feel guilt, old witch. I'm dead, remember? I don't feel anything. So, think on this ... you speak of beginnings? Well, fingers are only a beginning. After that, there is the wrist, the forearm, the elbow, the shoulder. And then you have another arm and legs. The human body can be an encyclopedia of pain, and unless you want me to read it to you the way you read palms, you better start telling me what I want to know."

"You won't ..." she started to say but choked off as I ground her bones together.

"Oh, but I will."

She looked at me then, maybe seeing me for the first time. Seeing me for what I truly was, for what I had become. For what Majoqui Cabrera had made me. So I let go of her hand, and she told me what she knew. It wasn't much, not as much as I needed, but it was all she had, so it would have to do for now.

41

J im Black was playing a dangerous game, and he knew it. Gil Mason was a loose cannon just now, and if things went south, it could easily cost Jim any chance of ever making chief and might even end him up in jail. On the other hand, Gil was the best cop Jim had ever seen work the streets. He solved more cases than most detectives. And the old adage of 'nothing ventured, nothing gained,' was firmly at play here. Because Jim did want to make chief and he didn't want to wait another ten years to do it. Of course, he had made some good cases over the years, enough to build a solid reputation, but it took more than that to make it to a seat on the Sheriff's office's command staff. It took a really big case. Like this one.

The scary part was what Gil would do if he actually found this Majoqui Cabrera. If he killed him, and Jim had little doubt he would try, it could turn out bad. If Gil got killed, it could also be bad.

Still, the investigation was going nowhere, and it needed a kick start. And if anyone could do that, it would be Gil. No one had more motivation to get to Cabrera than Gil. Murdering his wife and daughter while leaving him alive but paralyzed was the ultimate motivation. Which was another reason Jim wanted to bring him in on the investigation. But he had to keep it quiet, completely under the table. He couldn't even bring his partner, Ryan Nolan, in on it. No, this had to be between him and Gil and no one else, for three reasons. First was the courts; Gil's involvement, if known, would seriously jeopardize any chance for a conviction. Second was the department itself; the Sheriff would have a fit if he knew Gil was anywhere near the case. And third ... ah third; chief's positions didn't come open very often, but when the next one did, Jim planned for there to be only one viable contender for the job. If Gil, or even Ryan, were known to be directly responsible for catching Cabrera, the position could just as easily go their way. And that just wasn't going to happen.

The light sound of email landing in his computer *binged*. Opening it, he saw it was from the LAPD Gang Squad. A hit on Cabrera's alias of The Crow; it was the third one today. Already Gil's info was paying off. Jim had reciprocated by letting the other agencies in on Cabrera's real name, as well as his mug shots, fingerprints, and DNA. Jim figured this was just the tip of the iceberg, and he had a feeling the berg, when fully revealed, would be big enough to sink the Titanic. They had already linked him to as many as nine additional murders in locations ranging from San Salvador to California to New York. The guy was an elite killer, maybe on a level with the likes of The Jackal. Jim hoped so. The more, the merrier. All the more impressive for the man responsible for capturing him.

And Jim, through Gil, would be that man. He could feel it.

Another *bing* from his email. Jim smiled.

42

J ames Arthur Washington Jr. stood outside the 7-11 on the 6300 block of 72nd Avenue in Combat City. He watched, with hard eyes, as the police cruiser rolled past. The cop watched him back with equally hard eyes.

As soon as the cruiser was out of sight, he lit up a blunt and pulled the mixture of cigar and marijuana smoke deep into his being. He was no punk kid doper. He'd had his play with the hard drugs back in the day, and it nearly cost him everything. But that was a long time ago. Now he contented himself with the occasional drink and a nice blunt a couple of times a week.

One of James' lieutenants walked around the corner, and they went through the ritual handshake routine. Dashon had been one of James' most loyal dealers for over a decade. He was Crip through and through, although even Dashon didn't know James' real name. His real name was reserved for only his close friends and blood relatives, and most of them were long since dead. To Dashon and most of the Denver Crip contingent, he was 'Three-Eight', named after the snub-nosed .38 he always carried somewhere on his person. Sometimes he carried two, maybe even three, no one could ever be certain, and that helped keep him safe. Another thing that kept him safe was that no one ever saw the guns, not until they were needed, and then it was too late.

When James had been young and full of fire and battle lust ... as well as other lusts ... he had loved the moniker, a symbol of his acceptance and fighting prowess. But in the last few years, something had changed in him. He couldn't say what exactly it was, but it was there, and it was real, and he couldn't *not* notice its effect on him. It wasn't any one thing, really. It was more a series of subtle *shiftings* that had somehow crept into his subconscious and subtly played with his emotions and thoughts. For instance, he could no longer think of himself as Three-Eight. He thought of himself only as James. So much so that he sometimes wanted to shout at his underlings for calling him by the gang name. Sometimes he could barely restrain himself from pulling out a gun and blowing their fool heads off. He knew this to be impractical. They were only paying him the respect he was due, and besides, they didn't even know his real name, so they couldn't call him by it if they wanted to. But sometimes that didn't matter. Sometimes the anger boiled up in him so hot that he had to talk to himself on the inside to keep from erupting into unwarranted violence. Another thing, and this one was really bothersome; he found himself crying at movies. Not all movies, but some. Mostly movies where someone brave died. And when he cried, he noticed that his hand would tremble. His right hand. His shooting hand. Sometimes it would tremble when he was eating or drinking. Not as bad, but still, not a good thing. And then there was the deal he had made with the cop. Something he would never have done even a few months ago, but he had, and he didn't even feel bad about it. If any of the Crips found out, he would be killed. And not all of his years as a gangster or even his elevated position in the gang would change that. They would see him as a snitch, even though he wasn't. That was the way they would see him. No matter that he was doing it to save them, to protect them, to eliminate an enemy he wasn't sure they could eliminate on their own. None of that would matter. They would kill him. But first, they would make an example of him.

So why *was* he doing it? He couldn't say exactly. It was like the movies and the crying and the trembling and his name. It just was.

James hadn't seen Dashon in several months, and now he noticed something different about him.

"What happened to your lip and cheek?" he asked.

Dashon shook his head. "Spic with an antenna."

"A what?"

"Antenna," said Dashon. "Like from a radio. Used it like a sword or something. Almost took my eye out with it."

This brought back memories to James. Memories of the old days, back before the Thirteens had invaded. Back when the Mexican gangs were ordinary, like the Crips themselves. Back before there were so many guns. Back before even he had joined, when he was still too young. But he was not too young to see, even back then. In those days, fighting with antennas was an art. One mostly forgotten on the youth of today.

A thought struck him.

"What did this man that cut you look like."

"Small," said Dashon. "Wiry. But cool, very cool, and calm."

"Do you know his name?"

Dashon thought for a minute.

"No, but he's shacked up with some chick I was gonna pimp. Least he was."

James took another drag on the blunt; the smoke drifting up into his eyes. Behind him, the lights inside the 7-11 blazed. All around were the night sounds of the city.

"Is he a Thirteen?"

Dashon's eyes grew wide.

"Maybe ... I don't know ... but yeah ... maybe." He rubbed the scar on his lip. "You think maybe he's The Crow?"

"Do you?"

Dashon thought again.

"I didn't see no tats ... but he was wearing long sleeves like they do." And then his eyes got bigger. "His one eye was jacked up."

James dropped the blunt and crushed it under his blue sneakered heel.

"Where's this woman live?"

43

"Ziggy done seen the sons of Mara," said Ziggy. "Ziggy done seen 'em with his own two eyes, that he did, yes sir." His head bobbed about, eyes looking everywhere.

"Where?" I asked. We were at a sandwich shop up the street from Coors Field. There was a game underway, and every once in a while, I could hear the crack of wood meeting ball and the roar of the crowd. It was an afternoon game, and the sun was out, bright and warm. In the old days, I would have loved it; now, it was just another annoyance.

"Ziggy seen 'em crashing at a house out Aurora way, out by the old airport. That's what Ziggy saw."

He meant the old airbase, Lowery.

"How many?"

"Ziggy seen three, maybe four, yes sir, he sure did."

I watched him take a bite out of his sandwich, a Philly Cheese Steak, and then poke around at some fries. How he could eat anything was a mystery because he only had about five teeth. The heroin takes its toll and is impartial to what parts of the body it destroys.

I asked for the address, and he gave it to me, then went back to his food. I took out a hundred-dollar bill and laid it in front of him. He looked at me, and for the first time I could remember, his eyes weren't bouncing, and his neck and head stopped their movement.

"Ziggy was real sorry to hear what they done to you ... to you and yours. Real sorry." He reached out a bony hand and pushed the money back to me.

I held his eyes for a few seconds, nodded my head.

"Thank you, Ziggy." I pushed the money back to him. "It's the department's money, not mine."

He held the look for a few seconds more, and I saw that he knew I was lying, but the gesture had been made, and that was enough. He smiled sheepishly and scooped up the bill.

"Ziggy can take you there, yes sir, that he can do."

"No ... thanks ... but no. You've done enough for now."

"Ziggy can't say the real bad man was there, no sir, he can't say that. But the ones he saw were sons of Mara, that much Ziggy knows for sure."

I said, "It's good enough, Ziggy. It's a start."

* * *

I parked about a hundred and fifty yards from the house. It was in the cheap part of the redevelopment project. The house wasn't old, but it was already rundown. Nowhere near as nasty as the Santeria witch's house, but ugly just the same. The paint was faded, the shingles a mess, there were bars on the windows and a heavy metal storm door. Behind the windows, thick curtains completely blocked my binocular's view.

There was a white SUV parked on the curb in front of the house, and the cracked cement of the driveway was barren. I couldn't tell if there was a car in the garage, but there were no windows, so I wouldn't be able to tell even if I chanced sneaking up to the house. Which I didn't plan on doing till dark.

I saw a pile of about twenty, heavy-gage, thirty-gallon black trash bags on the curb—a lot of trash for three or four guys.

Pilgrim sat behind me, looking out the window, his giant melon resting on my right shoulder. I reached up and stroked his muzzle and ears. I was about to put him in harm's way, and even though he was accustomed to danger, I was worried about him getting hurt. Couldn't be helped, though. I kept telling myself that.

A big van with no back windows pulled into the driveway at around six-thirty. The garage door slid open, and the van disappeared inside. No one got out of the vehicle, and no one came out of the house. And then, the garage door closed as though the house had swallowed the van whole. Maybe it had.

I poured some fresh water into Pilgrim's bowl and waited till he lapped it up. That dog is the sloppiest drinker on the planet, and by the time he was done, there was a good-sized puddle all around the bowl. I mopped it up with a microfiber cloth and swabbed the back of the front seat as well. After that, I went back to surveillance, Pilgrim's jowls soaking my shoulder.

The sun went down around eight, and it was good and dark by eight-thirty. Time for some recon.

I still hadn't shaved, and my stubble was slowly turning to a beard and stash. I was dressed in black, lightweight sweatpants and a tight black body armor t-shirt covered by a black windbreaker—typical recon attire. Pilgrim followed at my side, gliding silently along, watching everything.

The houses out here were spaced a decent distance apart, with larger front and side yards than back. Most were separated by four-foot-high, chain-link fences that had seen better days. Three houses down from the target location, a stereo was blaring, and I could see two blondes, dressed in halter tops and jeans dancing opposite a twenty-something guy with no shirt and spiked pink hair. There was a big-screen TV, a dining room table, a couch, and some folding chairs. Not much else, including curtains, which was why I could see so much through the living room window.

Being one of the Titans of the dog world, Pilgrim wasn't the greatest jumper. Six feet was about his limit. He was better at going through walls than over them. But since the target house's fence was

no higher than the others, he made it with little effort. Together we
ran to the west side wall and hugged it tight. The closest streetlight
was maybe fifty yards away, and there were no lights lit on the exte-
rior of the residence, which was good news for me. Darkness is the
friend of recon.

Stretching on tiptoe, I tried to get a look through the barred side
window. Nothing. The curtains were thick, but still, if there was a
light on inside the house, I should see something. But it was
completely black. I tested the bars—no budge, and in contrast to the
rest of the house, they looked new. Interesting. Hmm. What was this?
Some top-secret Mara headquarters? A drug house? I looked for
cameras—none. No dogs. Unusual for a drug house. My experience
with top-secret Mara headquarters was limited, so I couldn't be sure
about that, but something weird was definitely going on here, and I
didn't like it.

I gave Pilgrim the forward command. He walked to the backyard
and stopped, ears high, nose straight, searching the night with his
eyes and the wind with his nose. Dogs have exceptional night vision,
roughly ten times more acute than humans, but their depth perception is lousy. Movement is what they are masters at capturing. Movement, sound, and scent.

By Pilgrim's posture, I knew the way was safe, so I went around to
the back. It was a carbon copy of the front. Bars on the windows,
heavy-steel storm door. No light at all. There were more of the black
garbage bags stacked along the north wall. A lot more.

On my belt, beneath the cover of the windbreaker, I carried a
holster with my Beretta, the one with no serial number, two extra
magazines, handcuffs, a door popper, and a mini Stream Light flashlight. I usually carry my badge too, but since I was being all *unofficial*,
I left it in the car.

I covered the flashlight's beam with my hand and ripped open the
bag that was closest to me—TV dinners, dozens of them. In the next
bag were more trays and torn clothes with what looked like blood on
them. Three bags later, I found a broken hacksaw blade covered in

dried blood and bits of meat. Perhaps this wasn't a top-secret Mara headquarters after all. I was liking it less and less.

My experience in cartel hostage houses was exactly zero, but I was beginning to think this just might be one. Human-slave trafficking is huge along the border states, and we'd been receiving tips from the Feds that it had spread to Colorado. But up till now, I'd never run across one. The thought that there might be men, women, and children in there, packed like cattle, being tortured and killed, made my stomach turn.

My anger told me to go in, gun out, ready to kill the first threat I saw. But reason said otherwise. No one knew I was here. If I got killed, there would be no one to save the people inside ... if there were people inside. I could be wrong, or I could be right, and they might have already moved all the people out. Besides, there was no way I could kick through that storm door. I'd need a heavy-gauge pry bar or at least a good ol' fashioned American steel tire iron. And even then, it would make such a racket it would alert everyone inside.

The smart move would be to call in the calvary. Problem was, I wasn't supposed to be here. I didn't have a warrant. I didn't even have probable cause to enter the curtilage of the property in the first place. And even so, all I really had were a bunch of soiled food packages, some *maybe* bloody clothes, and a bloody hacksaw blade that could have been used to carve up a roast. The bars, curtains, and storm doors could easily be explained away to a slightly paranoid security-conscious homeowner who was afraid of burglars.

Aurora could do a knock and talk at most with what I had. And all the bad guys would have to do is not answer the door, and that would be that. My mind was now racing with thoughts of what could be happening to hostages I had now convinced myself were in there.

I started walking back to my car and pulled out the cheap cellphone that I used for Dog. I called 911. A female dispatcher answered on the second ring.

"Aurora Police Dispatch, do you have an emergency?"

"Yes," I said, with my best scared-sounding voice and a heavy southern accent. "I heard screaming and a gunshot. I think someone's being killed."

"Where's it coming from?" asked the dispatcher, who sounded about thirty, black, and all business.

"Down the street from me."

"What's the address, sir?" A little annoyance, but still to the point.

I gave her the address.

"You're calling from a cellphone, sir. What's your name, address, and phone number?"

"Oh, I don't want to get involved, but hurry, I just heard a woman scream and a baby too, and now a man is shouting ... no ... two men and ... oh, did you hear that?" I started whispering. "It was another gunshot. Now it's quiet. Oh, why is it so quiet? Hurry."

I hung up. I was maybe fifteen yards from the house. The garage door opened. The van pulled out, backed into the street, and drove away as the garage door lurched downward on its chains.

Aurora was on the way.

I shook my head, turned, and sprinted, hurdling the four-foot chain-link fence. Pilgrim moved faster than I did and landed ahead of me without even being given a command. The door was at the halfway point. I kicked in the afterburners, made it to the sidewalk, dove and rolled twice, coming up in a kneeling position inside the garage as the door touched concrete. Pilgrim sat next to me, tongue lolling, smiling like this was the funnest game in the world. Maybe it was.

I'm no acrobat. Both of my knees were skinned, and the sweatpants were ruined. I checked my holster and other gear; everything was in place.

Now what?

I didn't have much time—Aurora was on the way. There might be twenty hard-nosed bad guys inside the house. There might be little kids. I'd read the reports, seen the pictures from Mexico. Little kids like my Marla.

There was really only one thing *to* do, wasn't there?

I quietly put my hand on the doorknob and twisted. It was locked.

I ordered Pilgrim into a down with a hand gesture. He would stay there, lying and watching, until I called for him. I stood back, seeing Marla's face, hearing her whimper. I raised my leg, kicked with all my strength. The door splintered, sending the reinforced door lock and pieces of the frame shooting across space. The gun was in my hand as I turned into the hallway and came face to face with Hell.

44

Tamera Sun was talking with Keisha when she saw Dashon walk in. She no longer worked at the diner. Majoqui didn't want her to work, and she was only too happy to comply, but she did go there a couple of times a week to see her old friends. It was nearly nine at night, and there were only two hookers at one table and a tired-looking businessman in a wrinkled suit sitting in a booth along the back wall. And Dashon.

A chill crept up her back at the sight of him. He had a nasty scar on his lip and another on his cheek where Majoqui had cut him with the antenna. He didn't say anything, just stared at her, his face a blank. She considered leaving, but she would have to pass him to get out the door, and she didn't know what he would do. What she did know was that he had a temper and that he thought all women were beneath him. She thought that if she tried to leave without at least acknowledging his presence, he might do something. Something bad. Besides, she did feel a little sorry for him. Dashon was a very proud man, and it must have been embarrassing for him to be shown up the way he was by Majoqui. Of course, she loved Majoqui for standing up and defending her, but still, a part of her did feel bad for Dashon. So, as soon as it was polite, she excused herself from Keisha and walked over to him.

"Hi, Dashon," she said.

"A coke," he said.

She looked over the counter, then back to him.

"I ... I don't work here anymore."

His eyes never left hers, and his expression didn't change.

"A coke ... and some fries."

She looked over the counter again, confused. She saw Keisha looking at her and was relieved when she came over.

"Can I help you, sir?" Keisha asked.

"Yeah," he said, his eyes sliding to her. "You can go away." His eyes slid back to Tamera. "A coke and some fries."

"You'd ... you'd better not do anything," she said, and there was a tremor in her voice. Her eyes started to well up with tears.

"And why's that? You gonna do something to me?"

She shook her head, her pigtails flapping loosely.

"No, not me," she said. She wanted to sound brave, but she didn't. Not even to her own ears.

"Not me," he mocked. "Who then?"

"Majoqui," she said, her voice cracking.

And now he did smile, nodding his head as though he had gotten what he wanted.

"Majoqui. That your new boyfriend? The one with the fast hands?"

She nodded, tears overflowing and running down her cheeks. Somehow she thought she had done something wrong; only she didn't know what. It reminded her of when she was little, and she'd splashed the milk from the milk pail all over the kitchen floor. Her father had just milked the family cow and was washing his hands in the bathroom. When he came in and saw the mess, he had looked at her in a way that made her feel the way she was feeling now.

"Where he at, this boyfriend of yours?"

"I don't know."

"He still be living with you?"

She hesitated, not knowing what to say.

"I don't ... think I should be talking to you?"

Dashon's eyebrows raised.

"Is that right? Why not?"

"You remember ... last time ...."

Dashon's hand flashed out, smacking her hard across the cheek. The impact snapped her back, and she almost fell down.

From across the counter, Keisha started toward them again. Dashon stopped her with a pointed finger.

"You go on back to pouring coffee and whatnot, or you'll get worse." He looked around at the meager crew of patrons. "Same goes for the rest of you. Mind your business, or I'll be in your business, and you don't want that."

The two hookers and the businessman quickly looked away.

Dashon grabbed Tamera by the arm, his fingers grinding down to the bone so that she yelped in pain.

"Now I asked you real nice like for a coke and fries, so get yourself back there and do as I say."

Tamera rubbed at the welt flaming on her cheek and staggered back behind the counter. She was dizzy, and there was a high-pitched whine in her ear. She dropped the fry basket into the grease and squirted soda from the fountain into a plastic cup. She set the cup in front of Dashon, rubbing her cheek and looking from him to the fries and back again, not knowing what to do but wishing Majoqui were here.

Dashon took a sip and smacked his lips.

"That's better. Now you showing proper respect. You and me used to be real tight, so I don't want you to think I hold what happened between me and ... Majoqui ... against you. I don't. But that don't mean you can disrespect me. Understand?"

Tamera nodded her head, still rubbing her cheek. She'd bitten the inside when he hit her, and the metallic taste of blood was sharp on her tongue.

He looked her up and down.

"I still say you could make some good money working the streets for me. I'd take good care of you, baby."

"I ... I don't want to do that," Tamera said.

"Girl, you don't know what you want. You still with that spic?"

That made her mad. Tamera hated that hurtful, racist term.

"Don't you call him that! Majoqui is good and kind."

"Maybe, but he's still just a spic. He's so fresh from swimming across from Mexico that his back's still wet."

"No, he's not," she said, her ire boiling. "He's from San-Salvador, not Mexico. And he has a lot of friends."

"What kind of friends?" asked Dashon.

Again, Tamera thought she had said something she shouldn't, only she wasn't sure what exactly. She lifted the fries from the grease, dumped them under the hot light, and sprinkled them with salt. She scooped out a plate full and set them before Dashon.

He picked up a fry and took a bite.

"They ain't Crips," said Dashon. "They ain't Bloods." He took another bite of the French fry. "So, who are they?"

Tamera shook her head, feeling more scared than ever. Dashon already knew Majoqui. They'd fought, and Majoqui had even threatened him. Still, she wasn't supposed to talk with Dashon at all, and he was supposed to leave her alone.

"I don't know who they are," she said. "Just friends. But Majoqui will be mad if he finds out that you ...."

Dashon jerked his head towards her as if he were jumping out of his chair. Tamera staggered back, her hand sweeping up as if to block a blow. Dashon sat back down, grinning, and popped another fry into his mouth.

"If he found out I hit you? I ain't afraid of your little friend with the antenna. Besides, it was just a lovetap—nothing like what I'll do if you get sassy with me again. But you ain't going to do that are you? Are you?"

Tamera shook her head.

"I didn't think so. Now tell me about your boy's friends."

45

Majoqui Cabrera walked out of the bar in Littleton, flanked by two of his best men. The gym bag he carried was filled with thirty, one-pound Tupperware containers filled with exceptional quality, freshly cooked methamphetamine. The crystals snow white and still wet. There were also two handguns in the bag.

A Littleton Police car stopped just behind the red, newer-model Lexus they were about to get into. Majoqui watched the car from the corner of his eye. He had personally inspected the Lexus before getting in tonight, having learned from his first encounter with Gil Mason. As little a thing as a faulty license plate bracket light could give police authority to stop you. The cruiser's headlights made it impossible to see the officer, but Majoqui could feel his eyes on him.

Once inside the car, Majoqui sat in the front passenger seat and instructed his driver to pay close attention to all traffic laws. They pulled out onto the narrow streets of downtown Littleton and drove west toward Santa-Fe Boulevard. The police cruiser pulled out after them and followed. The speed limit was twenty-five miles an hour, and "X-Ray," the driver, kept their speed at a smooth and even twenty.

A short distance later, X-Ray activated his right turn signal and, after a sufficient time, moved over to the turn lane for northbound Santa-Fe. The police car followed. Majoqui was not nervous. He understood America's search and seizure laws better than ninety percent of Americans did. And if that wasn't enough, there were still the guns and his blessings and amulets.

ANTHONY GONZALES WAS a veteran of eleven years on the Littleton Police Department. He was short and powerfully built, with a classic barrel chest and thick biceps and triceps. He could bench three-seventy-five and deadlift seven hundred pounds. Once, he'd gotten into the middle of a bar fight between two local professional football players who played for a team with a familiar horse logo when they both turned on him. One was a right tackle; the other played defensive lineman. When the fight was over, about twenty seconds later, Anthony had a bruise on the right side of his chin and a little swelling. The right tackle was shy three teeth and half his left ear. The lineman was a lot worse.

Gil Mason was a good friend of Anthony's. In fact, his previous dog, Samson, had saved Anthony's life one dark and stormy night. He'd been to Gil's house several times. He'd been fed by Joleen and had played with little Marla. He checked the pictures on his computer screen again. One was clear. It was Majoqui Cabrera, The Crow. His mug shot from after his arrest. The other was the picture taken at the convenience store. It was grainy and dull.

Anthony had seen the three men get into the Lexus. He thought the middleman, the one carrying the bag, might be Cabrera. He felt *more* confidant that all three of them were MS 13, and he was *certain* they were trouble. Over a decade of experience in dealing with trouble confirmed this last observation to his bones. He'd had the forethought to snap a couple of pictures with his smartphone, but they weren't great, what with the low light and distance and all.

He followed them onto Santa-Fe. The driver was being very careful. Anthony looked for a reason to pull them over. All lights were working—nothing hanging from the mirror. There was tint on the windows, but not enough. The muffler was muffling. No cracked windshield. He ran the plate; it wasn't stolen, and there were no hits or holds on it. It listed to a rental agency.

Anthony followed the car out of Littleton into Sheridan, through Sheridan and into Englewood. From Englewood to Denver—way outside his jurisdiction. He was mad at himself for not stopping them back in Littleton, but there was just no reason to pull them over. Nothing. He called a buddy of his that worked the streets of Denver, but he was tied up on a domestic and couldn't break to pull a traffic stop on such sketchy info.

The Lexus pulled onto northbound I-25, and Anthony had to let them go. He turned around and headed back to his city. He sent all the vehicle information and the description, along with the pictures he'd snapped, to Gil's personal email. He wished he could have done more.

MAJOQUI DROPPED the bag off at the apartment. It had taken a little while to double back to Gunwood, but they'd had no more following. He'd thought they would have to run from the police officer, maybe even kill him, but the saints had protected him.

Tamera was not in the apartment. He checked his watch, nine-thirty. Late for her to be out. But he knew she liked to go to the diner where they had met to speak with her friends. He decided to walk there and surprise her.

The walk took about ten minutes. Majoqui enjoyed the night. It was warm. Some might have thought it almost hot, but they had not lived through the summers in San-Salvador. Majoqui liked the hustle and noise of the city. Soon he would be the ruler of this place. Not just Gunwood, but all of Colorado, maybe more. The Crips were close to being finished, and the Bloods would pose little trouble. The ACLU, along with liberal politicians, were handicapping the police to such an extent that soon, they would not be able to stop Mara, just as the police officer was not able to stop his car.

He was across the street, waiting for a car to pass, when he saw the black man. It was Dashon. Majoqui saw the scars he had inflicted and grinned inwardly at his handiwork. He looked through the glass front of the diner and saw Tamera sobbing at the bar, another woman comforting her.

Majoqui did not doubt his power over Tamera, so the idea of her cheating on him did not even enter his mind. What did was rage. An emotion that did not very often affect Majoqui. But there was one thing he would not tolerate, and that was contempt of his power.

Dashon had been given clear instructions to stay away from Tamera. That she belonged to him now. And Dashon had decided he did not need to fear Majoqui's demand.

Talking on a cellphone, Dashon turned down the alley and walked away from the diner. Majoqui followed.

DASHON FINISHED TALKING and hung up the phone. He'd just elevated his position in the Crip hierarchy to an unknown degree. What incredible, perfect luck. Who would have thought that skinny white girl would be worth so much? And once the spic was out of the way, there would be nothing to stop him from making her work the street for him. Double cash in.

As he was putting the phone in his pocket, he heard the man's voice behind him. It was soft and calm, and it sent a chill traipsing up his spine. He knew that voice.

"I told you not to go near her and what would happen if you did."

"Yeah," said Dashon. "Yeah, you did." He turned, his hand still in his pocket. He looked at the thin man in front of him. There was no antenna. His hands were empty.

"Then there is nothing more to say," said the Latino.

"Nope," said Dashon, "Guess not." He pulled his hand out of his pocket. He was no longer holding his phone; he was holding a .22

semi-auto, sleek and black and carrying five rounds of carnage. He lifted the weapon gangster style, one-handed sideways, just like in the movies, and pulled the trigger. Only the gun was no longer there ... neither was his hand.

Dashon stood, staring at the stump and the gushing blood. He tried to shoot again and thought for a second that he could still feel the small trigger ... still feel his finger pulling back. But then he saw the thing in Majoqui's hand. It was some kind of funky sword. And there was blood on it. A lot of blood.

Dashon looked down at the dirty cement and saw his own hand, still holding the little gun, lying in the trash and dirt and grease. Something about that made him feel sick. His hand, lying in that filth. His blood, soaking up the germs and disease.

He looked up, trying to form words to say to the man in front of him. Words that would explain ... that would take it all back. But all he saw was a quick glint of light on the slashing steel as it swung toward his face. And then his perception halved and changed its angle, and he thought, for just an instant, that he saw his body standing there while his view fell down and down, forever down, and he saw nothing more.

46

J ames Arthur Washington Jr., AKA Three-Eight, hung up the phone. He had a decision to make. Dashon told him where the woman lived and that he thought her boyfriend was almost certainly The Crow and that he wasn't there now but should be within a few hours. His first thought was to round up about ten of his bad boys and head over to her apartment to set up a nice little surprise for him. But two things stopped him. First was his deal with the cop ... he'd given his word. Second was the failed trap his boys set up. The one that backfired, leaving eighteen men ... good men ... massacred. Even the Crips couldn't absorb losses like that for long. So, much safer to let the cops handle it.

Taking out the special phone, he hesitated. *Why?* It was the right call, the smart call; all his instincts said so. Still, something kept his finger from pressing the call button. *Pride.* As a leader of the Crips, it galled him to feel the need to have an enemy fight his fight. Who were these wetback nothings to cause all this trouble? Colorado belonged to the Crips and the Bloods; had for decades. Mexican gangs existed here, always had, but they were secondary, content to pick up the scraps left by the two major players. What right did Mara have to steal their turf? How dare they.

Slowly his finger moved away, and he dropped the phone on the pavement by his feet.

There would be no call to this police officer. The Crips needed no help, not from anyone. James ... no ... Three-Eight would kill this upstart himself.

The strange feeling that had been affecting him lately was taking him down a very dangerous path, a path that would eventually destroy him if he didn't quickly check its progress.

His teeth ground together at the thought of his dead men and the failed plan. Revenge ... *justice.* His head bobbed slightly, and his eyes narrowed to slits. Yes, justice for his fallen brothers.

The night air blew past him, bringing the scent of the city. The scent he'd lived with and known all his life. When he was young, they had seemed the very spice of life; tobacco, beer, whisky, pot, blood. But lately, they had soured, smelling stale and rancid and dead.

No, a warrior did not think like this. And above all, Three-Eight had proven himself to be a warrior time and time again. A warrior and a leader of warriors. So, no police, despite his word and the seeming uniqueness of the strategy and situation. The Crips would do as they had always done and take care of their own.

Before he could reach for his personal cell, it vibrated in his pocket. The voice of one of his lieutenants sounded from across the void and told him that Dashon's body had been found in an ally cut to pieces.

Three-Eight nodded to himself and slipped the phone back into his pocket. He paused, thinking and not thinking at the same time. Three-Eight nodded again, looked down, and saw the phone lying at his feet.

James Arthur Washington Jr. reached, picked up the phone, and pushed the button to call the police officer.

47

I've seen war. I've seen terrible things, evil things. But what I saw as I entered the house jumped to another level. Four men, all Hispanic, holding a woman of maybe eighty down on the floor. A tiny thing, wrinkled, nut-brown skin with wispy, pure white hair that had escaped a disheveled bun. Spread beneath her was a rectangular sheet of black plastic. A man knelt on her legs while two more stood with one foot each on her wrists. There were no fingers on her right hand and only three on her left. The heel of a filthy sock protruded from her mouth. The man standing on her right wrist held a blood-smeared pair of wire cutters. The man standing on her left wrist had a small butane blowtorch, a plume of blue flame jetting from the nozzle. Smoke still rose from the stumps of her thumb and index finger. Sitting on her chest, the last man had a phone in one hand and a small sledgehammer in the other. He held it raised over his head and was bringing it down in a savage arc as I burst in.

Before they registered my presence, and a split second before my mind could take in what I was seeing, the hammer landed, smacking with a sound that will live with me forever.

The old woman tried to move at the last second, her eyes wide, like the eyes of a trapped animal, but the hammer hit just above her eyebrow, crushing the ancient bones of her skull and leaving an indent in her flesh like a child's lump of Play-Doh.

I put two bullets into the side of the head of the man with the hammer, then two more into the man with wire cutters. One of the shots struck him in the neck, the other in the ear. Blood sprayed.

Nine-millimeter slugs aren't big ... but they were big enough. Both men crumpled, dead before they knew they'd been shot.

The other two looked at me, both flinching. The man with the blowtorch jerked it up as though to deflect a blow. I shot him three times in the chest. He grunted, looked at where the bullets had punctured his shirt, then back at me.

I changed targets and shot the man at her legs as he jumped to his feet. The first round took him in the belly ... low ... just above the pelvic girdle. Then I put a bullet in each thigh. He fell to the floor, screaming and bleeding.

The man with the blowtorch yelled something at me, but my hearing was gone, blanked by all the gunfire.

Five rounds left before I'd have to change magazines. I put three more in his chest. He took a step back. *Tough guy.* I looked down at the pitiful old grandmother and put one more in the center of his forehead.

Not tough enough.

I turned my attention back to the guy moaning and rolling a few feet away. I didn't kill him for a reason. He was going to tell me things. Things he didn't want to tell me ... things he shouldn't tell me.

For the first time, I took in the décor. The windows sported square sheets of plywood, heavily bolted to the walls, pinning dark curtains beneath them.

Everything about the place screamed hostage-house.

There were no phones, heavy triple-keyed deadbolts on the front and back doors, hardwood floors throughout the living room, hallways, and kitchen. No real furniture, just a few wooden chairs, two standing lamps, and a card table laden with used cups, paper plates, and an overstuffed ashtray.

Oh ... and five more bodies stacked along the north wall. They were all neatly packaged in black plastic, but I knew what they were.

Horrified muffled screams echoed from the cellphone that the man with the hammer had dropped. Picking it up, I put it to my ear and heard the unmistakable frequency of grief and terror vibrating through shrieked words, spoken in a language I didn't understand. What could I do? Even if I possessed the capability to make the woman on the other end of the phone understand me, I could do nothing to ease her grief, her terror.

I said, "I'm sorry," and set the phone back down, still connected so that maybe the police could make contact with them once they arrived.

Like I said, what could I do?

I walked to the man writhing on the floor. Blood flowed freely from both thighs, and a quarter-sized dot stained the edges of the hole in his stomach. Minimal bleeding from a belly shot meant some pipes on the inside must be spraying full out. He didn't have much time left, but then again, neither did I.

People say torture is wrong, and in my old life, depending on what you consider torture, I would probably agree. But my old life no longer existed, and now a zombie stood, looking down at the man who had just participated in cutting off an old woman's fingers after shoving a sock down her throat and then caving in her skull with a hammer.

Having been in the thick of one of the most brutal wars in history, I'd seen and even participated in a lot of hard things. I'd never personally tortured anyone, but I'd seen experts, mostly Taliban and Al Qaeda, but some others too. I never thought I would ever have to use any of that knowledge. I was wrong.

I kicked him in the face. Not hard enough to put him out; I just wanted to get his attention off the pain in his stomach and onto me.

"You speak English?"

He stared at me, blankly.

I shot him through the shin.

He screamed and screamed.

I kicked him in the solar plexus, stealing his wind. That shut him up, but he writhed worse than ever.

"If you don't speak English, you're no use to me. The police are on their way, so I've only got a few more minutes to waste on you." I pointed the gun at his forehead. "You're bleeding internally, but they can save you if they hurry. Only they won't get the chance if you don't let me know you can understand me right now, because if you don't, I'm going to put a bullet through your brain."

He gulped air now, coughing weakly ... blood slicking his lips. He nodded, his entire body trembling. "Si ... yes ... a little."

"Anybody else in the house?"

"Si."

"How many?"

He seemed to be thinking. "Treinta y tres ... thirty tres ..."

"Thirty-three?"

"Si."

"Where?"

He convulsed in pain, breathing hard and fast. With a trembling finger, he pointed down.

"The basement?"

"Si."

I knelt next to him, his breath smelling of onions and blood. I grabbed hold of the front of his shirt and ripped down, revealing scores of faded blue tattoos running his torso. "Mara."

He nodded, his eyes closed in pain. "Si."

"Where is The Crow?"

Opening his eyes slowly, I saw something I didn't like. Defiance. Ordinarily, I'd have to respect someone able to still show defiance after all he'd been through, but I didn't have time for defiance. I dropped my knee onto his broken shin. He almost passed out. I grabbed him by the jaw and shook him back and forth till his eyes lost their glaze, and the pain reestablished its hold on his nerves.

"I know you ... gringo, " he grunted and gasped the words from behind gritted teeth. The onion and blood smell washed over me in a swampy wave. He looked at the puckered scar on my throat where I'd been shot. "The Croneja ... Crow ... did that to you."

The defiance burned brighter, even through the pain.

"Pilgrim," I said softly, without inflection, and he responded the same way, padding from the garage in a low slinky crawl until his big head rested by my thigh. His eyes locked on the man's eyes, knowing prey when he saw it. "I'm going to ask one more time, and if I don't hear what I want to hear, I'm going to have this dog tear parts from your body, and I'm not going to stop him until you are dead."

As if on cue, Pilgrim yawned hugely, showing his forty-two knives, and then resumed his stare.

No more defiance, only pain and primal fear. He gave me an address in Byers.

I left him moaning where he was while I went to the basement stairs, Pilgrim guarding him. He would live or die depending on the police and his own determination. I am nothing if not a man of my word. The stairway seemed to go down forever. It was dark and cool, clammy, as though the walls themselves were sweating and dimpled with gooseflesh. The door, solid, not one of those hollow core deals, sported two deadbolts. It took four hard kicks to breach it, and when it went, it took most of the frame with it.

What I saw inside made me sick ... the smell and sounds were worse—mostly women and children, with a handful of broken men. I couldn't even begin to guess at how long they'd been held here. A bucket sat in one corner and across from it, another; toilets. Several clear plastic water bottles littered the floor, and a single bare bulb hung from the ceiling on a string. The windows were bolted down here, just like upstairs. The rest was bare concrete with a concrete floor: no chairs, no tables, no mattresses or blankets. A wraith of a girl of maybe four, covered in dirt and snot, waved her little hand at me. Two of her fingers were blackened stubs.

I went back up the stairs, called Pilgrim to me, and walked to the destroyed garage door. I could hear sirens coming from far off. The one surviving gang member clutched his abdomen with both hands and stared at me.

"The Crow will ... "

I shot him in the face and left.

48

Tamera Sun was packed and ready to leave. Majoqui sat on the bed, speaking calmly on the phone. She told him everything, of course. All about Dashon smacking her and what she'd said to him and how strangely he'd acted. Majoqui had nodded and said it was alright, that Dashon would never trouble her again, just as he'd promised. He said they had to move, that he'd found a new place for them to live and that they had to leave tonight, as soon as possible. He told her to pack what she needed for now and that he'd have his men pick up the rest within the next few days.

Majoqui wasn't angry with her or even upset that she'd told Dashon things she didn't think she should have. He just smiled gently, kissed her, and told her he was sorry Dashon had hurt her again and then urged her to start packing.

Outside, she saw several new friends of Majoqui's, all very quiet and serious, looking about with hard eyes and thin lips, as though expecting danger. Tamera didn't know what could be making them act this way. With this many tough looking guys, she couldn't imagine anyone trying anything. No one would have a chance. She counted seventeen men, and those were only the ones she could see.

Finishing, she plucked up Miranda and beamed a perky smile at Majoqui. "I'm ready."

He put away his phone and smiled back at her. "You are certain you have what you need?"

"You're all I need," she said. "You and Miranda." She snuggled the cat against her cheek.

He nodded and held out a hand, which she took. Together they walked down the stairs to a car, not her VW, a fancy black four-door with electric locks and windows and leather seats. She didn't know what kind of car it was; she'd never been good with things like that, but it was nice and smelled new.

At four-thirty in the morning, the streets were nearly deserted. The sun was just beginning to poke her rays through the wispy clouds painted across the sky from the east. Tamera loved the sunrise; it always reminded her of how much hope and promise each day held.

As she got in, she saw police cars coming toward them from way down the street. They didn't have their lights flashing or anything, but it looked like a lot of them. Majoqui got in beside her, and the car rocketed away before she could even put on her seatbelt.

In the past, Tamera would have been afraid of so many police. But not now, with Majoqui beside her, Tamera wasn't afraid of anything.

49

As I drove away from the hostage house, three APD cars slid into the area with their lights off. My lights were off too. I pulled into a driveway a few doors down and waited till the three uniforms made their way on foot to the house. They were being cautious, as they should be. One went to the back while the other two took up positions on either side of the garage door I'd left open.

Eventually, they went in, as I knew they would. I left the area fast.

My cellphone, the special one reserved for Dog, vibrated in my pocket.

"Go," I said.

"Your boy is downtown in Gunwood, shacking up with some white woman name of Tamera Sun." He gave me the address and apartment number and hung up.

Interesting.

I don't know if I really expected him to turn Cabrera over to me. I called Jim Black and relayed the information. I told him I wanted him to stake the place out until I could get there, but under no circumstance to go in. He agreed.

I wanted to go straight there, but I had a task to do first. I needed to get rid of the gun that I just used in dispatching three killers—the gun with no serial number. And I had to get rid of it in a way that would make testing for ballistics impossible.

Most people think that real life is like TV, where the crime lab, packed with the latest and most advanced equipment of science, trots out to every crime scene to suck up and analyze minute bits and pieces of evidence. The truth is that the vast majority of crimes never see a hint of the forensics teams. Usually, a standard burglary, or even an armed robbery, is processed by one or two responding officers. And, as long as no one was shot, they get stuck with everything, up to and including making sure the scene is safe, talking to the victim or reporting party, photographing the scene, taking prints ... if they even check for prints, taking statements, and writing the report. And always with the knowledge that their precinct or district partners are getting hammered with other calls, so they have to hurry to get back out there and help.

This, however, was a hostage house ... with at least six dead innocent victims and four dead bad guys, an entirely different animal. For this, they would call out everyone and utilize every hi-tech piece of scientific equipment in their arsenal to glean the smallest molecule of evidence. DNA, fingerprints, shoe prints, GSR (Gun Shot Residue). And it wouldn't just be the local police either. A hostage-house warranted the FBI since the hostages would likely have been smuggled in over state lines. Maybe even the CIA, and certainly ICE, since they came from out of the country. The gang aspect might draw in the DEA, as well as possibly the ATF.

Getting caught with the gun used to kill the Mara members would, at the very least, tie me up for days, and worse, could put me in prison for murder. I wouldn't chance either until I'd taken out Majoqui Cabrera. That meant I couldn't chance showing up in Gunwood while I had the weapon with me.

But what to do with it?

I couldn't just throw it out the window. It could be found and linked to the killings, and even if I gave it a thorough cleaning, it might hold a speck of DNA or somehow be traced back to the guy that sold it to me. Or it might be found by a thug who could use it to commit a crime, or worse, get picked up by a child.

Hiding it opened a whole set of new problems. The first being where? Not at my house. If a witness saw me or my car near the scene, it would be traced right to me and a warrant issued. As for my car, it wouldn't even take a warrant due to the exigent circumstance provision for motor vehicles.

Finally, I decided to just keep it simple. In the police academy, they use an acronym for writing reports, K.I.S.S. "Keep It Simple Stupid." I figured this to be the time to take that advice. I drove to a darkened underground garage, checked for a security camera system, quickly emptied the Beretta, and field stripped it. I grabbed a hammer from my toolbox and the barrel of the gun. Laying the barrel on the cement, I raised the hammer. Suddenly, I saw the poor old woman as the hammer swung down at her face. My stomach turned. I shook my head, feeling the blood pulse at my temples, and swung— hard. It turned in my hand with the impact and slid out from the main force of the blow. I knelt down and clamped it to the now chipped cement with my foot, putting as much weight as I could on it, and struck again—and again—and again. I inspected it ... no ballistic testing would be done on this baby.

Getting back in my car, I drove to a dumpster behind a strip mall. I chucked the bent and cracked barrel into the dumpster. Then I drove to another dumpster at another strip mall where I disassembled the hammer and trigger assemblies and dumped them into separate dumpsters. Hammers make distinct striking's on primer casings that can be traced back to a weapon, and since I had to leave the casings at the scene, it wouldn't pay to overlook the hammer. Finally, I cruised several side streets until I came across a neighborhood with trash cans lining the curbs in front of private houses. I wiped the frame clean of any possible prints and shoved it deep into a white trash bag before tying it closed with the red plastic drawstrings.

Not perfect, there could always be witnesses: an insomniac looking out the window wondering why a car would stop to throw trash into a neighbor's can, a bum, or a doper, or a prostitute by the dumpsters—a tagger looking for bare cement walls in an underground garage. But perfect isn't possible, not in this world, so the best I could do with the time and circumstances at hand would just have to do.

I took one of my spare guns, a Ruger five-shot, from my gear bag and tucked it in my waistband, realizing that, unlike the weapon I'd just taken such care to dismantle, destroy and make disappear, this gun did have a serial number and that it was on every file imaginable leading straight back to me. I'd have to be more careful, unless, of course, I came face to face with Majoqui Cabrera. If that happened, all bets were off. Trial, jail, prison, even death, none of it mattered. All that mattered was looking into that monster's eyes, and by my own hand, sending him straight to Hell.

Hitting Colorado Boulevard from I-25, I started north. Gunwood stood just up the road. The speed limit sign said forty miles an hour. I toed the accelerator and watched the readout climb past sixty.

I'd lost too much time already.

50

Detective Jim Black pulled up in the lead car, parking about thirty yards from the apartment building in Gunwood. Seven marked units, along with a SWAT van, stopped behind him. On a usual SWAT deployment like this, they would have "eyes" on the location for hours already, making sure the suspects were on scene and checking for lookouts or muscle. The "eyes" units were always snipers with powerful scopes and even more powerful rifles, ready to neutralize any threat that might materialize. But Jim couldn't take the chance on Gil making it to the scene before Majoqui Cabrera was either in custody or dead. Not if he wanted to receive the credit and keep from allowing Gil to murder the man and ruin everything.

The sun still hid beneath the horizon, sending purplish bands across the heavens, blanking out the stars overhead one by one. The dark offered a tactical advantage, which, coupled with surprise, manpower, and weapon superiority, tipped the odds strongly in their favor.

The SWAT agents dropped off the side running boards of their specially equipped van and formed into two perfect lines. They ran-walked toward his vehicle, rifles at the ready. K9 units moved and staged at the back of the building, along with another team of SWAT in unison.

Jim set this up quickly, and in so doing, there always remained the possibility of error. But, having been around as long as he had had its advantages. Experience knowledge. Having planned and participated, at least in some functions, on dozens of SWAT hits gave him the advantage. He didn't see any holes in the mission ... except one ... the one you could never plan for. Would the target be there? If he'd been able to set snipers in place, he might know, but then again, maybe not. Often you had to hit, even after a day or more of surveillance, with never having seen the target. You just had to go with the info you had and hope for the best. Still, the timing came in nearly perfect. Bangers and dealers were all cockroaches and rodents —vermin. And vermin lived and loved the dark. They did their work in the shadows of the night, always hiding, always evading the light. And when the sun rose, they scurried back to their little holes, like vampires seeking a coffin to sleep the day and light away until they were brave enough to venture out, back into the dark of the night.

Jim exited his car and flopped a heavy-gauge armor vest over his shirt and tie and then followed at a safe distance as the team passed him. He had the vest, but no helmet, shoulder, or groin protection. Plus, he didn't want to get in the way of the professionals.

The team slid through the door, up two flights of stairs, and positioned themselves outside the target apartment, three-quarters of them forced to line the stairs due to lack of space on the landing.

Jim had obtained the no-knock warrant through a judge he played golf with twice a month. Jim always let him win, not by much, just enough. That, and the fact they were going after a mass cop killer and torturer of women and children, made it easier. A no-knock meant exactly that. The SWAT team would breach the door with no warning, the safest method of entry since it put the element of surprise firmly in their court and gave the bad guys no chance for preparation.

The Entry Team Breacher stood next to the door with a thirty-pound, two-handled battering ram, waiting for the signal to breach.

Jim felt the hairs bristle on the back of his neck. He loved this part; the adrenaline surge, the raw, primal feeling of danger, and the hunt. Once they hit that door, anything could happen. The door could be rigged with explosives or tricked out with a shotgun on the other side, or a crew of bangers with guns behind couches and tables having spotted them on their way. There could be pit-bulls trained to attack or little kids playing on the floor. It was a roll of the dice, and snake eyes were as likely as a lucky seven—no way to know till the cubes stopped rolling.

The team leader raised his fist. Go time.

MAJOQUI CABRERA FELT RAGE, something he rarely allowed. He'd expected the Crips to attack and made arrangements for just such an assault. The first order of business had been to get Tamera to a place of safety. After that, it came down to sending another message, one that would put The Crips on notice that their time in Colorado was past and they needed to move along. What Majoqui had not expected or prepared for was the police. When he saw their cars cruising down the street toward her apartment building, he instantly knew that someone had betrayed them. No matter how fierce the rivalry between gangs, no one talked to the police. No one ratted to law enforcement. Anyone that did would receive a guaranteed death sentence. Not only them but their whole family, perhaps even friends. And the death would not come easily. The lesson he came to Denver to deliver to the bank president couldn't compare to what would be done to a member who sided with the police.

He wanted to go back, to be with his men, but he knew better. Killing police was bad business. He sat back in the car and squeezed Tamera's hand, letting his rage dissipate. His men were lost; nothing could be done about that now. He'd set the ambush to execute a squad or more of teenaged dopers, not trained professionals with modern weaponry and armor.

Despite his knowledge of the dangers of further involving law enforcement in his activities, a part of him hoped his men would acquit themselves well and take many souls with them.

Dismissing them from his mind, he began to plan his revenge against The Crips.

I SPOTTED the SWAT van first and felt my pulse start to race. What did Jim think he was doing? I told him to set up surveillance and wait for me, not stage a full-scale war before I could even arrive. Pulling in south of the apartment, I saw the last of the SWAT agents as they stormed the building, Jim in the rear. I couldn't let them kill Cabrera. It had to be me. Running for the front doors, I heard the first of the flashbangs go off.

That's when the war started.

JIM BLACK SAW the SWAT commander's fist go down. Simultaneously, the door breacher swung the heavy ram, disintegrating the lock, doorknob, and most of the frame. Two other SWAT agents immediately threw in flashbangs—basically low-powered cylindrical concussion grenades. Blinding flashes, accompanied by enormous thunderclaps and pulse-waves, slammed through the room and out into the hallway. The entry team moved instantly after the explosions, rushing the room and breaking into two diverging lines as they ran the walls.

Black loved tactics and the study of tactics. He'd read virtually every book on the subject, from General Tsing to Colonel John Boyd. He practiced "war-game" scenarios continuously while at his desk, an essential tool in Boyd's decision cycle framework, commonly referred to as the 'OODA loop.' The theory's main concept is that whoever can move through cycles of the OODA loop fastest during a competitive situation will be able to impose their will on an opponent. Utilizing the OODA loop, the person makes an observation, then orients the meaning or impact of that observation on their objective, then makes a decision on a course of action and institutes that action.

There are numerous ways to enhance one's ability to increase their OODA loop speed and reliability; practice, muscle memory, familiarity with tactics, weapons systems, architectural layouts, knowledge of opponents, surprise, distance. Black shot three times a week at the range, worked out five days a week, and was a third-degree black belt in Taekwondo. He'd never actually been on the SWAT team, or any special team, but he'd advanced to detective after only three years on the street and had an excellent record, as well as the second-highest case closure rate in the bureau.

Jim went through the entire scenario for maybe the fiftieth time as he climbed the stairs and saw it end in his mind just as the flash-bangs detonated.

The men rushed the room, Jim almost on their heels. Being a step behind saved his life. Holes punched through the ceiling, floor, and walls from four angles and the heavy barking of automatic gunfire rippled and bounced off the walls and stairs. Even so, three heavy thuds impacted his chest-plate, stopping his forward progress and knocking the wind from his lungs. He staggered back, seeing the sparks and puffs of disintegrating copper, lead and Kevlar smack and ricochet off helmets and vests of the men in the room. The door next to him splintered and chipped as bullets ripped up, down, and through. One of the SWAT agents took a round in the groin from below, another in the thigh. Confusion reigned for maybe three seconds before training, experience, and professionalism took charge. Realizing that they were being shot at from above, below, and two different sides, they moved into a square formation and started firing back, with two agents shooting straight up and another two shooting down through the floor. Together they moved toward the door.

Comprehension of the situation hit Black, and he sucked it up, ran down the stairs, and turned to the door directly beneath their target. He kicked the door, splintering the frame, and ran inside just as Gil Mason entered the building.

THE CHATTER of automatic gunfire assaulted my ears as I ran into the building. Bullets and splinters of wood and chunks of plaster and tile were zinging about like shrapnel from an IED. Smoke filled the hallway, and I saw Jim kick in a door and start shooting. I followed right behind, but two boys lay on the floor, blood dripping down their tatted bare chests, AK's lying close.

Together we waited until the all-clear came from the apartment above—strolling through the room only to have the SWAT guys upstairs send a few dozen rounds through the tops of our heads would be disastrous. Once it came, we cleared the rest of the apartment. SWAT finished mopping up the two other rooms. Total bad guy count came in at five dead and two critically wounded. Three SWAT agents were taken to the hospital for gunshot wounds, two serious. Another three guys had been hit in their armor but were fine.

Majoqui Cabrera was not there. Looking at the carnage, I turned to Jim.

"What happened? You were supposed to wait for me. And what's with SWAT?"

Jim shook his head. "They found a hacked-up Crip just down the street, and a witness said the cutter ran into this apartment. SWAT planed the whole thing without me. I was just lucky to get the word as they headed out and tagged along to look for your boy."

"Well, he's not here," I said. "Again."

We both put our guns away.

"Look, *you* need to not be here," said Jim. "I'll take care of the investigation, but if the brass finds out you had anything to do with this, we will both get hung out to dry. So beat it."

He made sense. I hadn't shot anyone, so no reason to stay and answer questions.

"All right," I said. "We'll meet up later."

Walking back to my car, I noticed drywall dust on my shirt and a thin, quarter-inch, jagged 'S' shaped chunk of copper in my shirt pocket. Hmm, wonder where that came from? Kind of made me think about how close we had all come to being shot back there. A pretty well-set trap, not good enough against elite SWAT agents, but it would have worked just fine against, say, a bunch of hotheaded Crips looking for revenge for their hacked-up buddy.

The whole set up had Majoqui Cabrera written all over it. And once again, he'd vanished before we showed up. The man was practically a ghost.

My teeth clenched. No ... not yet ... but once I found him.

The morning blossomed now, the sun bright and starting to put out some real heat. People walked past as I got into my car, rubbernecking the crime scene to see if they could catch a peek. Not that shootings and killings weren't commonplace in the city of Gunwood, because they pretty much were. Still, a shootout is a shootout, and who isn't curious about that?

I started the engine. I had a place to stake out in Byers.

MAJOQUI CABRERA HELD the door open for Tamera and led the way to the trailer just off Front Street in Byers. The South American and Hispanic population had increased in the small town over the last ten or so years, but still, three carloads might raise a few eyebrows. Majoqui didn't care. Byers was far enough removed from the big cities that he highly doubted word would get back to their law enforcement agencies. Besides, he'd acquired these five trailers nearly three months ago and made certain that nothing illegal, noisy, or disruptive took place so as to establish a very low profile with the local residents.

Right away, he'd learned of a smalltime meth lab in a trailer on the other side of the park and had a few of his men take out the cook, well away from their location. The last thing he wanted was to have cops or the DEA lurking around because of some cheap tweakers ratting to save their skins.

Outside, the trailer looked pretty much like all the rest, but inside it was beautiful—a seventy-two-inch flat-screen decorated an entire wall, fronted by a lush leather couch and love seat. A top of the line Bose sound system wrapped the listener in majestic waves of resonance while the small kitchen came equipped with all the modern conveniences of a state-of-the-art, high-end restaurant. The bathroom was ornate, and the two bedrooms had been converted into one master suite with a king-sized bed and hand-carved wooden headboard. The carpet flowed from one end of the trailer to the other in a tight weave of thick light tan.

The expression on Tamera's face told Majoqui all he needed to know. She deserved this. Of all his servants, she was his most loyal. Throughout his life, the women he had known, starting with his mother, were nothing but whores in one form or another. But not Tamera. She only wanted him, only cared about him. And she asked for nothing more. Not his money, his undivided attention, not even his time. She understood his responsibilities and respected his power. She trusted him completely.

And so, he had this trailer outfitted expressly for her. He'd even had her stuffed bear and many of her baubles—silly things like a snow globe with a dragon inside and a lamp that cast stars on the ceiling—brought over and placed in the bedroom just to surprise her. When she saw them, tears welled in her big eyes, and she hugged him around the neck. Exactly the response he'd expected and hoped for. Yes, Majoqui knew her, knew all of her, down to her exact thoughts, and this was why he could trust her completely. The first person in his life who had ever made him feel this way.

She needed to be protected. His enterprises had moved far beyond mere narcotics. Now, Mara had established Pollo-Houses— Chicken Houses—where kidnapped illegals were kept until their families were bled dry through extorted ransom. Once the payments stopped, they would kill the victim and dispose of the body. Majoqui had located an excellent area in Elbert County where mass-graves could be dug and buried over far from prying eyes.

Majoqui had also established shakedowns of various businesses and had instituted illegal gambling in his territory—although, because Colorado had three different parts of the state that allowed gambling, it was more difficult. Governments hated competition for their tax dollars. Still, he'd learned over his years that even when vices were legalized, there would always be an element that wanted something darker—deeper—more dangerous—and so back-alley gambling houses thrived. Majoqui sent tendrils of inquiry into the shadow worlds of prostitution, strip clubs, and escort services. He'd even started ventures into underground anything-goes-bare-knuckle-fighting—like MMA, but the fights could go to the death. These were still in the infant stages, but he was gaining ground and felt confident that soon Colorado would be his.

Of course, moving into others' territory had its difficulties, its dangers. The old rulers never wanted to give up and leave quietly. Examples needed to be made, new boundaries set, battles and skirmishes and wars. But these were the things Majoqui teethed on as a boy and grew to know well as an adult. Now a conquering general, he would assume his rightful place in this land flowing with such riches.

The Crips and the Bloods were but the beginning of his adversaries, and he understood this only too well. The Italian Mafia still held little pockets of power in Colorado, as did the Russians, the Asians, and the white-biker gangs. Each with their own little piece of the pie. A pie that Mara would completely consume. Their time had come and passed; they just didn't understand this yet. But Majoqui would show them. He would make them understand.

Bloodshed was inevitable, but that too was as it should be. The saints and the demons had to be appeased, and this would require blood. God always requires blood for blood. In the end, it is the only thing that truly matters. This Majoqui understood, perhaps better than anyone else, and he would not shy from his obligation to produce the sacrificial blood that would baptize and thereby justify his endeavors. He was and would always be the Virgin's servant, Maras' servant. And he would offer them up an ocean of blood.

Majoqui wrapped his arms around Tamera Sun and held her as she cried tears of joy into his chest. He would have to take her to the witch woman soon. Being his most prized possession, he wanted her protected. An amulet perhaps, or a charm, blessed and sprinkled and spoken over. Majoqui held her tighter and smiled.

51

Jim Black basked in the glow of the praise he received from everyone. Even the Sheriff stopped in to tell him what a great job he'd done in discovering this nest of MS-13 hidden in the very heart of the city of Gunwood. The chief of police of Gunwood was probably none too happy to have the County step in, showing them up, but since the county had jurisdiction over their city, there was nothing he could say about it.

Breathing a sigh of relief that no one seemed to have noticed Gil Mason at the scene, he sat at his desk. Having already gone over the story about a dozen times, first for his immediate boss, then for Internal Affairs, then the Sheriff, the Shoot Team, and for several of his partners in the bureau, he felt exhausted. And he still had a lot to do.

He opened an email from a detective friend in Aurora asking him to give him a call. Jim considered waiting till things quieted down, but something made him go ahead and call. The friend asked him if he'd heard about the killings in the old Stapleton area, and when he said he hadn't, he told him that a whole slew of MS-13's had been shot up and that a bunch of illegals had been rescued from a hostage house. The friend thought Jim would want to know because of the

Mara connection. Jim asked if the Mara boys had been cut up. His buddy said no, but that they had been taken out with some really nice precision shooting. He promised to email the crime scene pictures and copies of the reports once they were uploaded. Jim thanked him and hung up.

Precision shooting—MS-13—anonymous call—hostages left alive. Hmm.

Quickly finishing his report, he slipped into the bathroom, made sure no one else was in there and called Gil Mason. He answered on the second ring.

"Where are you?" asked Jim.

"Got a possible line on a Mara safe house out in Byers," said Gil.

"Really. How'd you get this line?"

A pause.

"From a friend."

"A friend?"

"Yeah," said Gil. "Why?"

"Might this friend have been located somewhere in the Stapleton redevelopment area?"

Another pause.

"No," said Gil.

"You sure?"

"Yes," said Gil.

It was Jim's turn to pause.

"You need any backup out there?" asked Jim.

"Not now. Strictly surveillance."

"You sure?"

"If you mean, do I need a SWAT team to help start a war, the answer is no," said Gil, and his voice sounded hard.

"I explained that," said Jim. "They were already on their way. I just tagged along."

"Coincidence," said Gil.

"They do happen," said Jim. "We need to trust each other, Gil. I didn't try and take Cabrera without you. Things just happened, and there was no time to clue you in. That's all."

Another pause, this time a long one, Jim waited him out.

Finally, Gil spoke.

"Okay, fine. Don't let it happen again. You let me know if you get anything—*anything*—I expect at least a call."

"Of course," said Jim. "Do you need me to fill you in on the dead men at Stapleton?"

There was that pause again.

"No," said Gil. "I heard about it."

"That's what I thought," said Jim. "Just so we're clear, I expect to be kept informed too ... about everything."

"Some things it might be best if you don't know," said Gil.

"Uh-uh," said Jim. "We are doing this legal, all the way. I'm already taking a chance on losing my job here, but I will not take a chance on going to prison. Do you understand that? Am I clear, Gil?"

"Yes," said Gil, and he sounded as sincere as he had when he denied any knowledge of the dead men at Stapleton.

The line went dead.

52

ajoqui received the news of his dead men with his usual calm. He'd known what the outcome would be the moment he saw the police cars. Still, the loss of some of his best men would hurt, both operationally and organizationally. The gang *business* was becoming more and more exactly that, a business. And in business, organization became vitally important—a fact that had been making itself abundantly clear to Majoqui in the last few months. Lately, he'd found himself thinking more like a businessman than a gangster assassin. Necessary, but also dangerous. He could ill afford to lose his edge; he had too many enemies.

A feeling of pride had accompanied his killing of Dashon. He felt grateful for the opportunity to prove himself still as capable as before his dealings with Gil Mason. The man had proven a true challenge. Majoqui had thought to let Mason live so that he could spend the rest of his life locked in a dead body. A body that could only remember his failure and guilt and that would have to visualize Majoqui's face over and over and over. Which was perfect and right. But then the man had awakened. He had gained the ability to move and walk, and who knew what else now?

Majoqui understood power, determination, and will, and he knew this Gil Mason to have great reservoirs of these qualities. Not only that, but he had some kind of protection, a protection that could not be seen, only felt. Majoqui had felt it. He felt it the night he shot at him and threw his great machete, the night the dog-monster attacked him. He'd felt it again at the bank president's house and once again at the nightclub. He thought he'd stolen that power the night he killed Mason and his family. Only Mason hadn't died as completely as he should have, and somehow, he still kept that power.

Majoqui suddenly wondered if maybe it was this man who was still causing him problems, and as soon as the thought struck him, it became a certainty.

Yes—yes—of course. He sat next to Tamera. She smoked the end of a marijuana cigarette and watched some movie on the giant-sized screen. Majoqui paid no attention to the movie, but he kept his eyes on the screen and on Tamera while his mind raced with this new realization.

A strange feeling crept over him. A feeling he hadn't had in a while. He was being hunted. Gil Mason was hunting him. That explained many things; the killing of his men at the pollo-house— the news said they were dead when the police arrived, and no one knew of these operations, not the Crips or the Bloods, no one. Besides, none of the black gangs dealt in kidnapping and ransom. In fact, the only human trafficking they were involved with was pimping prostitutes. It also explained the police raid at Tamera's apartment. The protected man was hunting him. And he was stronger than before, yes, stronger because he had a new power. Something that made him far more dangerous. Something that Majoqui himself had given to him.

He had hate.

Majoqui's eyes still stared at the screen, but his lips slowly curved to a smile.

53

I parked across the street from the trailer park around seven-thirty in the morning. The problem with doing surveillance in a small town like Byers or Strasburg or Deer Trail is twofold. First, there's almost no place to hide, and second, everyone knows everyone, so newcomers stick out like the proverbial sore thumb. However, that being said, it almost made it hard for new bad guys to hide.

I couldn't see trailer 23 from my location, but with only one entrance, it made it easy for me to observe anyone coming or going. I reclined the seat and sat back and low. Pilgrim sniffed my ear, and I petted his huge head and under his chin. I turned on the radio to an FM station playing pop-rock, not for me, for Pilgrim. I was past music. Past talk radio. Both things I loved in my old life. Back when I had a life and a wife and a child. Now there existed only hate, and the endless blackness of a life with no meaning save one.

Justice.

Others would call it revenge, and they might be right, but that in no way negated the fact that it was justice. If the God of all creation refused to do what was right, then I would, and He better not try and stop me. Nothing ... nothing would stop me.

I felt a pain in my jaw and realized I was grinding my molars. I made myself relax. I breathed deeply, in-out, in-out, in-out.

On the radio, Imagine Dragons' song, *Monster,* played quietly. The lyrics rang true to me. Speaking of what I was ... what I had become ... what God had made me.

A monster.

How could He do this to me? I'd asked that question a thousand, thousand times while paralyzed in the hospital and countless more times struggling and sweating and fighting to make my numb, useless limbs move and pump and pull until I came to the understanding that He would never answer me. He did what He wanted to do, mindless of the horror and pain and tears of His children so far below—like the myths of Zeus, using humans as nothing more than pawns in some silly game of the gods. Only there was only one God, and He was no myth.

My hands turned into tight fists around the steering wheel, and the leather covering creaked beneath the pressure.

He could have saved them ... *saved me.* It wouldn't have taken a lightning bolt from heaven or a parting of the sea of asphalt ... just a push ... a touch ... an instant of clarity one second before I saw that flash, that reflection, and maybe I could have done the rest on my own. Maybe I could have swerved or stopped or sped up, anything ... ANYTHING!

Pilgrim whined behind me, and my jaw was aching again. The steering wheel creaked and groaned. I was breathing fast and hard. Lights and sparkles flashed somewhere behind my eyes, and sweat ran down my face.

The monster raged inside me.

The whole Bible says how much He loves us, how much He loves me, but when I needed Him, when Jolene needed Him ... needed me ... when Marla ... Oh, Lord ... Marla ... when Marla needed Him ... needed me ... He ... I ... we ... we failed her ... failed them ... failed US!

Pilgrim pawed at my shoulder, and I turned on him ... *the monster turned on* him ... turned so fast and furious, the monster's hand leaving the steering wheel to swing at him, to hit him, to smack Pilgrim ...

I stopped myself ... *stopped the monster* ... still breathing hard, looking into his eyes ... Pilgrim's eyes. And suddenly, the monster was gone. I grabbed both sides of his face, pulled him close, and cried into his fur. He licked away the tears, and soon I calmed, feeling tired and weak and foolish.

The hate, though, the hate was still there. I didn't have to feel for it; I never had to do that. It burned bright and strong and hot and filled with promise.

The monster still lived ... buried just below the surface.

I turned to the front, and as I did, I saw the car pull out of the park. A small red Honda. Nothing unusual, except that it was filled with four MS13 bangers.

The banger I'd shot in the face hadn't lied. Majoqui was here.

54

James Arthur Washington Jr., known to all his men and peers as Thirty-Eight, watched the white cop through a pair of high-end binoculars. Fifteen members of the Crips sat impatiently in a string of seven cars along a dirt road nearly a mile away.

Shifting his view, he took in the trailer park. From his vantage point, he saw five Mara guards walking around a series of three trailers. They carried themselves with a certain look that bespoke discipline and maturity. He wished he could say the same about his men. Most of his best had been killed in the last few skirmishes with the 13s, and he had to take what was left. They were mostly young; two were fourteen and the oldest under twenty. Still, they sported fully automatic weapons, and they had the element of surprise on their side; surprise, and hopefully, numbers.

Scanning, he saw no signs of other cops. He'd watched the raid from across the street and had to admit his admiration for the SWAT team's professionalism and ability as they came under ambush. He knew they would have cut his men to pieces. He had no intention of coming up against that kind of firepower and tactics. If a squad of SWAT vans or police moved in, he and his men would stay put. But that was not his intention at all. He fully intended to end Mara's attempt to take over Colorado today, once and for all.

Moving back to the cop, he considered his options. James Arthur Washington Jr. didn't like the idea of betraying his word, but Thirty-Eight always did whatever proved best for both himself and his gang: lying, stealing, killing, betrayal, anything. The question that bounced around inside his mind now was, who exactly was he today? More and more, he saw himself not as an OG but as a man that might still make something of himself. Might, one day soon, take a wife and raise children. As a younger man, he never thought he'd live long enough to contemplate such things. He lived for the day and the money and the excitement. But somehow he'd survived, and now he found himself thinking more and more about a life away from the Crips. He had never allowed himself to care for anyone else because he didn't believe he would be around long enough to develop that kind of a relationship. Of course, the Crips, like most major gangs, had neither a retirement program nor an early out clause in their contract. Still, there were ways. And even in their most brutal days, long since passed, they were never as serious in enforcing the 'once in only death out' motto as Mara.

Some movement caught his attention, and he brought his focus back to the trailers. Four men got into a red car and drove slowly toward the main road out of the park. That meant four less in the fight. Time to strike. But what about the cop? The phone rested in his pocket, burning like a lump of guilt ... guilt at his betrayal of the Crips and betrayal of his word to this man. He could call him, tell him to leave, that he would make sure The Crow would fly no more, kill no more—forever. But something about the man made him think this a bad move. That maybe the cop had his own personal issues and that nothing would stop him from exacting his own punishment on The Crow.

If he called, what would the cop do? Either leave, call in reinforcements, or go in right away. He thought the last the most likely, even though such a move would be suicide.

Of course, that was the cop's business; his death meant nothing.

Only the betrayal of his men mattered. But if the cop went in for a fight, it would ruin his element of surprise and that he could not risk.

So, the only real question of any importance came down to who actually stood in his shoes today ... and perhaps from here on to the end of his life; James Arthur Washington Jr. or Thirty-Eight?

Sighing, he brought down the binoculars and pulled out his favorite gun. He snapped out the cylinder and watched as the brass casings spun about like a carousel. Popping it closed, he looked up with eyes that felt dead.

Thirty-Eight prepared his mind for battle.

55

Jim Black hit the accelerator and swerved around an eighteen-wheeler. Mile marker 321 swept past. He barely had time to catch it—nine miles out. At this time of day, I-70 carried mostly big rigs and out-of-staters either coming or going to or from vacations, not too crowded, but not exactly deserted either.

Jim left before finishing his reports or talking to the shrink, a departmental mandate after being involved in a duty-related shooting. But something in his conversation with Gil made him pack up and leave. It might have been Gil's shortness or vagueness, possibly even his tone or inflection; he couldn't say for sure. But something about Gil's demeanor pushed him to get up and leave, and in his years as a detective, he'd learned to trust his gut in matters like this.

Talking to the shrink might be a good idea, though. Jim had never shot anyone before, and killing two men, no matter how necessary or how much they may have deserved it, was taking a strange toll on him. He'd read of the psychological effect of killing people and the five stages of grief and all that stuff. He'd also thought of it as more or less a load of crap, but now, now he thought better of it.

The scene kept looping in his mind.

...the SWAT commander's fist pumping down, giving the "go signal," the breach, the bangs, the gunfire, bullets ripping through the walls and ceiling and floor. Blood and screams and confusion. The jar as his foot splintered the door frame and then seeing the two men, their rifles pointing straight up and casings flying out of their breaches in a continuous stream. He pointed his weapon as his finger pulled without him even ordering it to, and red mist erupted from the closest man's chest, leaving gaping black holes standing as the mist dissipated. And then the other guy came into his sights, slightly blurry in the sight picture, partially due to the dimness of the room, but mostly because of his concentration on the three green dots that decorated the small black posts. The recoil of the shots shivering through his wrists, forearms, and biceps. His body rocked marginally as his stance supported weight absorbed the concussive impact. The man started to turn, his eyes going wide, registering danger where there had been none an instant before. Then the missiles hit, eviscerating the strange beauty of the tattoos that looped and twined in gothic letters across his hairless chest, cratering the skin and shoving him back a half step before the life left his eyes and he fell. Dead. That fast. All he ever was or would ever be. Gone. Forever ...

A sheen of sweat slicked his forehead, and his eyes stung. He blinked several times quickly. Cleared his throat and tried to concentrate on the road. The scene looped again.

He shook his head roughly. "Knock it off!" he said out loud, and his voice sounded weak to his own ears.

Gil, he should be thinking about Gil and what he was sitting on. Had he found Majoqui Cabrera hiding out in Byers? Would he be too late to stop Gil from killing him or maybe even getting himself killed?

... the AK47 barked and coughed out fire as the ceiling disintegrated, and then the mist and holes—like black holes in a space darker than the darkest night—opened up right where his heart hid a few inches below the skin, and the second man turned, his eyes going ...

Jim slammed the steering wheel with one hand. *Stop it!*

It hadn't bothered him at first, but as the minutes turned into hours, it began to wear on him, like when someone sings "Old

McDonald." It gets stuck in your head—not the whole song—no—
no, that wouldn't be so bad—it's always just a small part of the song
replaying over and over and over—until you feel like your head is
going to explode. It was like that. He'd have a few seconds of relief
and not be thinking about it at all, and then—*BAM*—it would start all
over again. *Maddening.*

Jim knew he should probably call in some backup. There was
only one County car this far out east, and who knew where he was or
if he might be tied up on another call. Adams County bisected the
small town north of I-70. They usually kept a couple of cars in the
area, but again, it was a lot of territory to cover and no way to know
what their call load might be. If he and Gil ended up needing help, it
might take a while to get there.

*... plaster and dust and wood and metal traveling at incredible velocities
filled the air with deadly intent, his heart beat fast, and sound hit his ears
like needles so loud, far louder than their design parameters, and the door
gave so easily and there they were, right in front of him, in front of his gun,
the same gun he'd had for over a decade, the gun he practiced with every
week for just such a situation, and now it was here, and it kicked and
bucked and fire flashed from the barrel in slow motion and ultra-fast at the
same time, sending death and those holes—those magic black holes and the
blood mist and ...*

His chest heaved, and he let out a breath he didn't know he'd
been holding. *Stop it!* He commanded his mind ... and it did ... for a
moment anyway.

The whole thing struck him as curious. Annoying, bothersome,
but still ... *interesting.* That it could affect him this way. He never
would have believed it. Still, he could control it; he knew that. He
knew that for certain. He'd always prided himself on his willpower
and mindset. For now, he needed to put his full attention on the
matter at hand. And that was exactly what he would do.

*... eyes so wide, as though they couldn't comprehend how the game had
just changed, as though he saw the face of death sweeping toward him even
as the bullets punched him center mass ...*

Jim jerked the wheel hard to the right, overcorrected, almost fish-tailing into the minivan he'd just barely managed to stop from rear-ending.

Yes, he could handle it ... he *would* handle it! Still, he thought it might not be a bad idea to at least *talk* to the shrink when he got back.

56

The red car got onto the interstate and headed west. Four men. That had to be a sizable portion of Majoqui Cabrera's entourage, or at least I thought so. I scanned the area, still not much traffic, either foot or vehicles. The sun stood a little shy of midpoint overhead. I basically had two options; wait till night and go in to scout around or do it now. Dark was usually better, of course, but the idea of waiting all day in the car while Majoqui sat in there drinking cervezas and eating chips didn't exactly appeal to me. Not to mention the fact that Byers didn't lend itself to strangers, which made it highly unlikely I could stay here for any length of time without someone getting curious and calling the police or maybe tipping off one of Mara's lookouts, wherever they might be. After all, I had no way of knowing how long they had been in the town or how well set up their little empire here had come to be.

Add to all this that I just didn't have a lot of patience right now.

I decided on plan number two. But how to approach? The park entrance would have someone watching it, I was sure. I drove around to the far north side of the small gas station that sat to the east of the trailer park. I put ten sets of flex cuffs in my back pocket and got out. The building hid my car from view from the park and the main road that ran north and south. Pilgrim settled quietly at my side as I made my way around to the North West.

Would there be guards posted on the outer perimeter? That didn't seem like the kind of work young thugs would care for, so maybe not. On the other hand, when did it matter what soldiers in any battle liked or didn't like? No, it would depend on the command staff as to whether or not guards would be posted. So, what kind of general did I think Majoqui Cabrera was?

I decided there would be guards, so I proceeded with that mindset.

I spotted the first sentry about two minutes in and seventy yards or so from my vehicle. He was young, couldn't be more than fifteen, wearing a plaid shirt and loose, sagging jeans that looked like they had been handed down through nine generations. Who knows, maybe they had. Close cropped hair and beat-up sneakers. He smoked a hand-rolled cigarette and kept reaching into his pocket and pulling his hand out while squinting up at the sun and clouds and then searching the horizon. All in all, not doing a bad job as a lookout for a fifteen-year-old on the most boring duty in the creation of warfare.

It was about to get a bit more exciting for him.

I figured the pocket-grabbing to be a pistol of some sort; guards usually had weapons—otherwise, they were pretty useless as guards. Still, I couldn't very well just shoot him dead. He was only a youngster ... besides ... the noise would give me away.

Moving further into the trees, I gave Pilgrim the *platz* command using a hand signal. He went down, watching my every step. I made it to about twenty feet from the boy before my cover ran out. Any further and he would be able to spot me. I raised my hand, index finger pointing straight up. Then I pointed that finger at the boy. Pilgrim swept in like a heat-seeking missile. The boy saw him about thirty yards out. His first reaction was one of surprise; then a small smile curved his lips. He started to raise his hand in a wave, when it must have registered this wasn't a friendly dog—might have something to do with a certain look in Pilgrim's eyes when he's about to rip out the spinal column of his prey—and the boy's mouth morphed into a big oval as he tried to take a step back. He didn't make it because I was behind him, slipping an arm around his throat while simultaneously applying opposite pressure on my wrist, shutting off all blood flow from his carotid to his brain and putting him to sleep in under six seconds.

Pilgrim stopped at his feet and lay down. I did a quick pat-down and found a cheap .22 in his right front pants pocket. I peeled off his shirt, ripped the sleeves off, and zipped him up with his hands behind his back. I stuffed one of the sleeves in his mouth and tied the other sleeve around his mouth to hold it in. I stashed him in the trees and gave Pilgrim a head check. He moved silently forward, sniffing out the next guard and finding him about thirty yards to the west with his back to us. Another teen-angel, maybe seventeen, speaking in Spanish on a cell phone. I put him out the same way, used up another set of flex-cuffs, and gagged him with his socks. I found two knives and a .380 that looked cheaper than the .22. My pockets were getting heavy with all these guns.

Pilgrim sniffed out the third guard on the far west side of the park. I saw his nose notch up, testing—testing—testing, then he went into a slink, moving forward like a great cat hunting on the Savana. I'm sure he would have loved to pounce, but he was well disciplined and knew his job. He stopped before we were forced to break cover— a double-wide with a pair of bicycles leaning against the side of the trailer. Being careful to duck below the window, I edged an eye around the corner and saw the guard leaning a hip against a three-foot picket fence surrounding the next trailer. Older than the last two, with a barrel chest, beer belly, a scraggly beard, bushy black hair, and a unibrow. Handsome devil. Just then, two girls came busting out of the trailer, saw me, and yelled in unison, "Mom, somebody's out here!" Loud.

Unibrow looked around before I could pull back. No choice now. I rushed him fast, even as I saw him pull the gun from his pocket. No way I could beat him.

PILGRIM'S PATIENCE was being sorely tested. He'd spotted the first two guards but held back until commanded by the Alpha. And both times, the Alpha took action without him, leaving Pilgrim to stand by watching, his blood lust unsatiated. But this time, the guard saw the Alpha and attacked. Pack mentality took over, and Pilgrim instinctively moved to protect the pack leader.

Pilgrim flew at the man, his powerful body moving with the lithe grace of a jungle cat. Each step increased his speed until he was a streamlined missile locked on its target with unerring accuracy. Pilgrim launched from three yards out, covering the nine feet in a blur too fast for the eye to follow. Four scimitar-like canines sunk into the man's throat, piercing his fragile flesh with the ease of a hypodermic needle, slicing in and severing tendons and meat and veins as though they were wet tissue. But Pilgrim's teeth were only the beginning of the carnage. His massive weight struck an instant behind, jarring the man's frame and increasing the destruction to his neck and throat exponentially. The impact picked the guard off the ground and threw him into the air in a tangle of arms, legs, and paws.

The man was tough. He fought with all his strength. But he had tried to attack the Alpha.

I SAW Pilgrim hit him full on. A hundred and twenty pounds of muscle and teeth and fury. The teeth crushed down on the guard's throat while Pilgrim's body slammed into him at roughly thirty miles an hour. I heard Unibrow grunt as the air left his body, and he hit the ground with a meaty thud.

The two of them rolled and flopped, Unibrow ending up on the bottom, clawing and punching, and Pilgrim growling, low and deep, and crushing with those wolf-like jaws. Making it to them, I gave Pilgrim the 'out' command, and he instantly disengaged. A lot of blood poured from the ragged flesh of Unibrow's throat and neck. He staggered to one knee, looking completely disoriented. I kicked him under the chin. His eyes rolled up into his skull, and he went straight back and out.

Grabbing him by the shoulders, I quickly dragged him to the far side of the trailer that had the bikes up against its side. Pilgrim came to me at a finger wave just as the two kids came running down to the sidewalk. They looked about as if a magic trick just happened, and in a way, it had. I was there, and then I wasn't. They went running back to their mother.

I figured there must be at least one more guard, one for each corner of the compass, and that he probably stood, or sat, to the south. Question now was, did I take him out or just proceed to the trailer? If I wasted the time to track him down, I could be discovered; or, he could cry out like what just about happened with Unibrow. But if I didn't, and I ended up in a gun battle with Majoqui Cabrera, I'd be open to the rear, and he could back-shoot me.

Not much of a choice, really; I had to take him out.

Pilgrim slipped away from me, moving fast until he started his shark-like air scenting. I saw the fourth, and hopefully, last guard three trailers to the southeast. Again, he was older, early twenties, but no beer belly or unibrow. He looked hard and sleek, with streaks of prison-ink tattoos creeping up from beneath the collar of his shirt and licking the undersides of his jaw.

The guy looked tough and capable, but he hadn't heard the scuffle with Unibrow, or at least he hadn't associated it with danger to himself or his boss, so maybe he wasn't quite as capable as he looked. Either that or he was deaf.

He stood directly in front of trailer #23, and that presented a whole new problem. If I took him out in front of Majoqui's trailer, he was pretty sure to spot me. If I put him down fast enough and there weren't more bangers in the trailer with Majoqui, it might work out all right. But if not, it could turn bad really fast.

I decided the best course of action was to bring this last guard to me.

Slipping my head back around the side and hugging the trailer, I coughed three times. Not too loud, as though I was trying to suppress it, then another three, this time a little louder. Pilgrim lay at my feet; his head fixated on the front of the trailer where the guard would approach. I watched him closely. Knowing him as I did, I knew what to look for.

There! Pilgrim's head canted to the side, the way dogs do when watching television or listening to the radio. I swung just as the last guard rounded the corner. It was a solid punch, and it landed square on the chin. He went down, but as I thought, he was tough and jumped back to his feet, trying for a fighting stance. But he wobbled and staggered, his balance and equilibrium gone. He was pretty much out on his feet. I almost hated finishing him off, but it had to be done. I cracked him in the forehead, and that did the trick. A quick truss job, a stashing by the trailers, and that took care of business.

All that remained was to have a face-to-face with a monster.

57

Thirty-Eight watched from the safety and distance of the dirt road. He shook his head as the white cop took out the last of the guards. Now, how had he known he was coming round that corner? Thirty-Eight raised his eyebrows as the guard went out—impressed. And Thirty-Eight didn't impress easily. The guy had taken out four posted guards in about ten minutes, without any of them being able to sound an alarm and without even killing them.

He wondered at the man's game. What sort of vendetta did he have against the Crow, and why? Not that it really mattered. What did matter was that The Crow and his men had to die, here, today, now. Would the man's actions affect that? He certainly seemed capable and acquitted himself well, but the hired help was one thing, The Crow himself quite another matter.

Looking back at his men, he considered. Most of them were boys now, his best and oldest dead. Mara had killed many, but once the Bloods saw the Crips' weakness, they had joined in and taken out more of his soldiers. *The enemy of my enemy,* and all that philosophical history crap. The end result was that the bulk of his fighting force had been devastated to the point of near collapse.

So, what to do? If he charged down there now and The Crow expected it, as he did at the parking lot, then he and his men would likely be wiped out. If the cop had set him up, somehow working with The Crow, then again, they would be crushed. On the other hand, he didn't see how the cop could even know they were there, and the same went for The Crow.

If he let the cop go in alone and he failed, the worst that could happen would be that The Crow would try and escape. But Thirty-Eight had seven cars to stop that. Besides, if the cop managed to take a few of The Crow's men out, that left less to pose a danger for him and his boys.

He picked up the binoculars and prepared to watch the show.

58

Byers, Colorado, a sleepy little city, way out east in the boonies, where small-town America lived. A place where people still waved as you drove by and said 'hi,' or 'howdy,' with a genuine smile on their face and a glint in their eye.

Jim Black hated places like this. He was a city boy through and through and held a natural mistrust of anyone "too open." Just what were they hiding behind those smiles? And what did that glint mean? Were they plotting on him? They had to be up to something. More than that was the way they talked, not exactly Texan or even southern, but ... different. Like the 'howdy,' not uber country, but close ... almost. One of Jim's biggest pet peeves happened at cop conventions and award ceremonies where cops from the big states like New York or California would joke about Colorado being nothing more than a cow town. Some of these guys wouldn't even believe him that horses and carriages weren't a regular means of travel in the downtown area anymore. He couldn't count how many times he'd been asked where his Stetson was. It drove him nuts.

Towns like Byers were why the myth perpetuated.

Not that city life didn't have its pitfalls ...

... the ceiling exploded as bullets ripped through the wood and plaster. SWAT agents, caught completely by surprise reacted to the barrage by jerking and dancing back and forth, blood puffing in mist-like detonations as screaming lead tore into them ...

Jim shook his head, yes, pitfalls. He wondered if Byers might not come face to face with some of those city pitfalls before the day ended. He hoped not, or did he? If Majoqui Cabrera was here, they might be able to end this now, without the cavalry, just he and Gil Mason. If it worked out that way, Gil would say he'd never been there, leaving all the glory to Jim. Of course, Cabrera could have an army stationed out here, and they could easily be walking into a slaughter.

... the first man never even saw him as the holes—so black—so impossibly black—opened up as if by magic in the center of his chest—sucking the life away from him and leaving his dead body to crumple and fall and then the turn, ever so slight, just a fraction of movement and the sights lined up perfectly and the man's eyes growing wide and ...

Jim didn't want that, not again, not this soon anyway. *Give me some time,* he thought, *just a little time and I'll be right as rain.*

Maybe Cabrera was out there alone. Or maybe just him and his little chicky, this Tamera Sun, and their vacation home as it were. If that were the case, everything might go just the way it should. Easy and safe, with no one shooting or getting shot. No magic black holes *—how could they be so black—blood isn't black, it's red—red—red! —*no invisible assassins shooting through walls and floors and ceilings. Just a double-click of cuffs being set snuggly in place and a long ride back to the station. And from there, a few congratulatory drinks at the local cop shop and then a promotion and one step closer to the nomination as County Sheriff.

Taking the off-ramp, he curved first to the south, then back to the east, stopped at the light, and when it changed, continued north past the small gas station. He saw Gil's car parked on the far north side and pulled in next to it.

... the chatter of automatic gunfire stopped as he felt the jolt to his arms and the release of velocity from the barrel of his weapon. The gang banger's eyes grew wide—so wide—then death stole their power ...

Jim grunted and popped the magazine from his gun—*full*—then snapped it back in. Something told him he hadn't yet seen the end of today's death.

59

N o screen door on trailer twenty-three, just a cheap-looking hollow-core wood job with a doorknob lock. Not even a deadbolt. The windows were curtained, and the door bare of peepholes or glass. I reared back and kicked. The door banged open with little resistance. I stepped in, gun drawn and aiming. The sun would have killed my inside vision, but I'd anticipated that and had spent over a minute shielding my eyes with my hand before kicking.

Ten or fifteen gangbangers of various ages all turned to look at me. A cloud of marijuana smoke sucked past me and into the daylight—no Majoqui Cabrera. An instant of surprised stillness and silence ensued while we stared at each other. And then, as if on cue, they all started reaching for weapons.

One stood up, and I shot him in the hip. I grabbed the door handle and jumped back. The lock broken, I pulled hard enough that the hinges bent and the door wedged at an angle.

I'd left Pilgrim on the side of the trailer, and as I turned to see if he was still there, the guy with the beer gut and the ripped-out throat came staggering around the corner, waving a gun at me. He cranked off three rounds, none of them even coming close. There was a blur of brown and black fur as Pilgrim hit him with roughly the speed and force of an Intercontinental Ballistic Missile. Unibrow fell to the dirt, forming a mushroom cloud, as Pilgrim thrashed him back and forth.

I'd been about to shoot him when Pilgrim showed up and was just lowering my gun as something burned through my thigh. The sound of the gunshot registered an instant later, and I looked up to see Majoqui Cabrera standing on the porch of the trailer next door. He fired again, and I felt the slug slap me in the center of my chest, followed by two more that hit me high on the right pec and another that whizzed past my ear.

Pilgrim yipped, and as I turned, I saw him fall, blood wetting the side of his head.

Turning back, I felt perfectly calm, steady as a rock. I slowly lifted my gun and put the front sight in the middle of Majoqui's face. The blade and dot of the sight grew sharp for an instant, and then I let them go blurry as his face became crisp and clear—opposite of all my training, but oh so important to see his expression as the bullet obliterated him once and for all. His face lost all expression as he realized there was no stopping the shot. He grinned at me—*grinned*—and stretched his arms out to the side with the gun held away—inviting the shot.

I felt nothing, not the blood running down my leg or the bruising in my chest. Not fear or anger or rage or even relief—nothing.

I pulled back on the trigger as the door burst open, and a hoard of bodies swallowed me. The bullet meant for Majoqui Cabrera struck a man that moved in front of me as I crashed off the porch and crushed into the dirt, fists punching and boots and shoes kicking. I tried to fight back, mindless of them, of any of them, my only thought to get to Majoqui Cabrera.

A fist hit me in the kidney, and a boot caught me in the nose and lips. Blood poured, and I felt the gun wrenched from my fingers. I reached around and grabbed a pair of nostrils with my fingers and jerked, feeling the flesh tear and hearing a scream. I bit someone's forearm and spit out a chunk of hot meat. Something hard and unyielding smashed into my head, and I almost went out, but shrimped ahead and managed to kick someone in the groin before three bodies fell on my right arm, pinning it to the ground. Another two guys covered my left. A fat guy grabbed both legs in his arms and buried his chest over my knees while a big muscular guy with blood streaming from a damaged nose reared back and kicked me full on in the temple.

Everything went dark, and once again, I felt nothing at all.

60

Majoqui Cabrera heard the first gunshot and sprang from the couch with a panther's grace and fluidity. The gun in his hand felt like an extension of his being. Tamera had hardly registered the fact that the sound had come from outside the trailer and not the movie they were watching. Her head turned his way, a quizzical expression raising her eyebrows.

Majoqui eased out the door and saw Angelo, blood flowing down his front in a sheet of crimson, shoot at the Americano police officer who stood on the porch of his army's trailer next door. Holes punched uselessly into the thin skin of the trailer, and then Angelo was savaged by the dog that had attacked Majoqui on that first night.

Majoqui fired quickly—too quickly—hitting the American in the leg. Instantly, he calmed his excitement and took careful aim. He fired a shot directly into his enemy's heart. The impact rocked the man, and Majoqui fired twice more, both shots hitting home—and then a final time into the head of the dog that had finished Angelo, even now, as it was charging toward him from behind his master.

The dog went down, but the American did not die; he did not even bleed. He, too, had protection. Majoqui realized the saints and the demons were testing them both. Testing their faith. Majoqui held his hands to the side. His power was *the* power, and this American who had hunted him for months would not prevail. Puffing out his chest, Majoqui smiled.

The American aimed, and the air grew completely still, the sun blazing its gentle warmth down on the two of them as the breeze stopped and all sound muted. So very different than that day long ago when he had been beaten into Mara and had killed a man much older than him. On that day, the sun had raged, and the air, choked with water, had made his clothes stick to his skin, and his sweat run freely. Majoqui did not die that day, and he would not die today.

The door to the trailer exploded open, and his men enveloped the American. The man fought bravely, but it ended quickly, the only way it could.

The blessed Mother herself protected Majoqui, and not all the demons or saints, or even a bulletproof vest, could long save the American police officer from Majoqui's power.

Still, the man had single-handedly located his hidden refuge. The gunfight made it impossible to stay here, but relocating was something he and his men were well used to. The only question that remained was whether or not he had the time to dispose of the American the way he wanted to. To do so would require leaving with him now. His hatred and respect for the man were such that he actually considered it for a moment. But then his tactical mind took over. Knowing the true danger this man posed, he walked over and stood above the man's head. The others moved aside as Majoqui pointed the revolver. It would be so much better to make this moment last, like on the bridge that night when he had murdered this man's wife and child in front of his eyes. He sighed. Logic dictated he end it here and now. But still ...

The American opened his eyes, blood running from numerous cuts, crusting his lips and nostrils. He looked up at Majoqui and laughed.

Majoqui decided.

He clicked back the hammer and took careful aim.

61

Thirty-Eight saw a vehicle pull up next to the cop's car behind the gas station. A man got out and looked around. Obviously a cop. He scouted a bit and soon found something under a tree that seemed to interest him. From Thirty-Eight's position and distance, he couldn't see what it was. The cop continued to the northwest, keeping to the trees, and soon was lost from sight.

Thirty-Eight caught a flicker of movement toward the south and refocused in that direction. A flash of light followed by two more— gunshots—and then a wave of commotion as a mob of bodies swarmed out of a trailer. No sounds made it this far, only the rush of traffic from the nearby highway. The binoculars focused, and he saw the cop that he'd made the deal with fighting on the ground, completely swarmed by the men that charged out of the trailer. A brief but intense struggle ensued, ending when a big man kicked the cop in the head.

A figure detached himself from the porch of the closest trailer, and the crowd separated as he walked to the fallen cop. Thirty-Eight focused on the figure, and as he watched him, he came to the realization that this was none other than The Crow. Something about his bearing and manner bespoke authority. And the way the men parted before him left no doubt to his rank.

There he was, his mortal enemy, the one person who stood between The Crips and Mara's blood struggle for Colorado. So, what to do? He couldn't make an exact count of soldiers down there, but it seemed about equal to his own troops. He didn't like it. It was always better to have superior numbers on your side before going to battle. Add to that, it was on the enemy's home ground, diminishing The Crip's odds even further. If they attacked and lost, it would mean the war. Even if they won but suffered extreme losses, it might mean giving Colorado to The Bloods, and that was unacceptable.

Thirty-Eight looked back at his men, stuffed into cars and waiting for his signal.

He did have the element of surprise, but how much would that shift the odds? Impossible to tell. He looked back and saw The Crow stand over the cop, still lying on the ground.

The man was dead; there was nothing Thirty-Eight could do for him from this distance. Not that he cared about the cop, he didn't of course, but for some reason, he felt an unaccustomed pang of guilt. The sort of feeling he experienced more and more these days. He had made a deal with this man, and the man had kept his part of the bargain.

The Crow pulled a gun up from his side and pointed it at the cop.

No, nothing he could do, no matter how he felt. There was no way to stop The Crow from killing him. But ... there was always revenge.

James Arthur Washington Jr. motioned to his men, sat back in the front passenger's seat, and signaled his driver to go.

62

Jim Black found the trail of unconscious bodies as he passed through the trees and from trailer to trailer. He began to feel a little afraid. Not of the Thirteen's, but of Gil Mason. He'd always known Gil was tough and efficient, but what he saw now seemed more on a level with secret agent stuff. How had he managed it? And then he heard two kids arguing with their mother, who finally yelled at them to shut up and go to their room. Moving quickly and quietly, he passed the porch. He almost didn't see the banger lying on his stomach, his hands and feet zip-tied, pushed up tight against the scarf of the far side of the trailer. The dude was out cold and looked like he had a broken jaw. Who did Gil think he was, Chuck Norris? Jim lifted a lid, and the pupil was rolled up high, showing almost all white. He let it fall. *Maybe Gil is Chuck Norris*, he thought.

Jim did a quick spot check on his gun, then moved forward but stopped when he heard gunshots explode just around the corner. He ducked and ran ahead to the edge of the hedges and past a thick tree that looked half dead. He heard a burst of yelling and what sounded like a fight, more gunshots, and then silence.

Peering around the tree, he saw several gangbangers standing in a semi-circle. No sign of Gil. Jim went back around the tree in the other direction, jumped over a knee-high chain-link fence, and then moved around a child's tricycle and up against another trailer.

Majoqui Cabrera stepped off a porch directly across from him and walked slowly between the men who parted for him like he was some kind of king. He stopped in the middle of the small hoard and looked down. A few people stepped aside, and Jim saw Gil Mason lying on the ground. Gil looked like he had been run over by a truck. His clothes were ripped and torn, and his hands and face were a bloody mess.

Oh, this was bad. Jim did a quick count and thought there must be at least twelve, maybe more bangers. Gil was out of the fight, and Jim had no backup. That had to change. He pulled out his cellphone and speed-dialed his partner, Randy Nolan. He answered it immediately.

"I'm in Byers. Majoqui Cabrera is here with a bunch of bad boys. Get the cavalry here quick."

"Where in Byers?"

"Trailer Park on the north side of I-70."

"Which trailer?"

Jim saw a gun in Majoqui Cabrera's right hand, riding the seam of his pants. Suddenly Jim heard laughing. It sounded like Gil Mason.

"Just listen for the gunfire," Jim said as he clicked off.

Jim thought the odds might be too great, even for Chuck Norris. He pocketed his cellphone as Majoqui Cabrera lifted the gun and pointed it at Gil's face. A revolver, not big, but big enough.

... *Jim saw the holes open in the man's chest, and the vacant look of death glaze over his eyes as he fell back. His sights moved, and the second man, still shooting, lined up perfectly ...*

He slammed his eyes closed, then back open. His gun was pointing across the expanse at Majoqui Cabrera's heart. A last vision of black holes filled with eternity stabbed at his brain.

Fine, he thought as he took up the slack on the trigger, *let's go all Star Trek and make us some singularities.*

The gun barked, and he felt that familiar jolt to his wrists.

63

The nothingness exploded into a bolt of pain as the boot connected with my temple, detonating like cannon fire inside my skull. I awoke to see Majoqui Cabrera standing over me. I couldn't have been out long because everyone still stood around me. He looked down into my eyes and pointed a gun at my face. I laughed, not because I was brave, but because I knew that no matter what he did, I would kill him. He could empty that gun into my face or heart or brain, and still, I would drag whatever was left of me to him and claw my way to his throat before I let myself die.

I rose my shoulders up off the ground, bending at the waist, coming for him. He clicked back the hammer. I didn't stop; nothing would stop me. As I pushed my palms against the hard-packed dirt, I saw his index finger slowly pull back. The gunshot broke the sudden silence that had fallen over the battered men and boys surrounding me, but I felt no impact. Instead, a bright spark flashed off the cylinder of the gun, and Majoqui Cabrera's hand snapped to the side like it had been cracked with a whip. Two of his fingers went spinning through the air in a spray of blood.

Before anyone could react, I was on him, my hands gripping his throat, my body pushing him down to the ground. He hit hard, me on top. The breath evacuated his lungs, and my fingers stopped him from finding another. His eyes bulged grotesquely. I squeezed in, feeling the flesh pulp and bones grind and pop. For an instant, a high-pitched squeak slipped past his lips. I crushed in even harder, and nothing escaped at all.

A man fell next to me, blood squirting through his fingers in an arterial spray as he tried to clamp it shut at his throat.

I ignored him.

Gunshots—a lot of them—a gun battle raging over me.

I ignored it.

Majoqui Cabrera twisted and turned beneath me, his life fleeing his body as I dug my thumbs into his Adam's apple, destroying the tissue and fibers that made up the muscles and tendons of his neck.

A screech of tires and shouting and screaming and bursts of automatic weapons. Men falling and fighting and shooting and dying; ballistic missiles scorching the air and screeching past the ears.

I ignored everything ... everything but Majoqui Cabrera. I had him. Here. Now. Within my grasp. In my hands. I saw my wife's face, my daughter's smile. Tears poured down my cheeks. An inarticulate scream burst from my soul. I gathered all the strength in my shoulders, biceps, triceps, and forearms and brought the tips of my fingers together around his neck. I felt his spinal column, saw his lips go from blue to purple-black. His eyes rolled back till nothing but the whites showed.

And then something crashed into the back of my head.

I ignored it.

Blood dripped down my forehead, and I was hit again ... and again ... and again. The dripping changed to a flow and then a river.

The world grew dark and dizzy, mixing with my wife's face and her voice and Marla's sweet fingers and lips and hair, and Majoqui Cabrera, so close to death, and someone yelling for me to stop and to let go, and that crashing of metal against my head. I turned and saw Jim Black, pulling back his hand, a bloody pistol in his fist as his lips moved, but I couldn't hear him anymore. I could hear only the sound of the blood pulsing in my ears. I snarled at him as he struck me in the ear with the gun, and I forced my hands tighter and tighter. It felt so good, so right, so just. And then the heavy metal hit me in the temple, in the same place the boot had caught me, and I was falling and falling and falling.

64

Thirty-Eight's seven cars worth of soldiers poured into the park and entered a war zone. A squad of MS 13 warriors was shooting at a white man dressed like a detective. He was shooting back at them as his men jumped out of still-rolling cars and started blasting. The 13ers backs were to them, and 38's troop's first volley took out a good five of them before they realized they were in a crossfire and adjusted.

He saw the cop he'd made the deal with on top of The Crow, his hands around the smaller man's throat. Still, the cop looked like he was one foot out of the grave, and Thirty-Eight didn't know if he could finish the job. He decided to give him a hand. A big guy slashed at him with a machete, so Thirty-Eight pumped three bullets into his stomach and chest. The big guy folded, blood gushing from his mouth. Another Mara shot at him, missing. He tried to shoot again, but his gun jammed, and Thirty-Eight calmly put a round into his forehead. He still had it, that ability to stay cool in the midst of chaos and death. It was this, more than anything else, that had kept him alive through the decades when so many others had died.

His men were doing well even after that first edge of surprise had worn off. But they were taking casualties. He saw Little Bee take a bullet in the cheek, and a machete hit Tre-Tre in the shoulder, flaying his flesh like butcher's meat. Thirty-Eight fired at the man with the machete, missed, took better aim, and hit him in the groin. He didn't go down, but he limped away from Tre-Tre and was quickly lost in the fog of battle.

The cop still maintained his position on top of The Crow, but he didn't look good. Thirty-Eight emptied the cylinder of his pistol and reloaded. He felt a sting just above his belly button and looked down. A neat little hole stared back at him. And then an ever-growing red flower began to spread from around the hole, staining his shirt. Thirty-Eight couldn't quite figure out what had happened. Where had the hole come from, and why was his shirt wet and red? It just didn't make any sense. He closed the cylinder of his .38 and walked over toward the cop and The Crow. Something punched him in the back of the shoulder, and it made him a little mad. He touched the hole in his shirt with his left index finger as he walked toward the two men fighting on the ground and saw that his finger came away bright red. So strange. He was close now, maybe ten yards away. He lifted the gun and pointed it at The Crow.

A bullet swept past his face, and he thought, *that was close,* and then he felt another punch, this time to his right kidney, painful, but not terrible. He felt weird, he couldn't exactly explain how, but sort of unfocused, not dizzy, but out of it. He saw the gun in his hand, and he couldn't remember why he was holding it or who he was pointing it at. Something about a bird, or was it a cop?

He looked up and saw the sky and realized he was lying on his back. He didn't know why or how he'd gotten there, but he didn't feel like getting up. It was nice here. Quiet and cool and peaceful. An airplane left a contrail way up high, and he thought how beautiful it looked. He'd never been on a plane and wondered what it must be like.

The .38 fell to the grass as James Arthur Washington Jr.'s eyes closed for the last time.

65

Majoqui Cabrera felt the gun rip from his hands. A fragment of metal hit him in the chin, and two of his fingers disappeared. Before he could react, the Americano police officer was on him, his fingers like steel bands wrapping around his throat and crushing off his breath. Then he hit the ground, and lights flashed behind his eyes, his air gone. He fought to suck in a breath but managed only a sip, and then the pressure turned into a living vise. He felt the bones creak and bend in his neck. Pain, greater than anything he'd ever imagined, exploded as vertebra compressed against nerve bundles.

The warrior inside his soul tried to rally, and he struck at the man's elbows and wrists, but Majoqui was an infant facing a giant. The man's strength was that of a demon from Hell itself. Desperately he tried to reach for the sword belt, but the man was pressed too tightly on top of him. There was no room and no time as the pain multiplied a thousandfold. Sparks and flashes popped like exploding light bulbs in his brain, and things grew bright and dark at the same time.

His mother's face came to him from long, long ago. Long before the men that kicked him and used her, before Mara, before death and blood. She smiled at him, kissed his face, and sang soft words, her breath like a gentle breeze that soothed and relaxed and promised hope. He wanted to touch her, to tell her he was sorry, that he loved her and that he wished he'd protected her, but the police officer's eyes burned through the image of her face. Mason was above him, blood dripping down his forehead and into Majoqui's face. In a darkening haze, he saw a thin man behind Mason, hitting him again and again with something. There was no sound now, just popping flashes as his synapses snapped closed like circuit breakers, one after another.

Death swept over him. He felt its cold dark fingers, like the American police officer's, around his throat, pulling him closer and closer, and not all his amulet's or blessings or curses could stop it now.

The man hitting Gil Mason could not hope to stop him. The saints could not stop him. Even the blessed Virgin herself could not stop him. He was death, and he was unstoppable, a juggernaut of immeasurable power, devoid of feelings or mercy or pain. Majoqui remembered that he had considered just driving away from the American police officer on that first night, and now he understood that he should have heeded his instincts. No one could stand against a will like this.

Something gave in his neck and spine, and another shard of pain speared his being. His vision blurred around the edges, sweeping in with horrible speed. And suddenly, the fingers around his throat were gone, and the weight on top of him vanished. He saw the thin man that had been hitting Gil Mason stand over him, pointing a gun. A breath made it into Majoqui's lungs, and he coughed, a racking horrid grinding sound that caused agony to spike and flair and burst in his back and neck.

The man was saying something. But before Majoqui could make it out, the man took a step back, as if off-balance and blood spread from a hole high on the left side of his chest. Majoqui turned, even though the pain it cost him was considerable. Tamera Sun stood on the porch, a smoking pistol held tightly in both hands.

Majoqui smiled and forced himself to his feet.

66

T amera Sun heard gunshots as Majoqui left the trailer. She went to the window and saw the man that had said those horrible things about Majoqui. That Majoqui had killed his wife and daughter. He was a muscular man, and he held a gun, aiming it at her man, but Majoqui's friends tackled him. The threat seemed to be over until the shooting started again. Then the men in the cars arrived, and it sounded like the fourth of July back in Kansas. People were running around and shooting and being shot. She saw people die. There were screams and blood and giant knives.

Now the muscular man was on top of Majoqui, choking him. She ran to the couch and picked up the gun Majoqui kept in the crease between the cushions. Throwing open the door, she lined up the sights just like Majoqui had taught her. The only real target was the man's head, so that's where she aimed. But then another man started hitting the muscular man in the head with the butt of a gun, and she didn't know what to do. Majoqui writhed beneath the man, and it looked like he didn't have long. She squinted one eye, took careful aim, and squeezed the trigger, just as something ran between her legs. The movement upset her aim, and instead of hitting the muscular man on top of Majoqui, she saw the thin man with the gun jerk back, blood spreading and wetting his white shirt.

The muscular man fell to the side, and Majoqui groggily looked toward her ...

Tamera looked down and saw Miranda shivering between her ankles, frightened to death at all the noise and confusion.

She leaned down to pick up her cat when she noticed that the thin man she'd accidentally shot was standing over Majoqui. He still held the gun, blood sopping his shirt all the way to his belly. He looked at her as she gripped Miranda in one hand and stood back up.

Tamera hadn't meant to shoot him; she didn't even know who he was. She held up the gun and was going to say she was sorry when he pointed his weapon and shot her in the throat.

Miranda jumped from her arms and landed on the other side of the railing before running under the trailer.

Tamera looked at Majoqui ... saw the horror on his face. She'd never seen him look like that before; he was always so self-composed and confident. It scared her. She tried to tell him it was okay, but blood gushed from her mouth, and she couldn't take in a breath. It felt like she was choking ... drowning.

The gun still sat in her hand, heavy. She wanted to show the man she hadn't meant to shoot him and raised it toward him. He fired again, and the bullet hit her low on the cheek at an angle. The impact took her vision in the left eye and the hearing in the left ear. She fell back against the trailer, hot liquid spilling down her front. She tried to speak again, but her teeth were shattered, and her jaw wouldn't work right. It didn't hurt exactly; there was just a strange feeling of blunt force concussion and disorientation.

Majoqui screamed. She heard it in her right ear, and he sounded so sad and hurt. She wanted to tell him it was okay that *she* was okay and that *they* would be okay, but nothing seemed to work quite right. She saw Majoqui turn on the man, whipping the sword belt from his pants. He swung, and the blade, suddenly long and stiff, sliced into the man's hip just above the thigh.

Tamera Sun wondered where Miranda had gone. She needed to make sure the little cat was safe. She thought she should ask Majoqui to get her; Majoqui would always keep them safe. He loved them, and he would always keep ...

67

I hit the ground on my shoulder, feeling dizzy and confused. Blood ran down into my face from my hair and into the dirt, making it muddy and dark. I saw Majoqui roll over to his knees, coughing and hacking, and he looked toward the trailer and screamed. I reached for him with one hand, but he was too far away, and he was sliding that sword belt from his pants. He swung around, and I saw the steel slice into the meat of Jim Black's hip. Jim yelled and staggered away a few steps, the sword sliding soundlessly free. Jim's leg buckled, and he flopped awkwardly to the earth.

Majoqui Cabrera tried to stand up, fell, tried again. I pushed myself off the ground, blood pouring down my neck and face. I made it to my feet just as he did. He saw me from the corner of his eye and swung that three feet of flexible death at me. But I was close, so instead of trying to evade, I stepped into him, wrapping his wrist and forearm up in the crease of my elbow, trapping it tight. The sword continued its momentum and cut me just above the left kidney. Not deep, but it stung. I wrenched down—hard—and heard his forearm snap. His eyes went wide, and the blood left his face. I came in with an overhand right, catching him at the back of the jaw below the ear. The bone crumpled beneath the blow. I pulled back, still trapping him with my other arm, and hit him in the eye—the bad eye. The cheek shredded, and blood flowed. I hit him again and again and again and again—not hockey punches—each one starting in my thigh and hips and building force as they rocketed up through my body, past my shoulder, and into my fist. His head flopped back and forth, loose and boneless as though his neck was no longer connected. I hit him once more, and the sheer force of it ripped him from my grip. He landed face-first in the dirt and lay there, completely still.

But my rage knew no end. I went to him and kicked him in the side. I stomped his ankle, breaking it, moved up to his knee, and stomped it twice. I went into a frenzy, kicking and stomping his back and kidneys and shoulders.

The sound of sirens screamed onto the scene, and through the clamor and fury, I somehow heard Jim Black's voice behind me. He was screaming, begging for me to stop. But I could no more stop than I could stop seeing my dead wife's face and hear my little baby girl's screams.

I'd made it to his neck and head, and I saw the perfect kill shot, right where his spine connected to the base of his skull. I raised my foot ... aimed ...

I didn't hear the shot, but I felt the impact as the slug of copper-jacketed lead took me in the shoulder and shoved my one-legged stance off balance. I landed on my butt and saw Jim Black, tears streaming down his face, holding the gun he'd just fired. I tried to get up on my feet, but two cops grabbed me by the arms and pulled me back.

Jim yelled for them to cuff me, and they pushed me facedown and dragged my arms behind my back. I wanted to fight, to claw my way back to Majoqui Cabrera and finish what I needed to finish. But there was nothing left.

They carried me to a police car and drove me to the hospital.

68

T he cavalry arrived, and the war ended. Both gangs had been pretty much decimated, leaving the playing field clear for the Bloods to reassert control ... that whole thing about nature hating a vacuum and all, I guess.

I lay in the hospital bed, reading the after-action reports of what was being dubbed the Front Street Trailer Park Battle. Nine dead, seventeen wounded. Among them, James Arthur Washington Jr., the Crip I'd made my agreement with. I recognized him from his picture. Tamera Sun, former owner of the yellow VW and girlfriend of one Majoqui Cabrera, also dead. Jim shot her after she shot him.

Except for Jim, Pilgrim, and me, no law enforcement officers had been injured or killed. In a trailer on the other side of the park, one woman had a bullet pass through her wall, stinging her left cheek and leaving a cut about a quarter inch in length and a sixteenth deep, before denting her refrigerator and falling to the floor. All other casualties were gang members.

Pilgrim somehow made it through with just a grazing flesh wound.

Majoqui Cabrera rested in a drug-induced coma under twenty-four-hour guard in the Denver Sheriff's Department's prisoner section located in the basement of Denver General Hospital. He'd suffered multiple broken bones, a massive concussion, a ruptured kidney, lacerated spleen, and the loss of an eye. He was expected to live.

I'd failed again.

I had two bullets removed; one from my thigh where Majoqui Cabrera shot me and the other from my shoulder where Jim Black shot me. The vest had stopped the two to my chest. I suffered three broken ribs, a broken nose, two broken knuckles, a concussion, about thirty stitches, a thousand or so bruises and abrasions, and I was still peeing blood nearly a week later. Other than that, I felt fine.

Only I didn't.

I'd had my chance—three really—after he'd shot me, when I had my hands around his throat, and when I was trying to stomp the life from him—and I'd failed. Maybe he was demonically protected.

The door opened, and my father-in-law, Nathan Bale, walked in.

"We've got to stop meeting like this," he said. He looked a decade older to me.

"I didn't ask you to come," I said.

He sighed, his shoulders slumping resignedly. "I'd hoped you'd come to terms with their deaths."

"Their murders," I corrected.

He nodded. "Yes."

"I have come to terms with it. I told you my terms the last time you visited me."

He looked at me from under thick gray brows. "You're a fool."

That one surprised me.

"Just leave," I said.

He walked over to the bed and picked up the controller, the one for calling the nurse. He set it out of my reach on a cabinet.

"No," he said. "Not this time."

I shook my head. "Really? All I have to do is yell."

"Are you so afraid of what an old man has to say to you?"

"I'm not afraid. I just don't want to hear it."

"Why not, have you got something else to do? Someplace else to be?"

I set the papers down on my blanket-covered legs. "God let them die. You know that. He could have stopped it. He didn't. He let that monster murder your daughter and granddaughter right in front of me. All he had to do was give me the strength to move, and I would have stopped him. Instead, he made me live with this. And you can accept it? You?"

"I accept it, yes. Because I understand why He allows it."

"Right," I said, "right. It's all for His glory. I've heard it before."

"No," he interrupted. "No, Gil. This didn't happen for God's glory. God didn't want this to happen. He's grieving *with* us over this. He hates that this happened. He hates that you and I have to suffer and that we will have to wait to see them again one day. He hates all of this."

I felt the rage build and burn through my passivity. "Then why did He let it happen?"

Nathan took a step closer. "Because the alternative is worse."

"Worse? WORSE? What could be worse than my life ... my love ... my wife ... my little baby girl being ripped away from me ... murdered while I had to watch and listen ... powerless to stop it or go to them or help in any way? You tell me what could be worse than that."

He looked at me from those bushy brows again, his blue eyes, still so bright and powerful, blazing at me. "To have never known their love at all. That's what would be worse, and that's why God allows bad things ... allows sin ... to happen in the world. Because the alternative is to make us a bunch of puppets, playthings, toys that He manipulates, placing every thought and word and action into our minds and hands and mouths. God could easily take away our ability to sin; to make it so that no one could ever do anything bad or harmful again. But to do that, He would have had to make us without free will. To not have the ability to truly love and care and feel love in return. And that's not what He wants. That's not why He made us. He made us to have an eternal relationship with Him, with the real, true

ability to share and interact with Him because we *want* to. Because
we see that His way is THE way and that we want to be like Him."

I shook my head, the rage boiling like molten lava. I didn't want to
hear it. I didn't want there to be a reason.

"Look," he said, "before you and my daughter decided to have a
baby, you knew there would be risks. You knew there would be bad
days. That Marla would get sick, disobey you, and who knows, maybe
even grow to hate you, or turn to drugs, or maybe even murder someone. You had to know those possibilities existed because they did. No
matter how good you and Jolene might be as parents, there was
always the chance. A bad friend, drugs, a child molester, bad choices,
whatever. You, being a cop, had to know that better than anybody.
And not only that, but since this is an evil world with evil people who
do evil things, you had to understand that there was always the possibility that Marla might get sick or hurt. She might have an accident.
She might die or even be ... murdered."

I clenched my teeth and my fists.

"So, knowing all that," he continued, "why in the world would
you take the chance of having her? Why not just go buy a nice, safe
doll? I'll tell you why. Because you're just like God in this instance.
Because you didn't want a *plaything*. You wanted to be able to love
and be loved. To be able to shower your child with all the treasures
and happiness you could possibly give her and for her to be able to
actually experience and enjoy those treasures. Not just pretend, but
for real. And that is why God took the biggest chance in all of
creation and breathed His very spirit into us. He gave us life ... true
life ... sentience ... and in order for it to be real and true, for *us* to be
as real and true as He is, He gave us what He *has* ... free will. Because
what would Marla's happiness be, what would her love be if she
didn't have free will? The ability to not be happy, to not love ... even
you?" He held out his hands. "It would be a lie ... pretend ... make-
believe. And how can you have a real relationship with that?"

He walked right up to me, and I saw tears in those eyes. I saw
pain.

"That's what would be worse than losing my daughter and granddaughter in such a horrible way. Worse by a million times. That they never had the ability to really love. That they were nothing more than dolls and that we are all just playthings of God's mind. That we ... who we really are ... are nothing more than God's thoughts. That my Jolene was never really mine at all. That she never loved me. That I never loved her or Marla or you. That this is all make-believe. A game. That ... that is what would be worse."

The tears spilled, and I felt ashamed that it was me that had caused him to have to say what he was saying. That it was me that was costing him so much.

He put a hand on my shoulder.

"God knew, from the very beginning, that we might fall. That we might choose to disobey him, to hurt Him, ourselves, and each other. He hoped it wouldn't happen. He hopes all things good, just as we do. Just as you and Jolene did when you decided to create Marla. You knew the dangers, the possibilities, but you chose to hope because of love ... because of love. And now there's pain ... such horrible pain. But I ask you, if you could ... would you take it all back? Would you choose for them to have never existed at all? Would you?"

I tried to hold onto my hate—my fury—my rage—I tried—I tried so hard—I wanted to hate God—for it to be His fault—His fault and not mine.

I shook my head, my own tears falling now. I saw Jolene. I felt her. I heard her laugh. I kissed Marla's sweet face, her tiny lips, feeling her breath against me. My voice sounded like grinding boulders to my ears. "No. No, not for anything."

69

F our months later, I sat at my computer looking at pictures of
Majoqui Cabrera in a courtroom, wearing a business suit, as
a woman judge announced his sentence. He'd refused to
waive his right to a speedy trial and was found guilty on all counts in
record time. The article's headline announced, "Seven Consecutive
Life Sentences for Mass Murderer." Seven lifetimes ... that was a long
time for me to have to wait to get another shot at him.

I felt better. Most of my injuries had healed ... the physical ones at
least. The departmental psychiatrist said I was a mess—his actual
words—but that I was finally showing some progress. I rubbed
Pilgrim's big melon as he slept at my feet, a fresh scar running from
the edge of his eyebrow to the top of his thick skull. The gunshot
wound hardly affected him at all; tougher than a Sherman Tank.

My war with God was over. He'd won. It took a lot of soul-
searching and several weeks of arguing and discussion with both God
and Jolene's father. But in the end, I caved. My father-in-law's logic
was too solid. God's character too good. I think I'd known it all along,
but the pain and guilt had been too great. Thankfully, He's a forgiving
God.

The Sheriff's Office, on the other hand, is not so forgiving. Earlier this morning, I received my final disposition of the Internal Affairs Investigation concerning my involvement and attempted murder of Majoqui Cabrera. The basics boiled down to this; they would forgo criminal charges if I resigned without protest and agreed not to talk with the press about the case. Jim Black wanted to take it all the way, attempted murder, the whole works, but the Sheriff and the District Attorney shot him down, and they offered the deal.

My lawyer wanted to fight it, but I said no. Too many memories. It was time to move on. The Sheriff let me keep Pilgrim, and that said a lot.

So here I sat. Inactive Marine, former cop, house on the market. No job, no family, no prospects. Then the phone rang. I looked at it for three rings, wondering if I should answer it.

"Hello?"

"Gil, it's Sam Ponsiago. Do you remember me?"

Sam was my first Field Training Officer back when I started with the Sheriff's Office. He had retired shortly after.

"Of course," I said. "How's retired life?"

"Who knows," he said. "Not my style ... yours either, if what the Sheriff tells me is true."

I went on guard.

"Really, how's that?"

"We're close, me and him. He told me everything—quite the ordeal. I'm truly sorry for your loss. I'm sorry you didn't get to kill the piece of garbage too. But hey, it doesn't sound like it was for lack of trying."

I didn't know what to say to that, so I just stayed silent.

"You still there?" he asked.

"Why are you calling, Sam?"

"I want you to work with me," he said.

"Work with you," I echoed.

"Yup."

I certainly hadn't expected that. "Doing what?"

"Private Investigation. Philip Marlow stuff. It's a blast."

"You're a P.I.?" Most cops placed P.I.s about one step above security guards and bounty hunters.

"Have been since I left the department. Took my retirement and invested it in a small agency. I've built it up pretty nicely if I do say so myself."

"I appreciate the offer," I said, "but I can't quite see myself spying on cheating husbands and wives—no offense."

"None taken," he said. "I farm those cases out for a small referral fee, but that's not what we do here."

"So, what do you do?"

"I help people."

Again, I stayed silent.

"Really, I mean it. I specialize in missing persons. I also help out police departments and other governmental agencies on certain types of cases. I think you'd be a good fit."

"Look, Sam, I appreciate the offer, I really do, but ..."

"I'm not offering you a job, Gil; I'm offering you a partnership."

That set me back.

"A partnership? Why?"

"I've gotten too big, or the agency has anyway. I can't handle all the cases by myself. I've been looking for a partner, the right kind of partner, for a while now. And here you are."

I started to say no, then paused.

"Look," he continued, "I know the man you were back when I trained you. The Sheriff says you're still that man, only better, more mature. I'm sure the Marines were a challenge, just like being a cop. Those jobs give you the chance to be a ... well, sort of a real-life superhero. You come work with me, and I promise you, we'll take that to the next level. You won't be sorry."

I told him I'd give it some thought, and we agreed to meet on Monday. I hung up and sat there, thinking. Pilgrim came over and stuck his cold, wet nose into my palm. I snuggled his massive head.

A stage of my life was passing away. That's always hard. I looked at the phone. Superhero? I didn't feel like a superhero. I didn't feel like any kind of hero. Heroes don't try and murder the bad guys. I looked at the pictures of Jolene and Marla lining my hallway, then back at Pilgrim. Yes, one stage passing away, but another was just beginning.

The End

ACKNOWLEDGMENTS

Hello dear readers, here we are again at the end of another book. I know some of you might have been disappointed that Max didn't appear in *Feral Instinct*, but I had always planned that the third book would explain Gil's past and the tragedy that has plagued his life.

A few readers have suggested that *Feral Instinct* should have been the first book in the series, but there is an important reason that I didn't start with this one. The Gil Mason series isn't just about Gil; it's about Gil *and* Max. That's it, plain and simple. It's about the two of them and the development of their relationship. Of course, the series is also about Pilgrim and Sarah, and others past, present, and future, but the nexus of the story is about Gil *and* Max.

If I had started with *Feral Instinct*, you might not have continued reading to discover there was a Max, and wouldn't that have been a shame? For all of us?

Instead of thinking of Gil and Max the way I do, you would be thinking, Gil and Pilgrim. Don't get me wrong, I love Pilgrim, just as I hope you do. He is fun, happy, playful, and loves to be touched and hugged, and petted. And in his day, he was a great warrior.

But even on his best of best days, Pilgrim was never Max.

Only Max is Max.

He's one of a kind.

Like Gil.

And that is why we had to start the journey with *Sheepdogs* and not *Feral Instinct*.

And now, on to the rest of the acknowledgments:

As with all my books, I had a lot of help writing and making *Feral*

Instinct pretty. I didn't find and catch bad guys by myself, and I don't publish books by myself either. It's a team effort. This book entailed efforts from my wife (editor), my oldest daughter, Athena (she does all my covers), and my dear friends, Barbara Wright and Betty Fisher, who help correct my many mistakes. I would also like to thank my son, Anthony, who has taken over my business matters (publishing, internet, stores, etc.), allowing me to focus on my writing. I'm not very good at all that other stuff anyway, so luckily for all of you, he will streamline the entire process.

I thank God (not an expression of speech) for allowing me the enjoyment of writing, the encouragement of my fans, and for being able to introduce small pieces of His Word to reach and encourage others (iron sharpens iron).

All of that being said, any blame for incorrect, outdated, or misapplied information is wholly on me, either because it worked for the story or because I messed it up.

And finally, it comes to you, dear reader. Thank you so much for buying and reading Feral Instinct. I hope to be seeing you soon as the adventures continue in upcoming books. Thanks for being a part of The Dog Pack, and please join me in our next hunt, Old Dog New Tricks.

Until then ...

ABOUT THE AUTHOR

About Gordon D. Carroll

Gordon Carroll is the author of GUNWOOD USA and The Gil Mason Sheepdog series. Gordon grew up at the foot of the great Rocky Mountains in Colorado. Joining the United States Marine Corps at eighteen, he served for seven years, achieving the rank of sergeant (selected for staff sergeant). After that, he became a police officer in a small (wild) city nestled snugly in the middle of Denver, Colorado, before moving on to become a sheriff's deputy.

Gordon became a K9 handler, trainer, and instructor, training and working four separate dogs for over three decades (a hundred-twenty-pound German Shepherd named JR, a ninety-pound Belgian Malinois named Max, a fifty-six-pound Belgian Malinois named Thor, and a sixty-pound fur-missile named Arrow). Gordon retired from police work in 2020 to focus on writing and spending time with his grandchildren. K9 Arrow retired with him.

Over the years, Gordon and his K9 companions assisted the DEA, FBI, and numerous other local, state, and federal law enforcement agencies in the detection and apprehension of criminals and narcotics. Together, Gordon and his K9 partners are responsible for over two million dollars in narcotics seizures, three thousand felony apprehensions and were first responders to both the 2012 Aurora Mall shooting and the 2013 Arapahoe High School shooting.

He has been married to the same wonderful woman (his high school sweetheart, Becky) for over forty years. Together they have four adult children and a whole *pack* of grandchildren.

Gordon's love of books began while he was in sixth grade when he became captivated by Jack London's *White Fang* and *Call of the Wild*. From there, he branched out, gobbling up everything from Robert E. Howard to Steinbeck to Brand, King, Wambaugh, Irving, Craise, Hunter, Rothfuss, Lowry, Card, Emmerich, and on and on.

After years of telling stories to his children and friends, his wife insisted he write some of them down. After that, he just couldn't stop. Sending short stories out, he was quickly published in several magazines in genres ranging from Si-Fi, horror, mainstream, mystery, and Christian. He then wrote GUNWOOD USA, followed by Sheepdogs (Book 1 of the Gil Mason and Max series), fictionalized compilations of real-life scenarios that he has seen, heard of, or been involved in over his years with law enforcement and military service.

The Sheepdog series, as well as GUNWOOD USA, became instant bestsellers.

Gordon is a member of Rocky Mountain Fiction Writers (RMFW) and served on speaking panels for years, as well as performing K9 demos at the annual conferences.

ALSO BY GORDON CARROLL

Gil Mason Book 1: Sheepdogs

Gil Mason Book 2: Hair of the Dog

Gil Mason Book 4: Old Dog New Tricks

Gil Mason Book 5: Sleeping Dogs

Gil Mason Book 6: A Dog Returns

GUNWOOD USA

Bone Hill

Made in the USA
Monee, IL
11 May 2023

33522343R00166